One Man's Purpose

A Novel

Stephen D. Senturia

◆ FriesenPress

Suite 300 - 990 Fort St
Victoria, BC, Canada, V8V 3K2
www.friesenpress.com

Copyright © 2015 by Stephen D. Senturia
First Edition — 2015

ISBN
978-1-4602-7468-2 (Hardcover)
978-1-4602-7469-9 (Paperback)
978-1-4602-7470-5 (eBook)

1. *Fiction, Literary*

Distributed to the trade by The Ingram Book Company

Author's Preface

Readers familiar with Cambridge, Massachusetts, may recognize the Cambridge Technology Institute as a thinly disguised version of the Massachusetts Institute of Technology. Indeed, the CTI of *One Man's Purpose* shares a location and a number of physical features (as well as a few organizational ones) with the real MIT, the place where 'you are what you do,' and where I parked my hat for thirty-six happy years as a member of the faculty. I owe an enormous debt to the hundreds of faculty colleagues, the thousands of students, and the many members of the staff and administration with and among whom I was honored to ply my craft as a teacher. But that's where it ends. CTI and the people who work therein are fictional. I can be a bit rough on CTI and on some of its minions, but that doesn't mean I bear corresponding animus toward MIT. And while faculty members everywhere share the stresses of work *versus* family in the midst of professional overload, the agony of tenure and promotion, and the often acrimonious debates over educational policy and practice, the story-teller must make these stresses concrete; hence, CTI.

Similarly, Bottlesworth College in the town of Brimfield Junction, Maine, is a fiction, bearing only the most superficial resemblance to Bowdoin College, and even the Harvard in these pages has had some minor surgery, but without a change of name because Harvard just is.

Some of the names, events, book titles, and dates are historical or, like DARPA's contracting procedures, have been plausibly modified in service to the story. Most, however, are made up. For example, the Metropolitan Opera in New York might not actually have presented *Siegfried* on one particular Friday night to be followed the next day by a matinee production of *Cosi fan tutte*. On the other hand, the theft of nominally secure information followed by posting on the internet is now an everyday occurrence, so it is only a matter of time before the confidential letters collected as part of a university tenure decision become compromised. Perhaps by the time you have read this book, it will already have happened somewhere.

Stephen D. Senturia

One Man's Purpose

Part I: Spring Term, 2013

* 1 *

The thermometer said her body was ready. The doctor said her body was ready. But was Martin ready? Really ready? He had been so nervous last time. Overly solicitous, almost patronizing, acting the role of doting husband instead of being one. And she could smell his relief after the miscarriage. Was he really ready to try again?

She could understand his nervousness. She, after all, had been plenty nervous before JJ was born. But George had taken such obvious delight in her changing shape, in JJ's first kick, so gentle and loving, coming home early from work, massaging her feet. She blushed as she remembered the making of JJ. It wasn't planned, like this, with an early-morning basal temperature test. No, it was spontaneous and joyful, and thoroughly orgasmic for both of them.

Jenny looked over at her husband, still asleep, just as the sun crawled up to start its final January traverse, spilling a cloud-filtered dawn onto the putty-colored house Martin had bought during his fourth year on the faculty and which, now that he had made Full Professor, they could afford to move out of. But Martin liked living near Harvard. He would even do without off-street parking and only one car in order to live near Harvard.

The two-story house had an attic gable facing the street, a pair of bay windows, and two snow shovels on the tiny front porch. Within, the furnishings told a story of displacement — the displacement of Martin's taste for simple clean lines and off-white walls by Jenny's preference for the elegance of eighteenth- and nineteenth-century furniture, or, in deference to budgetary realities, well-done replicas, all tempered with softer wall colorings and textured papers. It was still a work in progress, this displacement. The kitchen, for example, remodeled by Martin using his tenure raise, still had its black-front appliances, Shaker-style cabinets and faintly pink granite countertops. But when Jenny wanted to replace Martin's Danish-modern teak dining set with a beautifully rebuilt and restored Queen Anne oak table and matching replica chairs, the teak dining set got Craigslisted away. They compromised on the living room: the furniture could be styled to Jenny's taste, but it had to be light enough to be moved out of the way when Martin had one of his chamber-music sessions.

Upstairs were three bedrooms. In the largest, the one with the two faux-Chippendale bureaus, tousle-headed Jenny lay nestled up against Martin's thigh, wondering. She had tried to warn him off by saying she wanted another child, but instead of running the other way — what she had both expected and dreaded — he had grinned and said, "A child? Great! So how soon can we get married?" And when Dr. Rosen said it was now safe to try again, Martin had said, "By all means, let's." She took a deep breath, smiled at his angular face with that shock of brown hair flopping over his eyes, and started shaking his shoulder. "Martin, love. It's up two tenths. Wake up. Two tenths."

Martin opened one bleary eye. "Wha? What time is it?"

"Six-thirty. C'mon. Wake up. It's up two tenths. I need your pearly essence. C'mon, love. Up, up, up."

Martin groaned. "Christ a'mighty!" He stifled a huge yawn. "Okay. I'm awake."

Jenny rolled over, put her head on his shoulder and reached under the covers to massage the appendage that held their future, if not in its hands, then perhaps in the little jewel sack it always carried around. She cooed, "C'mon, Jean-Pierre. Wake up. Wake up so Martin can be a daddy. JJ needs a little sister."

"Sister? You've chosen a sister?"

Jenny laughed. "Or brother. I'll take either one."

Martin closed his eyes and imagined Jenny as Salome, dressed in seven gauzy veils, then six, then five… Jenny, not being particularly gauzy, but nevertheless having thus aroused Jean-Pierre many times in her quest for motherhood, felt his response. "C'mon Martin. You're doing fine. Keep it up."

He chuckled. "Jesus, Jenny! Get it up. Keep it up. There's just gotta be a better way."

She giggled. "This is the natural way, you goofus. And you're almost ready. Me on top?"

"Please."

She mounted him, guiding his tumescence where it needed to go, and with her well-schooled motions gradually brought Martin to deposit his little DNA-carriers deep inside her, hoping that maybe, this time, maybe...

After a short snuggle, Martin rolled out of bed, pulling on his ragged sweat pants, his swamp-smelling sneakers and the treasured *Pocari Sweat* T-shirt he bought during his 2010 trip to Japan. He descended to the basement to do his three miles of treadmill and ten minutes of weight lifting on the home gym.

Jenny lay still for a while longer so that Martin's little gene bundles would not be expelled by gravity. She imagined this swarm of micro-guppies following some mysterious emanation that would guide them to her cervical opening, swimming up the path of life in a race for the egg her thermometer told her was on its fallopian journey toward a gametic rendezvous. In a country where the son of a Kenyan goatherd had been elected president, now for a second term, Jenny felt that whichever one of Martin's sperm won the race would create an embryo of great potential. Maybe this time it would take proper hold in her uterus and turn into a baby.

Enjoying that thought, she edged herself out of bed, took a shower and began dressing. She picked out a brown and tan tweed skirt, a tailored white blouse with a round collar, a pale green cardigan that was loose enough to keep her shapely bosom hidden from her blue-stocking clients, cream-colored panty hose, brown flat-heeled shoes, and an amber bead necklace and matching earrings.

By the time Jenny put Martin's plate of scrambled eggs and toast on the kitchen table and poured juice and coffee, he was on the way into the kitchen, sweaty and hungry.

"I'm sorry I had to wake you like that. I know you hate it. Good workout?"

"Good enough, considering. My headphones are just about shot. They make Pavarotti sound old and creaky, and that's sacrilege." Martin took a big bite of toast, and started talking through the mouthful. "And I don't actually hate those pre-dawn awakenings. But, y'know what I miss?" swallowing the toast, and taking a swig of juice. "Slow cuddly fucks. Nibble-your-boobs fucks. Kiss-your-sweet-pussy fucks."

Jenny blushed and replied, "Shush. JJ will hear you. And, yeah, I know, it's not all that exciting. But you come to bed so late. We used to really enjoy…"

Martin cut her off. "Speaking of timing, I have to edit a thesis this afternoon and might be a little late getting home. How 'bout I call you this afternoon with an ETA for dinner?"

Jenny frowned. "What's a little late mean? Oh, never mind. Just don't forget to call. I'll manage." She plunked her dishes in the sink and went upstairs to wake JJ and get him ready for the Montessori pre-school near the Belmont line. Martin, oblivious to Jenny's dish plunk, skimmed the *Globe* sports section, noting that the Celtics' point guard had turned up with a strained hamstring, but the Celts had won anyway. He finished eating and went upstairs to shower just as Jenny was starting downstairs with JJ, a tow-headed energy quantum, blue-eyed like Jenny with bright-red chubby cheeks.

Martin was a careful dresser. He had an image to maintain, positioning himself between the scruffiness of his grad students and the overly suited and necktied Department Heads, Deans, and other wastrels, all the while still being presentable enough not to embarrass the surprise visitor from Japan or Taiwan who might appear at his office door on any given day, requesting fifteen minutes of his precious time. It was almost a uniform: slacks, a shirt of an appropriate pattern and color *vis a vis* the slacks, sometimes a tie but mostly not, a blue blazer or tweed sport coat, and loafers, except when the weather required boots. By the time he got downstairs, Jenny and JJ had gone.

With a serious chill in the air and the threat of what the TV weatherman loved to call a 'wintry mix,' Martin opted for boots, his navy blue L.L. Bean down coat, the small green knapsack he used as a briefcase and a black and yellow wool cap that Jenny had knitted. The cap made him look like a Bruins fan, not a bad thing when one lives just a block from Somerville. Suitably swathed, he went out the front door and was surprised to see a robin foraging in his patch of yard. "Don't you know it's still winter?" asked Martin. The robin looked up, tilted its head, and resumed its hop-and-peck search for food.

Martin took the longer path to his office, cutting across the Divinity School, past Mem Hall and through the Harvard Yard to Massachusetts Avenue, where he turned left toward the Cambridge Technology Institute. His path would vary from day to day, but he usually managed to traverse at least a corner of the Harvard campus. It connected his present to his past, a soupçon of coherence and calm before the stresses of his typical day. The ebb and flow of classes, exams, and undergraduate advising was one thing — what one might expect in a professor's life — but what made him work his hardest was the endless cycle of supervising his graduate students' research, reporting the results at conferences, and writing new grant proposals to fund the next set of students. Martin had long ago given up figuring out which was the chicken, the pullet, or the egg in this cycle, but in spite of its many irritations, he was an expert at managing it.

Jenny would ask him, now that he was tenured and a Full Professor, why he continued to labor so mightily in this arena, especially since he repeatedly told her that he was getting tired of having to produce new and revolutionary ideas to justify the next round of grants. He had no crisp answer. How do you find the words to justify your addiction to the perks that flow from a high position in the professional pecking order, the invitations to give plenary talks at conferences, appointments to journal editorial boards, requests for consulting services, even (once) testimony before a congressional committee? His twelve-person group was generally considered among the two or three best in the world at modifying the surfaces of semiconductors to give them special and highly desirable electrical or optical properties. But Martin knew, deep down, that his group's actual rank was number one. Like making first-string center forward with the whole world as cheerleaders.

Ego-stroking by colleagues notwithstanding, Martin's deepest passion was for teaching. He thought of himself, first and foremost, as a teacher and a teacher of teachers. If he could only set aside enough time to write, he knew that his planned book on the essential role of live conversation in education, now just a glimmer within his busy brain, would be a wake-up call to all those zanies who think that massive online education is the wave of the future.

-　-　-

Massachusetts Avenue is the backbone of the skeleton of Cambridge, but only the tourists ever use its full name. Over the years, development along Mass Ave has resulted in fewer Irish bars, more coffee bars, some box-like apartment and office buildings, gradual encroachment by retail chains, and a jumble of low-cost ethnic restaurants in Central Square, a major intersection a bit more than half way to CTI: a frenetic mix of rich and poor, Irish and Italian and African and Caribbean, sober and not. As Martin walked this well-trod path, his thoughts floated back to his morning with Jenny and how predictable and forced their sex life had become.

He recalled their first time, after a lovely dinner in Jenny's condo, with JJ put to bed and asleep. Jenny had taken the lead. She insisted on undressing him with the lights on so she could see and feel and smell that he wasn't George, and then she held her arms out and said it was his turn to undress her, which, with shaking hands, he did. The effect was volcanic. Not only was Jenny bold like that, she was totally comfortable with her body and could say exactly what she wanted — touch me here, kiss me there — something that Martin had always struggled with. Was the sex in other marriages like his? He had never talked about such things — not with Sumner, not with Horatio, nor with anyone else. With a four-year-old child in the house, sex was necessarily different. But consciously trying to conceive another child? On demand stud service? That's really different.

- - -

Martin reached the edge of the campus and turned toward the chunky concrete box that was the Semiconductor Technology Lab. He took the stairs to the fifth floor, greeted Felice, his assistant, already at work in the outer office, and entered his private sanctum.

Firing up his email, he noticed cc's of several messages between Miles Callaghan, the Editor-in-Chief of *The Journal of Semiconductor Materials Technology,* and Wolfgang Schultz, an author, whose paper Martin, as one of the four Associate Editors of *JSMT,* had rejected four days earlier. The gist of it was that, according to Schultz, Martin had completely misunderstood not only the paper but also the referee comments and therefore had wrongly rejected the paper. Callaghan's view was that Martin was in charge and he would get involved only after Martin sent the paper out for a new set of reviews, which, via cc, he was asking Martin to do. Martin silently cursed the pair of them, acknowledged to both via email that he would pursue a new set of reviews and opened the pdf of the paper to think about what to do.

He thought about Phelps at Purdue, someone he disliked but whose reviews were usually prompt and more or less thoughtful. To find another, he examined the reference list in the paper, picking out S. J. Chang, co-author on the key reference. This would be something of a gamble since Martin knew nothing about him. He called, "Can you come in for a minute?"

Felice Albright, thirty-something, coal black and seriously overweight, with corn-rowed hair surrounding a broad and usually-smiling face, came in and took a seat on the little pumpkin-colored sofa, pad in hand. A native of Sierra Leone and a graduate of UMass-Boston in communications, she had worked at CTI for three years and as Martin's assistant for the past two. Her work was accurate and her manner friendly. Martin knew almost nothing about her life outside CTI, other than that she lived with her mother and a seven-year old daughter near Central Square.

"We've got to send the Schultz manuscript out for new reviews. A clean re-review. No copies of the two we already have. I've selected Arthur Phelps at Purdue and a new guy, S. J. Chang. He is co-author on reference seven, and you might have to do some web-searching to track him down. Before you send it out though, let me check his web page to see if he's appropriate. Okay?"

Felice smiled as she wrote notes. "You don't know his organization?" she asked, with an imprint of her West-African heritage in her speech.

"Not sure, but I think he's the Chang in Materials Science at Texas A&M. Try there first."

"I'll try to have this before you get back from lunch," she said as she rose to leave. "Oh yes, one more thing. Your calendar was clear, so Peter moved today's squash game to eleven."

-    -   -

Peter Dempsey, ten years Martin's senior and an expert in transistor physics, had been playing squash since his prep school days at Groton. Thirty pounds overweight, paunchy and turning gray, Peter was court savvy. In spite of his paunch, he could move with catlike speed in the short bursts needed within the confines of the court, and because of his paunch, he was impossible to dislodge from the T, the strategic central position. Peter had introduced Martin to the game. It took about six months for Martin's athletic skills to catch hold, but he was now able to provide good competition for his more experienced partner.

Today's match followed the typical pattern. Martin would clobber the ball and Peter would find a way to return it. Martin managed to win the first game in a tie-breaker, but Peter won each of the last two by a handful of points. As they headed to the locker room, panting and sweaty, Martin asked, "What are you teaching this term?"

"The grad device physics," wheezed Peter. "And you? Doing the usual Broadway show?"

"If you mean C&E, then yes." Martin reached his locker and began stripping.

"We need natural actors like you on the faculty," said Peter as he and Martin went for their showers. "Most of us are boring. If I was teaching C&E, the lecture hall would be empty after two weeks. But you seem to keep 'em coming. How do you do it?"

"It's not acting, you asshole. It's teaching. I engage their brains."

"Sure, sure, teaching. But you can tell me the truth — you get off when those freshmen girls fall in love with you, don't you?"

"Jesus, Peter! Is sex all you ever think about?"

"No," Peter chuckled. "Sometimes I work."

"Very funny. Speaking of work, did you send me your DARPA stuff?"

"The dreck is in the mail," said Peter, as they finished their showers. They dried off and dressed in silence, and Peter went off to the campus bookstore.

Martin decided to grab lunch in the student center. The rigors of the squash match entitled him to pizza, two slices with pepperoni and onions. He went to a table in the corner of the noisy dining room, wiping off some spilled soda with a handful of napkins before he sat down. Two bites into the first slice he found himself pondering the sting of Peter's teasing. Freshman girls? Bullshit. It was much deeper than that. When Eddie Cranshaw had his heart attack, he had volunteered to take over the huge Circuits and Electronics class even though he didn't yet have tenure. Once he took it over, enrollment steadily increased and was now up by thirty percent, all from out-of-department students choosing to study with him. And they weren't just freshman girls, goddam it.

"Can I share the table?" Martin looked up to see a familiar face, but he blanked on the name.

"Sure. Have a seat," said Martin, eyeing his slight, owlish, wispy-haired companion.

"Is that Martin? Martin Quint? Hi, I'm Julian Kesselbaum." He extended a hand.

"Oh, yes. Hi," shaking hands, but still confused. "Sorry, but I didn't expect to see you on campus. Out of context, I guess."

"But I'm here quite a lot these days. IT security department. I help them out when they have problems."

"So you're still in Cambridge?"

"Oh, yes. I run a blog and do some consulting, and, of course, lots of teaching. Different places around town. I'm giving a seminar here, today, for administrative staff, on safe use of the internet."

"Well," said Martin, "I'm sorry about the tenure. I thought you did a great job for us."

"The truth is," said Julian, chuckling. "I'm not a research type. At least not the kind of research you can publish. Internet security, bugs and viruses and all that, is a tough field for academics. I mean, the weakest link in any network is the people who use it. Try publishing that in a journal. Most people will fall for a well-designed Trojan horse. Anyway, I heard that Ken Fitzgerald is headed to Washington. Doesn't this affect you?"

"Yeah, I just heard, but I'm not a candidate for lab director, so I don't think it will change my life all that much."

"You never know," said Julian, a remark that puzzled Martin. Did Julian know something?

Martin finished his lunch, said a brief goodbye, and walked toward his office, wondering why that odd duck would have chosen to sit with him, or with anybody, for that matter.

* **2** *

Before Martin could get to his thesis reading, he had to run his kickoff C&E staff meeting: four faculty colleagues who each taught two sections, eight Teaching Assistants and four undergraduate homework graders. With practiced efficiency, he got everyone introduced to everyone else, assigned each to their sections, primed them for his first lecture, Tuesday at eleven, described the subjects to be covered by the faculty in the first set of Wednesday sections, and announced the time for the weekly staff meeting, noon on Thursdays, following lecture. Meeting adjourned.

On returning to his office, he learned from Felice that S. J. Chang was an Assistant Professor of Materials Science at the University of Minnesota with a short but highly relevant publication list. Decision made. Send him the Schultz manuscript for review. Finally, he turned to the business at hand: what Martin referred to as the Wojtowicz Catastrophe, or the WC.

It was a gnarly source of irritation that Martin's American-educated students often wrote less well than his foreign students. Khalil, for example, his Algerian post-doc, wrote flawless English. Kevin Wojtowicz, on the other hand, born and bred in the good old U. S. of A., sputtered and flubbered through even the most elementary exposition. With Wojtowicz now on draft number four of his PhD, Martin was reasonably convinced that the science part was finally okay, but awkward sentence structures and grammatical hiccups persisted. He wished there was the equivalent of a spell checker for general writing, sort of a Hemingway button: simple declarative sentences with no extra words would survive; everything else would be erased. He also wished his students knew how much of their professional lives would be spent writing English. Perhaps, then, they would work harder at it. But in this age of computer literacy and language illiteracy, it felt like a losing battle. The thesis defense was already scheduled for the end of March, and here he was still correcting English. Phooey.

By four o'clock, with forty pages to go, he was Wojtowicz-saturated. A wet sloppy snow had started. Not delighted at the prospect of either walking through ankle-deep slush or giving in and taking the Number One Bus up Mass Ave, he extracted the waterproof knapsack cover, custom-made for him by the lady who did repairs at Eastern Mountain Sports, zipped it over the backpack and stuffed his iPad and the WC inside. Then he picked up the phone to call Jenny.

-     -   -

The walking wasn't too bad. As he picked his way north, Martin's thoughts drifted once again to Peter's teasing, which, he admitted, had struck a nerve. His sister used to taunt him the same way when she was feeling pissy.

"You're nothing but a big phony," Helen would scream, with the self-righteousness only a fourteen-year-old girl can muster. "You just want to play first string so the girls'll fall all over you. If you really loved soccer, you wouldn't care what position, you would just play. You'd play for the sake of the team. But no. You gotta be first. Alla time first. Dad's wrong. It's not that you're a jock, it's that you're a stuck-up phony."

Martin, driven to fury by the taunting and nearly eight inches taller and fifty pounds heavier than his sister, could have done real physical damage had he wanted to. Instead, he would suddenly grab her in his arms, and hug and tickle her until her taunts became laughter. But it was true. He did want to be first — at everything. When Sumner got him to try out for crew in college, Martin couldn't take the rah-rah, the all-for-one and one-for-all crap. He quit the freshman crew and rowed singles to satisfy his Phys Ed requirement. Peter's taunt, too, was on target. He did enjoy the fact that the freshmen girls fell in love with him. Was that so unusual? Was it preventable? Was it wrong? And it wasn't just freshmen. He had more female graduate students than most of his colleagues, and some of them clearly had crushes on him. What's wrong with that? Women students need good mentors. It's not like he fucked them or anything.

- - -

By the time Martin reached home, it was dark and the slushy snow was turning to snowy snow. He opened the front door, dropped his dripping backpack inside, called out a "Halloo" to Jenny and ducked back outside, where he grabbed one of the shovels from the front porch.

Shoveling snow gave Martin a lot of satisfaction. There was the pragmatic fact that if he got it out of the way before it froze, life would be better for him, for his neighbors and for the mailman, but it was mostly that he liked the feeling in the muscles of his back, arms, and legs when he was shoveling, hoisting, and tossing. No matter how much he worked out on his home gym, something real like snow shoveling was energizing, both physically and mentally.

With the walks temporarily cleared and the street side of his car shoveled out (unless, of course, the Cambridge Snow Plow, a rarely seen object, showed up to plow it back in), Martin was satisfied and nicely sweaty. As he entered the house, JJ pounced. "Daddy, Daddy," grabbing Martin's legs. "You got home early. Read me a story tonight? For bedtime?"

Martin chuckled. "Sure, bud. Give me a minute to get my wet stuff off. Of course I'll read you a story. Which one?"

"*Wild Things. Wild Things.* Rumpus, rumpus." And he ran off shouting, "Mommy, Mommy. Daddy's home. Daddy's home!"

Martin took a quick shower before joining Jenny and JJ at the kitchen table. Getting home in time to share a midweek meal with his now-adopted son had become a rarity. JJ had already started fisting ketchup-slathered hotdog slices into his mouth.

Martin was hungry, and he dug into the food while Jenny reported on her day. "I landed a new client today. Very exciting. Big job. Total re-do — furnishings, wall-coverings, the works."

"Very cool," mumbled Martin with a full mouth, as he wiped ketchup smears from JJ's face. "Do you like these folks?"

"They're really nice. Husband is an investment banker downtown. Says he knows Sumner, by the way. And she is, as she put it, a philanthropist. Serves on boards. Writes checks. That kind of thing. But not snooty at all. The house is on Berkeley Place, that little cul-de-sac off Berkeley Street. Late 1880s, I think."

"Do they know what they want?"

"We'll just have to see," said Jenny, putting some melon on JJ's plate. "The schedule for the planning phase is pretty tight. And she mentioned a trip to New York to look for antiques. With me, I mean. Budget is apparently not an issue."

"Whoa," said Martin. "Budget not an issue? Must have made you drool."

"Oh stop it, silly. I'm sure there's a budget. So, anyway…"

"But you haven't seen it?"

"Not yet. She told me not to worry about that now. Anyway, are you ready to start the new term?"

"Yeah. Staff meeting went well. All set." Martin, a fast eater, got up to clear his plate and noticed that JJ had already gobbled his melon. "Hey, little guy. How about a bath and a story?"

- - -

JJ was in one of his cooperative moods and went smoothly and quietly to bed. Closing the door to JJ's room, he went downstairs to do his thirty minutes on the piano, tonight practicing a trio by Menotti that he, Sumner and Vladimir were learning. He then extracted the WC from the now dry backpack and took it to the third bedroom, their shared study, crammed with two small side-by-side desks, an easy chair and a small sleep-sofa, all arranged with a precision and functionality that only an engineer married to an interior designer could devise.

Jenny was at her computer, working on CAD drawings. "Is this for the new project?" asked Martin.

"Yeah," she said, not looking up. "I need rough layouts in time for a meeting next Tuesday."

Martin went to his desk and found a yellow card on the seat of his desk chair. "What's this?" he asked, turning to face Jenny.

Jenny pushed her keyboard back on the desk and swiveled in Martin's direction. "I want to try something. A signal."

"A signal?"

"Think of it as a yellow traffic light, a caution. I don't want to fight. I just want you to pay attention. One of the things I love about you is that we can usually talk through things. But we've both so busy lately that we miss the chance, and then things get bottled up or we end up snapping at each other. I want a signal so you will talk with me without feeling attacked. Does that make sense?"

"I actually like the idea. I never want to fight with you. But what did I do to earn a yellow card?"

"This morning. You complained about our sex life. Okay, I understand that. I really am a noodge about getting pregnant, and it does interfere. I miss those nice sexy times too, those whatcha-call-it fucks. But when I started to talk about it, you changed the subject, and not to something nice. You just dumped 'might be a little late' on me. Now I already do all of the chauffeuring, most of the shopping, and most of the cooking. The least you could do is be considerate about my schedule for a change, and not just assume that your schedule trumps everything. I've got my own work to do, not just as maid and nanny."

"Yeah, I guess I was a bit abrupt. You're right. I'm sorry." He held up the WC. "This goddam thesis, well, the kid just can't write, and it's bogging me down just when I need to be working on the new DARPA grant."

"Okay, but you're not the only one. I need to make a completely new set of drawings by Tuesday, all between cooking and chauffeuring and spending some decent time with our son. It's not a question of who has the most work to do or the most important work, it's about awareness of each other's feelings. You've gotten sloppy, my love, and it's best if you hear it direct from me when it happens. I hate fights. But I hate being dumped on, too."

Martin stared at the floor. "Okay. You're right. This is much better than fighting." He took a deep breath followed by a poofy exhale, then looked up at Jenny. "Yes, you're right. I earned a yellow card today, and I deserved it." And with a puckish smile, he added, "But it takes two yellows to be disqualified, and I'm going to be a pussycat from now on."

"You are such a goofus!" giggled Jenny. "I was thinking of traffic signals, but okay, if you understand yellow cards from soccer, so be it. It's sort of cute. And now I've got to work on these drawings."

Jenny turned back to her computer. Martin moved over to the easy chair, adjusted the reading lamp, and opened the WC.

After almost an hour, Jenny got up from her desk. "That's it for tonight. I'm heading for bed." She cocked her head to one side. "I'm not sure if you're, shall we say, up for it, but I would be happy to accept your donation tonight and then I wouldn't wake you so early in the morning."

Martin, expressionless, looked toward his wife, wondering. "I'll join you soon." Jenny smiled and left the room.

Martin pressed ahead to finish the final Wojtowicz pages, got up from his desk, turned out the study lights, and went into the hall. He could hear that Jenny was in the shower, a very different and familiar kind of signal. In spite of having already showered, he stripped quickly and joined her just as she had finished rinsing. As soon as he got wet, she grabbed the soap and started washing him, from his shoulders, down his back, then carefully, gently, in the crack between his butt cheeks. Turning him around, she soaped his arms and armpits, chest, and stomach and, finally, his now rampant erection. "My boobs want a nibble," she said, as she got out of the shower.

Martin shot back, "And your sweet pussy?"

"That too. Finish up and come to bed."

* **3** *

Tuesday. With Jenny's ovulation window now passed, Martin was not called to stud service at six-thirty. He was, nevertheless, roused by Jenny shortly before seven because it had snowed six inches overnight and, thanks to what the locals call the Montreal Express, the temperature was heading down into the teens by mid-morning. Jenny needed the car liberated before the salty street slush turned to ice.

The Cambridge Snow Plow had made an appearance during the night, and it took a full thirty minutes for Martin to deal with the impacted car, all the while wondering how that poor robin was doing. Knowing he wouldn't be walking to CTI today, Martin indulged himself with an extra twenty minutes of the *Globe* and the *Times*, after which he selected a white shirt, regimental-striped tie, and blue blazer to honor his first class. Bundled up and with eyes on guard for icy sidewalks, he minced his way over to Mass Ave to pick up the Number One Bus. The snowy conditions reduced traffic to a crawl, so he arrived at CTI with only an hour to spare before his lecture.

He found an email from Rebecca in Department Headquarters asking him to drop by at 3 PM, no explanation offered. Professor Wong needed to see him. After confirming that he would see Wong at three, Martin used what was left of his free hour trying to assemble the first complete draft of a preliminary grant proposal, called a White Paper, for a huge seven-investigator program on advanced semiconductor materials. DARPA was going to create two such centers this year, and with five million dollars on the line, the competition would be fierce. In addition to his own group (CTI, Purdue and Berkeley), there were teams from Stanford-UCLA-Cal Tech, Michigan-Cornell-Georgia

Tech, Penn State-Columbia-Maryland-Illinois, and maybe one involving several of the University of Texas campuses. The White Paper was due at DARPA on Friday of the following week, and it still needed a lot of work. Three of his collaborators were late with their revised submissions, so Martin had to send nagging emails and work around the gaps. Then he went to class. At least this part of his day would be fun.

Martin entered the lecture amphitheater at eleven sharp, pleased that several of his TAs were already clearing the white boards. He scanned the room to find and nod to each of his four section instructors, put his one sheet of notes on the lectern — not notes really, just a few bullet points — and looked around at more than two hundred fifty eager faces. Well, maybe only ninety were all that eager. The rest were computer science students who had to take C&E as part of their core requirements. To Martin, computers were a bunch of high-speed electronic switching circuits. It was the moral duty of anyone who worked with computers to be curious about that, or at least to know something about it. After quieting the crowd and introducing himself, the section instructors and the eight TAs, and outlining what was expected in terms of homework sets, laboratory exercises and exams, Martin began his lecture.

"You are all about to embark on the study of engineering, so it's reasonable to ask: what is engineering? My answer is both simple and complex. The words are simple: engineering is the purposeful use of scientific knowledge." He paused to let that sink in, then wrote the word 'PURPOSEFUL' on the board in large caps and underlined it twice. "The problem, and it is a real problem for each and every one of you," as he glanced almost menacingly around the room, "the problem is that one man's purpose, or one woman's purpose, can be another person's anathema. Consider drilling for natural gas by the method known as fracking. To those worried about running out of fossil fuels, fracking has been more than a blessing, it has been a boon. To those worried about the environment, it is the devil incarnate, polluting the water table and risking earthquakes, all for the sake of some profit-hungry oil company." Martin paused to scan the room, now dead silent.

"Society needs to debate these issues. Each of you, as a member of our society, must come to your own decision about what is purposeful and what is not. It is your moral duty as a citizen and as a human being. But, even more, as engineers you will be equipped with a power that ordinary citizens won't have. You will have the tools to imagine, design and build whatever society might need. This places on your shoulders a more intense moral responsibility to be aware of and attuned to the impact of your work.

"In this particular course, Circuits and Electronics, we're not going to spend the rest of the semester in debates over what is purposeful and what is not. But I want each one of you to be aware that the tools you will learn here make it possible for you to do good in the world or to do evil. I want you to commit to benefitting society. Get as broad an education about the human condition as this fine institution offers. Take your humanities courses seriously. Read newspapers or blogs or opinion pieces. Or, failing that, at least watch the news on TV, although much of that is now just overblown propaganda for one point of view or another. Learn to recognize where technology offers choices to society, and what those choices mean when measured against your ideas of what is purposeful. In other words, grow into true citizenship, but as an engineer-citizen, superbly responsible for his or her actions."

Martin paused long enough for a murmur of whispers, neighbor to neighbor, to begin to build across the lecture hall. He waited patiently for it to reach its peak and then subside back into silence before continuing. "Many of you were checking with your neighbor about what I just said. That's good. I want you to talk to each other, but, of course, not while I'm talking." Laughter. "I'm not a philosopher, but I do have a strong sense of what makes for good education. It's communication between people. When you," pointing to an auburn-haired woman in the third row, "can explain something to him," pointing to pony-tailed man seven rows back, "and he can then tell you, in his own words, what it means to him, you have not only helped him learn, at the same time, you have intensified your own understanding of the ideas you were talking about. Learning is, at its root, a social as well as an intellectual experience, a conversation. Face to face. Person to person.

"But," he went on, waving a finger, "this is not a license to copy someone else's work and turn it in as if it were your own. You are responsible for doing your own work. You can ask anyone for help. You can even look up the answer to a homework problem in a book, if you can find it. My only requirement is that you cite your sources." Martin wrote 'CITE YOUR SOURCES' on the white board, underlined. "If you get help from a friend, tell me which friend, and if you find the answer in a book, tell me which book."

Martin once again paused, waiting for the cadence of whispers to grow and then subside before continuing. "Okay, gang. Let's get to work. I'm sure you all expect to see a lot of facts about electric circuits, and you will. These circuits and their behavior create the infrastructure for our modern electronically-linked and computer-intensive society. But even more important, I want you to learn a methodology of problem solving. And since I expect you to cite your sources, I will now cite mine.

"George Polya, a mathematician at Princeton University, wrote a wonderful little book called *How to Solve It.*" Martin wrote Polya's name and the title of the book on the white board. "According to Polya there are three ways to solve a problem. The first…" Martin paused, assuming a Benny-esque pose, with one hand on his cheek, supporting the elbow with his other hand. "By far the best way," pausing again to tilt his head and look askance at the class, "is to know the answer." After a brief burst of laughter, the room went silent, but Martin held his pose as the silence again rippled into laughter, then quieted.

Martin relaxed his posture and said, "Yes. There is nothing so satisfying as knowing the answer to a problem. Failing that, the second-best way to solve a problem is to transform it into one for which you do know the answer." Silence.

"Let me give you an example. In physics you all learned about the vibration of a mass attached to a spring. You then analyzed the swinging of a pendulum, and you discovered that, at least for small-amplitude swings, the dynamical equations for the pendulum reduced to those of the spring-mass system that you had already solved. So it then became trivial to write down an expression for the period of the pendulum.

"We're going to be doing the same kind of thing here, but at increasingly sophisticated levels of complexity. I call it the method of solved cases. We're going to learn in exhaustive detail how to solve a few simple problems. After that, we will take more complex problems and cut them into pieces. Each piece corresponds to one or more of our solved cases, one for which we already know the answer. We then reconstitute the original problem, often writing down the final answer without having to do any actual solving. The methodology can be used everywhere, especially in programming, where you draw on subroutines and functions calls — the solved cases."

Martin paused again. "Any questions before we move on?"

The auburn-haired woman in the third row raised her hand, and Martin nodded to her. "I thought you said there were, like, three ways to solve a problem," she said. "What's the third?"

Martin grinned. "Thank you for asking," he said. "The answer is what Polya calls brute force." Another pause, punctuated with nervous laughter. "Yes. Really. Brute force. Write all the relevant equations and solve by whatever grungy method you can find. We will continually run into new cases where we can't do the partitioning into pieces, and this will lead us, perhaps by brute force, to a new class of solved cases we can then use for even more sophisticated problems. It's a never-ending process of knowledge and skill building, and once you get the hang of it, it's really fun.

"Now I have a question for you. How many of you know how to ride a bicycle?" After a puzzled silence, nearly every hand went up. "And when you learned to ride a bicycle, did you just read a book about it?" Bemused murmurs. "No, of course not. You had to get on a bicycle, feel what it's like when you are properly balanced and then train your muscle systems to find that balance without having to think about it. Riding a bicycle went from being an unsolved problem to a solved case. When you ride a bicycle, you might have to think about where you are going to turn, but not how to turn. The solved case of riding supports your higher-level action of deciding where to go.

"Along the same line, how many of you can play a musical instrument?" About a third of the hands went up. "And when you learned to play that instrument, did you just read a book about it? No, of course not. You had to suffer through the process of teaching your body to produce the sounds you wanted. Once you did that, though, you could play Bach, or acid rock if that's your taste. Making the sounds on the instrument became a solved case, one you could apply at a higher level to make real music.

"I think you get the point. When learning a new skill, you need to practice. Here in C&E, we are going to be teaching you a new skill: partition, solve, and reconstruct. To become proficient at this process, you will have to practice, practice, and practice. The homework sets will feel long, occasionally tedious, and eventually somewhat repetitive. But that's the point. Once you recognize that a problem is repetitive, you can jump for joy, because that problem has now become one of your personally owned solved cases. As we embark on this adventure, be aware that tedium might be a sign of success. When you can look at a new problem and just write down the answer, you will have arrived. We will start with the simplest solved cases on Thursday."

Martin thanked the class, the roomful of students applauded, and Martin smiled.

* **4** *

Martin's research group met every Tuesday at 1 PM. His seven graduate students, two post-docs and three undergrads, representing a mix
of genders, racial features, raggedness of hair and number of pierc-
ings, drifted in to the conference room and took seats around the long
rectangular table. It was a little United Nations. Khalil was Algerian;
Ahmed, Egyptian; Yu-Chong and Ming-Wu, Chinese; Byung,
Korean; Latisha, African-American; Arnold, Kevin, Michael, Evan
and Christina, Caucasian-American; and Natasha, a native Caucasian
from the Ukraine. Christina wore her usual uniform: a short skirt with
black panty-hose and a much-too-revealing tank top set off with bangle
earrings. Everyone else was dressed in shapeless clothes — standard
CTI grunge. It always puzzled Martin that the women students would
choose to dress as sloppily as the men. Only Christina dressed with any
flair, and she overdid it.

Martin stood at the head of the table with the white board behind
him, bearing a list in deep-blue marker entitled 'SMSC PAPERS.' The
list had three names: Khalil, Yu-Chong, and Christina. He rapped the
table briefly and started the meeting.

"Okay, gang. This will be a short meeting. First of all," handing
Kevin his thesis manuscript, "I've finished what I hope is your penulti-
mate draft. The things marked in red still need some attention. Let me
know if you can't understand my scrawl."

Kevin took the document and Martin continued. "The deadline for
the Semiconductor Materials Specialists Conference is a week from
Friday, the fifteenth. Since it's in Boston this year, we have to make a
good showing. I've gone over your draft abstracts, and I've decided

these three have the best shot at acceptance." He pointed to the list. "Khalil's is about done. Yu-Chong's is technically fine and just needs editing to clean up a bit of creative English." Yu-Chong smiled and looked down at his hands. Martin turned toward Christina and added, "Christina, we still need one more confirmation of the surface reconstruction correlated with the reflectivity." Christina nodded.

Martin continued, "The critic teams are Byung and Ahmed for Khalil's, and…"

Byung, a new Master's student, barged in. "But sir, you really think I can help? I barely know what the paper is about."

This was Byung's first time through the paper-submission process. Martin said, "It isn't a question of whether you can help, Byung. We always do this in teams. This is how you learn. You and Ahmed go over Khalil's paper with a microscope and help fix any problems — references, commas, whatever."

Martin paused for effect. "Natisha and La…" A chuckle and a pause. "Sorry," continuing syllable by syllable, "Na-Tash-A and La-Tish-A. That's a mouthful, isn't it?" Pointing, he said, "You two." Everybody laughed, including Martin. "You two work with Yu-Chong on his English. I'll help Christina. Any questions?" He waited the obligatory fifteen seconds. "Okay. We need to get this done right now, so let's cut this short. We'll pick up with the normal cycle of project reports next week."

As the room emptied, Martin beckoned Christina to stay. He asked, "Have you got a sample ready to go?"

"Yes, Professor," she said, a glow in her cheeks. "I've got three good samples, and I already did the scan on the first one. It looks really good."

"Great. Let's go see."

They went to Martin's laboratory, to the bench holding the atomic force microscope, a tool that can actually 'see' the arrangements of individual atoms on a surface. "See that sir?" asked Christina as she pointed to the video monitor. "The hexagonal arrays repeating across the probed field? Just like it should be?"

Martin studied the display. "This looks good. So do the optical measurements and the analysis. Bring the results to my office when you're done."

Martin returned to his office and once again worked on the White Paper. He was assembling the revised Purdue section when Christina knocked on the door and, mouse-like, opened the door, poking her head in.

"I got the data, Professor. Can we go over it now?"

Martin, without looking up from his computer, said, "Yes, grab a seat. Give me half a sec to finish this." He continued to work as Christina sat on the sofa. A few minutes later, he turned back to her. "Okay. Done. How did it turn out?"

Christina was wistful. "I'm not sure. There's a systematic difference between the model and the data, and I can't figure out why."

Martin got up from his desk, and wedged himself into the little sofa so that he and Christina sat hip to hip. "Let me look."

Christina put her papers and charts on the coffee table and leaned forward to point at the columns of figures, displaying more bosom than Martin thought appropriate. He wished he could find a way to tell her to dress more modestly, but failing that, he did what most other males might do. He snuck a peek. "This column is the measured reflectivity," said Christina, "and this one is the simulation. The shape is mostly right but there's a factor of 1.4 between the two results, and the baseline seems too slanted. Here. I've got the graphs."

After studying the results, Martin asked, "Did you run the standards before and after the reflectivity measurement?"

Christina raised her hand to her mouth, and blushed. "Oh, shit!" After an embarrassed pause, she continued. "Excuse me. Sorry, Professor. No, darn it. I guess I was rushing and I forgot. I used the standard from this morning's measurement. How stupid!"

Martin loved these gotcha moments right after a student's mistake. In his most professorial tone, he said, "When facing a deadline, we need to be swift but careful. Always careful. Do it over with the standards.

Then you'll have to repeat the simulations with the new values."

Christina, nearly teary, answered, "Yes, I know. I'll get on it."

Martin gave her a big smile. "Now don't worry. There's still plenty of time. I'll check in with you tomorrow." As Christina exited, Martin smiled to himself, happy with the thought that for the rest of her career, she would never forget to run the appropriate standards.

Martin glanced at his watch, turned to scan his e-mail and, finding no emergencies, went out to the east-side stairs and down two flights into the third floor of the connecting building, which housed, among many things, the newly-renovated Department Headquarters. Just inside, he greeted Rebecca, a thirty-something zaftig brunette with long and luxurious hair, the kind Martin would see in shampoo ads on television. She looked up from her desk with a grin and said, "Hi, Martin. Grab a coffee and rest your butt. He's got someone in there."

Martin grinned. He and Rebecca often joked about being in the same class, each joining CTI eleven years earlier. He was a frightened but outwardly cocky Assistant Professor, having been recruited by CTI after a three-year faculty stint at Carnegie Mellon. She was the junior assistant to Professor Fitzgerald, Associate Director of the Semiconductor Technology Laboratory. They enjoyed an occasional chat together, and when the occasion permitted, ribbed each other with feigned venom, except for that brief time some years ago, when, because of Martin's misbehavior, the venom directed his way wasn't feigned. Fitzgerald was now the STL Director, and Rebecca had worked her way up through the administrative assistant ranks to become the assistant to the Department Head and had added a wedding band to her jewelry.

He went into the kitchenette, selected a Sumatra K-cup for his coffee, brewed it, and took a chair in the waiting area near Rebecca's desk.

"Know what this is about?" he asked.

Rebecca smiled and shrugged. So Martin waited.

* **5** *

Morris Wong was the epitome of the second-generation American Dream. Born in Westchester County to immigrant parents who ran a successful fabric import business, he was educated at Fieldston and Yale, finishing with a PhD from Berkeley. At 3:20, he emerged from his inner office escorting a tall but very young man in a tee shirt, jeans and sneakers, set off with an ill-fitting blue blazer. They shook hands and the visitor exited the office area. Morris, in a subtly pinstriped gray suit with a white shirt and paisley tie, ran his fingers through his brilliant white hair shaped into what his colleagues (but only behind his back) called the Seiji Ozawa cut. He turned to Martin. "Sorry we ran over. Can you believe that the kid is worth 450 million? A dot-com plutocrat."

Martin got up and shook hands with Morris. "That's a lot of lettuce. I assume you're trying to eat some for him?"

"Of course," he answered. "He's thinking about funding a chair. Six mil, up front, is what I told him. The leeches in Development will work him over now, a named professorship and all that, with some good discretionary money as well. I think we'll get it. Anyway, c'mon in. I've got a job for you."

They entered Morris's office. Martin took a seat in one of two black leather chairs while Morris sat on the black leather sofa, a small walnut coffee table between them.

"Let me get right to business. I assume you've heard that Ken Fitzgerald has been asked by Obama to serve as co-chair of a new Technology Assessment Task Force."

Martin nodded. "Yeah, I'd heard."

"Well, because of that, he'll be in Washington a lot, so last week he asked me if he could get off the Personnel Committee. He specifically recommended that you be his replacement. In fact he insisted on it, and I agree. Unless you jump up and down and scream in protest, you should consider yourself appointed, effective today. The only requirement, besides the honest employment of your good judgment and absolute discretion, is that you hold Wednesday 3-5 PM open every week starting in three weeks. I think that's the twenty-seventh."

Martin's eyebrows shot up. Of course he wanted it. It was the only truly important committee in the department. The PC consisted of fifteen of the most senior and trusted members of the department, the first string. Martin had assumed it would be years before he got asked to serve. Faintly aware that he might be risking another yellow card from Jenny, he said, "Of course I'll do it, Morris. It will be an honor."

"I was hoping you would say that. By the way, we don't post the membership on the department website. It's not exactly confidential, but we don't advertise. Okay?" Martin nodded, and Morris continued. "Now for the more important part of the job. Kat Rodriguez is coming up for mandatory tenure review in the fall. With the Gillespie disaster looming, it's essential we get her through."

"The Gillespie disaster?" asked Martin. "What's that?"

"This is confidential, okay?" Martin nodded. "Your first bit of confidential PC business. Looks like Sharon Gillespie in Mechanical will be denied by her department. There's sure to be a big stink once it goes public — demonstrations, lawsuits, the works."

"But isn't she one of the best teachers at CTI? I mean, her January robotics contest gets national TV coverage. How could she be turned down?"

"It's a department decision, and I don't know their reasons. But, whatever the reason, we don't want to end up like that with Kat. With Ken suddenly gone, I must ask you to be Kat's Case Manager." Martin sat in stunned silence.

"Yes, I know this is kind of sudden, but it's what we need you to do. Get her through. No turndown by the Dean, no demonstrations, no lawsuits. Tenure. Please meet with her right away and get on it. Rebecca will give you a copy of her CV. We'll be starting those discussions on the twenty-seventh, but we'll hold off on discussing Kat until after spring break to give you a few extra weeks to get organized. Welcome aboard, and get busy."

Morris stood up, so Martin did as well. Still dazed, he accepted Morris's handshake and was ushered out of the office. Rebecca was waiting for him, holding forth a blue three-ring binder with his name prominently printed on the spine. "This is for you," she said. "It has the CVs for all the Assistant Professors plus I put in the old one I have for Professor Rodriguez. I don't have her update yet. Do you have a lockable file cabinet?"

Martin nodded. "So you knew about this?" he asked.

"Of course," she said, arching one eyebrow.

"Can I take it home? Looks like a lot of reading."

"Just don't lose it. Eventually, when we get letters on the cases, they will go in this notebook. Don't carry it around campus, and don't leave it lying on your desk. If it's not in your hands, it needs to be either in your house or in a locked drawer."

Martin floated out of Department Headquarters with the notebook securely tucked under his arm, feeling like he had just been asked to join the elite society of elders. Was this what Julian Kesselbaum had hinted at last week at lunch? If so, how did he know?

When he reached his office, he told Felice about his new appointment and the associated time constraint on Wednesday afternoons. He also asked her to set up a one-hour appointment with Professor Rodriguez, tomorrow if possible, in her office.

Then he forced himself back to that DARPA White Paper.

-    -   -

Just as he was loading his backpack to go home, the phone rang. Felice had already left, so he answered it himself. It was S. J. Chang. After the usual politenesses, Chang said, "I'm sorry, Professor Quint, but I cannot do review of Dr. Schultz paper."

"Is it because of the subject area, Professor Chang," asked Martin, "or something else?"

"Something else. Dr. Schultz has things in manuscript from my work three years ago. Is no citation."

"But," said Martin, "I thought he did refer to your work. That's how I got your name as a reviewer."

"Different paper. Schultz equations three and seven, he says he derived. Not true. I presented them at SMSC in 2009, and Dr. Schultz was at my talk. Is from my PhD."

"Well," said Martin, "is it possible that it's a simple error and could be easily corrected?"

"If he cite me for equations three and seven, paper has no original content."

"Ah," said Martin. "This sounds difficult. Listen, Professor Chang, I would very much like you to do the review and say in writing what you just said to me on the telephone."

"But he will know I am reviewer. SMSC paper is not in journal. Only conference paper. He is senior person. I am only Assistant Professor."

Martin paused before answering. "I see. Perhaps I do need to find another reviewer. Can you think of a more senior person who was also at that SMSC session? Perhaps I can do the review that way."

"Andersen at UCLA was there. And Cal Tech guy. Name begins with K, I think."

"Koppin. Is that it?"

"Yes, Koppin. Him."

"Thanks so much for your help, Professor Chang. But one important thing: please email me a copy of the 2009 paper. I want to see everything myself. I will not do anything that will allow Dr. Schultz to learn your identity. Thank you very much for bringing this to my attention."

Martin was perplexed. Schultz was a senior scientist at ChipsOnDemand.com, a competitor to the company Martin consulted for. He had a big reputation as an expert in advanced atomic deposition techniques for control of semiconductor structures. If what Chang said was true, and he had no reason to doubt it, then Martin would have to reject the paper. Chang was surely right about something else: when a junior person crosses a senior person, even in the nominally idealistic arena of science, the junior person might get squashed. Care was needed. He decided to send the manuscript to both Andersen and Koppin, but he would wait until he could look at Chang's paper.

- - -

Martin walked home as fast as the slush underfoot would permit — it was chamber music night. As he opened the door, he heard JJ in the kitchen asking, "What does Daddy really do all day?"

He heard Jenny laugh. "Well, he's a teacher like Miss Cornelia at your school, but he has lots of other things to do also. He works with grown-ups to discover completely new things."

"What kind of new things?"

"Why don't you ask him? I think I heard him come in."

Martin came into the kitchen and gave Jenny a quick kiss. JJ was stuffing mac and cheese into his mouth. After a big bite, he asked, "What new things do you discover?"

As he paused to collect his thoughts about how to explain semiconductor surface engineering to a four-year-old, it struck him that at places like CTI, you are what you do. Jenny was simultaneously a mom, an efficient homemaker, and a pretty successful interior designer. She managed to keep all three roles balanced and afloat, and was recognized in those various roles by her friends and colleagues. What was Martin? A teacher, a semiconductor expert, a husband and stepdad, a performing musician, a decent athlete, and an occasional helper at home, especially around JJ's bath and bedtime. But the title 'Professor' cast a long shadow over everything else, and it skewed his priorities as well.

Martin took a seat at the kitchen table. "Good question, little guy. Let me see if I can explain. Have you heard of atoms?"

"They're little, right?"

"Yes, little specks of stuff. Everything is made of lots and lots of atoms."

"Even me?"

"All of us. Everything. In the special stuff I work on, called semiconductors, most of the atoms are organized, like when you line up your toy soldiers in perfect rows. But the atoms at the ends of the rows, on the surfaces, they can get out of order and this ruins the semiconductor. My job is to tickle the atoms back into the best possible arrangement?"

"You tickle them? With your fingers?"

"Not our fingers. We use other atoms, and some heat. If you do it just right, the material works better for making computers and things like that."

JJ giggled. "I'm gonna tell Miss Cornelia about how atoms are ticklish. She won't believe me, but I'm gonna tell her anyway."

- - -

Twice a month, on the Tuesday evenings not otherwise taken up with Martin and Jenny going to hear the Boston Symphony, their living room became the music room. Tonight's group included his old Harvard roommate Horatio Billington, now a Professor of Linguistics at Boston University, his other roommate, Sumner Collingsworth III, who had become a successful investment counsellor, and Vladimir Tchernoff, a musicologist from CTI who played both violin and viola. Depending on the choice of music, other friends would be invited to join in, but tonight the agenda was the Brahms *Opus 114* trio for clarinet, cello and piano and the Menotti *Trio* for violin, clarinet and piano.

Horatio, who lived just three houses away, arrived first, with his cello case, a music stand, a portfolio of music, and two books, one brand new with a bright blue cover, the other, well-worn with a red and black cover. He handed them to Martin as he removed his slushy boots in the foyer. "Langacker finally came out with a more readable version of his *Cognitive Grammar*. Just published. You'll find it easier than the first one. I brought you my copy to look at, hot off the press."

"Oh, great," said Martin. "His stuff is so neat, but hard to read. What's this other one?"

Boots off, Horatio began setting up his stand in the living room. "When we were talking about your theory of education as conversation, it occurred to me that you needed to read this guy Clark, especially *Using Language*. He talks about what he calls signaling as an essential part of every conversation. It's like there are two things going on simultaneously — a set of signals between participants and then the actual content. It seems to overlap your idea of the social and intellectual components of teaching. Same basic concept with different words. I thought it might help you with your article."

"You're a hero, Roy. Thanks a lot. Can I keep them until our next session? And pick your brain once I've read some?"

"Sure, no problem," said Horatio, unpacking his cello. "We're doing one-fourteen tonight, isn't it?"

The doorbell rang. It was Vladimir and Sumner, who drove together from Brookline. Vladimir had a hand out into which Martin pressed the guest parking pass. Sumner entered, removed his shoes, and began assembling his clarinet as Vladimir returned from the car with his oversized violin-plus-viola case. Martin moved the floor lamps so that each player had good light. The musicians took their seats and warmed up, noodling through scales and arpeggios, and then asked Martin to sound an A on the piano for tuning.

Jenny came in, greeted everyone, and asked what they would be starting with. Hearing that it was the Brahms, one of her favorites, she stretched out on the sofa by the bay windows to listen. Vladimir, who didn't play in the Brahms, held the score and followed along, humming the themes *sotto voce*.

Playing music is not, as so many think, an escape *from* things. It's an act of exploration, an affirmation, a journey *into* a magical world, a world without DARPA deadlines or tenure committees or even freshman girls. It's a world in which the scrawls on a page, set down by Brahms more than a century ago, map a captive set of sounds that need to be liberated by the players, realized anew at each playing, breathing one more life into Brahms' vision.

Opus 114 was familiar and well-studied. Their first performance of it had been over twenty years ago in the Eliot House Junior Common Room after a Sunday noontime dinner. Tonight, they simply played it, end to end, to keep it fresh. Jenny thanked them for the lovely little concert and went up to her study. Attention shifted to their first run-through of the Menotti. The piece was challenging in spots, so it was hard work, following the usual steps that all chamber players must traverse: first, learn your own part, which each had done; second, learn how the other parts fit with yours; third, make it into music. Tonight, they were on step two. Vladimir swapped seats with Horatio, who, with score in hand, was an integral part of this process, catching errors, explaining, and coaching.

After making as much progress on the Menotti as a first playing would permit, Martin got out beer and snacks. The four friends sat around the Queen Anne, discussing the program for their next concert. It was scheduled for the end of April in the CTI Little Theater, so named not for its size but for a man, Peter Little, although it was little, seating only one hundred and twenty. The Menotti was too new to the group for an April concert, so Vladimir proposed that they do one of the Beethoven string trios, perhaps the *Archduke*, which they had already reasonably well in hand, with maybe one or two of the Bruch *Trios* to complement the Brahms. They agreed not to decide yet, and called it a night.

When they left, Martin took Horatio's two books to the study, paging quickly through Clark, tantalized. He thought about signals, reminded of how Jenny used all kinds of signals.

-    -   -

Some men enjoy pornography. Not Julian Kesselbaum. He got his late-night jollies looking inside other people's hard drives. Just about the time that Horatio, Sumner, and Vladimir were saying their goodbyes, Julian was hunched over one of the six computers in his North Cambridge condo, assembling the final details of what he expected would be a new untraceable route into CTI's computer network.

The son of a Stanford computer science professor, he had hacked into his father's machine at age eleven and was the only kid in middle school who knew exactly how much money his father made. By the time he reached high school, the Arpanet had become the internet, and he had invaded all of his schoolmates' home computers. Then, with aid of a well-constructed bogus web link, he breached the entire computer system of the Palo Alto Department of Education.

Julian was careful not to destroy anything. His obsession, which was what it had become by the time he entered Stanford as a sixteen-year-old freshman, was just to read other people's emails, diaries, finances and browsing histories. He gravitated to the on-campus hacker community, sharing some of his tricks and learning many more in the process. When he applied to the CTI PhD program in Computer Science, his application demonstrated such deep insights into computer security that he was offered a fellowship.

He did his PhD thesis on the problem of phishing — hooking people with phony emails and web pages, a technique at which he was already quite expert. His doctoral research was on why it works; why even computer-savvy users fall victim to phony emails and phony web pages. He did a study with volunteers and learned that neither gender, age, educational level nor number of years of computer experience had any bearing on the probability that a particular phishing attack would succeed. A well-disguised web page or email would hook even the experts.

CTI hired him onto the EECS faculty after his PhD with the hope that he would build on that thesis work in some important way. Now in charge of a classroom, he discovered that he could, for the first time in his life, engage with people instead of just computers, albeit from a superior position. He was the authority, the source, and people wanted to hear from him. His efforts on behalf of 'safe-sex' computer use were legion. He not only taught the graduate internet security course, he offered seminars for undergraduates, for staff members, even for the coaches in the athletic department. He proselytized on how to protect logon IDs, passwords, virus prevention, warning signs when a computer is infected, and how to detect and remove spyware and malware. Even the CTI computer-system managers would consult him on security problems. He loved it, but it didn't earn him tenure. In January of 2011, he learned from Morris Wong that he would not be offered a permanent appointment.

Most people would be crushed and angry by a denial of tenure. Julian was angry, for sure, but not crushed. He started a consulting business in an office above The Crustacean, a cutesy restaurant in an office block up Mass Ave toward Central Square, and the CTI Information Technology people immediately put him on retainer at the level of a second-in-command. To bring in more business, he mounted a blog, BiteTheBot.com, which gradually gathered readership, landing him three local banks as clients. From there, while he didn't exactly prosper, he certainly could afford to live and eat in modest comfort. To satisfy his compulsion to teach, he took Adjunct positions at UMass-Boston, UMass-Lowell and Bunker Hill Community College for twelve hours a week of in-class instruction on how the internet worked, web pages and their discontents, and how to avoid the most common intrusions.

Tonight's goal was to see if he could use his private botnet, a network of twenty-eight hundred already-infected machines located mostly in Romania and Bulgaria, to set up an untraceable bogus account at CTI. He sent the instructions to the botnet and after only a few thousand tries, ten minutes worth, wormed his way into the CTI Computer Accounts server, creating a new account with logon ID mark.felt, chuckling as he did so. With that success in hand, he created six more accounts, each with a clever alias, and like the acorn woodpecker of his native California, he stored them up.

The plan, at least for now, was to wait, testing whether anyone at CTI would discover the intrusion. If it was discovered, he was ready with an instant solution, building his reputation as a security wizard. If not, he had a new set of platforms from which to work his way around the CTI network on the sly. It was, in his view of the world, win-win.

* **6** *

CTI's student newspaper, *The Widgit*, comes out on Wednesday mornings. Martin usually picked up a copy to scan for that occasional item worthy of a read. This morning there was a short opinion piece by the Associate Editor.

CTI SHOULD OFFER CREDIT FOR MOOCS
by Emmanuel Encarnacion

The recent explosion of MOOCs (Massive Open Online Courses) offered by Stanford, CTI, Harvard, and elsewhere creates new opportunities for education everywhere in the world. Everywhere, that is, except at the colleges and universities that are creating these courses.

Last semester, 120,000 students from around the world signed up for the online version of Circuits and Electronics offered by the Free Internet Education (FIE) consortium. According to Professor Hoo-Min Huang, who led the course, more than 7,000 students completed it, most of them earning passing grades entitling them to a certificate of completion. Among those 7,000, according to Ahmed Masouf, head TA for the MOOC, thirty-five were CTI students. Among those thirty-five, more than twenty, as Mr. Masouf put it, "aced the class."

At this point, these students are not entitled to any credit or modification of their degree programs because of the successful completion of the FIE C&E. We think it is time for the Educational Policy Committee to explore this issue and find ways for our students, who clearly can learn from either the MOOC version or the regular in-class version taught by Professor Quint, to get proper credit for completion.

Martin put down the paper, lit up his email, and sent a query to Morris asking whether there was any push within the administration to give CTI credit for MOOCs. He also sent a note to Hoo-Min asking to discuss the issue over lunch. Before getting to work on DARPA, he scanned the fifty or sixty new emails that flooded into his inbox daily, looking for those few that actually needed replies. One, from Carl Urquhart at Southampton University in England, caught his eye:

> From: c.urquhart@soton.ac.uk
> Subject: Plenary Invitation to ESM 2013
>
> Dear Professor Quint:
> As you know, the European Workshop on Semiconductor Materials (ESM) will be held in Istanbul, July 21-24, 2013. The Program Committee would like to extend to you our invitation to be the Plenary Speaker at the opening session, a 45-minute address on a topic of your choice.

The message continued with details about expenses, the length of the abstract that would be needed, and a request for a quick reply because the official call for papers would go out soon. Martin's response was immediate:

> Carl - Very interested in (and honored by) your very kind invitation. Need to check with my wife and clear out any calendar conflicts. Istanbul is on my bucket list, so I'm hoping I can accept. Any chance for a side trip to Troy as part of the conference? And is it raining in Southampton, as usual? Will your football team be able to dodge relegation? Looks dicey. - Martin

By this time, Hoo-Min Huang had replied:

> Martin - It's pretty clear that CTI is going to have to bite this bullet, especially since the good students really do learn the stuff. We need a way of waiving the C&E requirement if MOOC students pass a suitable test or something like that. Lunch today at noon is good. See you then. /Harry

Felice knocked and brought in a note saying she had set an appointment with Professor Rodriguez at three, so before getting back to the DARPA White Paper, he got the PC notebook from the locked file and paged through until he got to Kat's CV. In spite of the many hours he had spent with her in the six years since she joined CTI, helping her with classroom technique and with the grant game, he had never really studied her CV with an eye to faculty promotion. Ken Fitzgerald had been her official faculty mentor and the Case Manager for her first promotion, the one to non-tenured Associate.

He already knew the basics: undergrad in EE at Merida, PhD with Andris at UCLA. The research record, though, proved to be a bit thin: two journal papers out to date, two in review; one PhD graduated, another about to finish and two others in progress; a half-dozen conference papers; only five invited talks at various conferences and universities; and one patent application. He wondered where she would rank among the other tenure candidates. In a few hours, he would know much more.

— - -

"I'm kind of surprised you turned the Dean down last spring," said Harry, seated across from Martin in the faculty lunchroom. "So was he. Figured this was right up your alley, legendary lecturer and all that."

Martin drew a long breath. "I guess I'm old-fashioned. I may only be forty-two, but sometimes around here, I feel like I'm seventy-two. All this emphasis on using computers to do what humans do much better. I'm a person-to-person type teacher, face to face. I can feel my students' reactions and adjust in real time. No way that's going to happen over the internet."

"It's true, I guess," said Harry. "Student interaction is actually our biggest challenge. I spent all last summer writing programs to generate and grade homework problems, and most of the fall making up test problems as well as taping the lectures. There wasn't much time available to worry about student interaction, but we got through it okay, and quite a few students did really well."

"How did Ahmed do?" asked Martin. "I'm still sort of pissed off that you stole him. I had to scramble like a maniac to find an acceptable head TA."

"Sorry. He was terrific. Managed all the online student forums. I know that losing him was tough for you, but he came to me, you know, not the other way around. So, technically, I didn't steal him."

"True enough. He said he wanted experience with online teaching before he returns to Cairo, which is smart. Online stuff probably provides something useful for the less-developed world. Anyway, what does 'quite a few' mean? And 'really well?'"

"Like it said in *The Widgit*, we had a bit over a hundred and twenty thousand students, about seven thousand finished and most of them qualified for a passing certificate. About eighty of them absolutely aced it. Got almost everything perfect. What I want to do for the spring is improve the student interaction, and that's where I want your help. Not just me. The FIE people too."

"How did the program get that silly name?" asked Martin.

"FIE? Stands for Free Internet Education," said Harry.

"Sounds like a Falstaff belch. Fie on't." Martin chuckled at his own joke, then grew silent, iron-faced. "You know what pisses me off about FIE and its claim of free online education?" asked Martin.

"No, what?"

"Nothing is free. To the Dean and Morris you're something of a hero for stepping up, and I guess they think of me as a cantankerous old goat for saying no. But there are real costs. I assume your research was put on hold while you prepared the MOOC, yes?" Harry nodded. "That's a huge cost, a personal cost to you and to your students. And while you're doing the MOOC, you're not available to teach in the classroom, which shifts all those responsibilities to the rest of us."

Harry started to speak, but Martin waved him off. "I'm not blaming you. It's really Prendergast and Ricci and the Deans pushing this. But it is a cost. And it's not your fault you need help with student interaction, which is the most critical thing in education. There's no real-time conversation between teachers and students. Unless you're using personal interactive video like a Skype call, the communication is fucked up. It's either one way, via video, or faceless, using text. Either way, the intellectual engagement is lacking. Canned lectures are just that: canned. Technology for canning lectures has been around since movies were invented, and, lo and behold, people still need live teachers." Martin paused, then added, "Sorry for the speech. I get wound up. What is it you want me to do?"

Harry stifled a laugh, "I was expecting a speech. Once your motor starts, everybody stands back."

"Touché. It's true." Martin smiled. "Bad habit, getting on my hobby horse. Anyway, what's the drill? What can I do?"

"I would like you to go to the FIE website and sign up for C&E. Take a look at what we're doing. Once you see what we have, you'll probably be boiling over with ideas."

Martin cackled. "I gotta hand it to you, Harry. You've got the biggest brass balls around, even bigger than the Dean's. You know I hate the idea of these MOOCs, and here you are asking for help. And you're so goddam nice about it. Of course I'll help you if I can. But just to be clear, it's to help you, not because I have much faith in the online thing. I think it's a lousy way to do quality education."

"Maybe so," said Harry. "We'll only know if we try, and try hard."

-   -   -

When Martin returned to his office, he set up a Gmail account in the name of Quincy P. Martin. He then logged onto the FIE website and registered Quincy Martin for C&E, muttering to himself, "Time to see what the enemy is doing."

He found in his email the final tardy materials for his DARPA White Paper, but before he got to work assembling all the various parts into a single draft, he sent off an email to Emmanuel Encarnacion at *The Widgit*, inviting him to set up a meeting sometime next week to discuss MOOCs.

Martin was making decent progress on the White Paper when he was interrupted by a knock on his office door. It was Christina.

"I finally got everything to work right," she said. "Can you look at it now?" Once again, they sat hip to hip on the sofa with the data spread out on the coffee table. Once again, Christina over-displayed her endowments as she leaned forward and, once again, Martin noticed with a mix of silent disapproval and equally silent glimpsing.

This time, the match between their model and the data was excellent. Martin was delighted and raised his hand for a high five, saying, "Look's like you've got it. Good job."

Christina blushed, raised her hand for a gentle high-five smack. "So what now? Is the abstract okay?"

"You need to do an edit to include the fact that we have this additional confirmation, but, fortunately, none of the conclusions need changing. Give it a try and email it to me. I may not get to it tonight, but we have plenty of time to finish before the deadline. Good job."

Christina left and Martin, with a glance at his watch, turned back to the DARPA proposal for the thirty minutes remaining before his meeting with Kat.

* 7 *

Katarina Rodriguez was waiting for Martin, wondering about this no-explanation-offered 3 PM meeting. Since they often crossed paths at lunch, official meetings like this were rare. Something was up. But what? A new call for research grants? A student complaint? Maybe an invitation to join the Program Committee for the Electronic Materials Conference? Regardless, today she had some good news to share. The National Science Foundation had just sent her confirmation of a three-year grant, enough to support one more student. Now she had to find the student. By the start of the spring term, most of the PhD students, and certainly the best ones, had already been snapped up and given Research Assistantships. Still, there were always students on Fellowships and TAs who would be shopping, and she was hopeful that Martin would have some suggestions. At worst, she might have to wait for the new crop of fall admits.

As she waited, she thought back to the many ways Martin had helped her along in her career, especially with her teaching. By the time she joined CTI, she spoke excellent English with only a light Mexican accent. In her first semester, she was assigned to teach recitation sections in C&E, with Martin as lecturer. She knew the subject matter well enough, but she would be so nervous that she would run to the ladies room to throw up before class.

Martin was her department-assigned teaching buddy, someone she could ask for help. Kat remembered sitting on the sofa in Martin's office, blushing enough to redden her light brown skin, saying, "I have a class full of the smartest kids on the planet, and I'm somehow supposed to be teaching them. I get so nervous, I not only lose my lunch before class, I lose track of what I'm doing. And I'm sure half the class knows more than I do."

He had smiled, saying that she knew plenty and chuckled that it had taken a full year after he started teaching for his nerves to settle down. He asked, "But didn't you ever do a TA at UCLA?"

"No, I had family support for the first year and then an RA after that. Professor Andersen didn't want me teaching. Said it would slow me down too much."

"Ah, yes, that's how Andris would think," said Martin. "I make all my grad students teach at least one term. It's good for them. It would've been good for you. But, hey, I've got an idea. Why don't you develop a fake case of laryngitis and I'll teach your Friday sections. You can sit in and we can talk afterwards."

It was mesmerizing. In the first section, Martin started by asking if the students had any questions. He waited through the nervous silence until one student finally volunteered a question. He wrote it on the board, saying, "I want to collect as many questions as possible before we start. Then I'll design a path through them that covers the material. So please, more questions."

After collecting a short list, he assigned numbers to them, picking an order that corresponded to the material he wanted covered in that section, and then invented examples to address each one in turn. The classroom sparkled. In the second section, he repeated the procedure, got a completely different set of questions, but was nevertheless able to construct a sequence, with examples, that once again covered the required material. To Kat, it was stunning.

Kat and Martin had gone to the faculty lunchroom after the second class. "How do you do that?" asked Kat, as she nibbled on her tiny portions from the buffet table. "Make up examples, like that, I mean, on the spot. I've been planning everything out before hand, and then I get flustered and it doesn't work."

"I wanted to give you a target to shoot at," said Martin. "I know it takes a lot of brass to lead a class that way, making up everything on the fly, but I've done this for long enough, I can just do it. The real point is that from the students' point of view, it's their questions that are driving the class. That gets them engaged. They talk. They think. They lose their shyness about asking, so they learn better."

Martin had then launched into what she would later learn was a stock speech: a discourse on the two components of education, intellectual and social. How the social part was a conversation, and that effective education not only required the conversation, it required that the conversation be two-way, even if the students were simply nodding from time to time. When illustrating a circuit, for example, draw it by hand so the students' empathetic motor systems would be engaged. Go for eye contact. Face to face. Get the students talking. Do that, and things would improve.

It had taken time, but she followed his advice, got her students talking, and things did improve. She was now comfortable in front of a class. But the teaching struggle had accrued other costs. Her research goal, a novel and bold idea, was to use quantum interference of atomic beams to deposit special impurity patterns in semiconductors that, if her theory was right, would improve transistor speed. But progress to date had been slow, and her tenure clock, like the clock on her wall while she waited for Martin, was ticking.

Martin finally arrived, ten minutes late. "Sorry for the delay. How's things?"

"Good news," said Kat. "The NSF came through yesterday. One student, three years. So I'm hoping you can help me find a student. Any ideas?"

"Wow! Congrats. Getting anything out of NSF these days is something of a miracle. Is this for the quantum interference demonstration?"

"Yes," she answered. "Both the new atomic-beam source, the experimental proof of principle, and the modeling. I guess that's three things, not two. But, anyway, it's pretty exciting."

"Great news," Martin beamed. Without missing a beat or suggesting any students, he continued. "Did Felice tell you why I wanted this meeting?"

"Not a word. What's up?"

"Ken Fitzgerald is off to Washington, at least part time, and Morris asked me to replace him on the Personnel Committee. He wants me to be the Case Manager for your tenure. So it's time for me to get even more inside your skin, if that's possible, and just so you know, I'm one hundred and thirty percent committed to success."

Martin paused to give Kat a chance to digest the news. She sat mute, expressionless. "I thought we could start today with a review of your CV just to see where things stand. Sound okay?"

"But," said Kat in anemic protest, "it's not up to date. Rebecca asked me for it, but I haven't had time."

"No problem. I have a copy of the one you put in last February, and I'll take notes."

"Okay, I guess so." Kat went to her computer and opened the file containing the CV. "Where do we start?"

"Did Ken give you the speech when you went up for Associate? The one about excellence and impact?"

"Yes, but he wasn't really convincing. All that stuff about how the numbers don't count as much as the impact. No matter what he said, I don't have enough journal papers, and I don't have enough money to do things right, so everything is going slow. The NSF will help, but the whole thing makes me nervous."

"Well, I'm new to this, but extrapolating from what Ken did when he managed my tenure case, I think the first thing is for me to get familiar with each student's project, one by one. Once I have that, we can think about what's next. You have, what, four students? Three for PhD?"

"It's five now. I took on a new Master's student. Leah Wiesenthal is writing her PhD thesis and will finish this term. She's really good. Nice demonstration of atomic-beam interference, and the depositions seem to be working. Very careful experiments and a good model for the strength of the effect. She's interviewing at Rutgers and Purdue for faculty positions so far, and she's also on the post-doc job market just in case. The others won't finish for another year, so the best I can hope for is two complete by the fall, Leah, and Frank Carillo, who finished last June. He went to COD to work for Wolfgang Schultz. Something in process technology development."

"Is there a journal paper on Carillo's work?"

"Oh, yes. We submitted two to *JSMT* in September. One is already revised and in second review. The other I'm still waiting on."

"And is Leah's stuff published?" asked Martin.

"She's given papers at each of the last two Quantum Materials Conferences — one of those should be on the CV you have — but right now, she has to get her thesis done. And I already know what you're going to say. Journal papers are important. They are. But so is finishing up her doctorate."

The rest of the hour was spent on Kat's itemization and description of her five students' projects, the technical goals, the accomplishments to date, the conference papers that had resulted, and the prospect of getting refereed journal papers out. By the end, she was a bundle of nerves.

Martin asked his final question: "I notice you only have five invited lectures, at least as of last February. Are there more? Any plans?"

Kat sagged. "No," she said. "And no plans."

"You look a bit wiped out. We'll continue this another time, but I'm going to recommend you get yourself on the lecture circuit. Let's have lunch next Wednesday after your class and talk about it. Maybe I can explain the strategy better when you're not so tired." Kat nodded. Martin got up and left, and Kat put her head on her desk and wept.

Later that afternoon, she got an email from Martin.

```
Kat -- Sorry if I wore you out this afternoon. This
Case Manager thing is new to me. Anyway, I've had
an idea of something you could do before lunch next
Wednesday. Make a list of the top ten people in your
field, world-wide, regardless of age and regard-
less of university or industry (or even government)
```

affiliation. It will help us figure out a strategy for
the coming months - for the lecture circuit, I mean.
Congrats on the NSF! Good show. -- Martin

My God, she thought. They want the top ten people in the world?
To ask for letters? They don't know about my stuff. They'll eat me alive.

* **8** *

One of the reasons Martin preferred to walk between his home and CTI was the chance to muse on whatever came to mind. As long as he remembered to keep his head up and stop at crosswalks, he could ponder anything his whimsy served up. Sometimes it was a remark he heard, sometimes a new idea for research, sometimes whether he really wanted to have a child with Jenny. They were already at occasional dagger points over the amount of time he spent working, and adding a child to the mix would be a huge perturbation. Today, though, as he ambled north, he drifted away from Jenny and babies to relive his own promotion cases.

His tenure case was only moderately stressful because he had made a huge splash internationally and everybody knew it, and the promotion to Full Professor last year had been a breeze. But that first promotion, from Assistant to non-tenured Associate, that one had been ugly. While he had invented what looked like a promising method of treating the surfaces of compound semiconductors to improve the performance of certain kinds of laser chips, he had been unable to get it to work consistently. He had reported the method in two well-received conference presentations and had filed several patent applications, but not only had he and his students faced problems with the experiments, no one else had managed to reproduce his results. The only journal publications he had on the books were based on his PhD thesis, and his conference papers, normally the bread and butter of an Associate case, were in short supply. Fortunately, he had already made a hit within CTI as a brilliant classroom teacher, taking over the lectures of C&E under emergency conditions and growing its enrollment. But more important, perhaps, Ken Fitzgerald had seen his lab results in person and was prepared to push hard for Martin, even with a thin CV. He was consumed by nervousness that year, nervousness that led to poor eating and to more drinks than were advisable.

It wasn't just his academic record. His whole life was fucked up. The house he had bought, even with mortgage assistance from CTI, drained his finances, and with the pressures of making good on his promotion, he couldn't do enough outside consulting to keep the coffers full. Nor could he spend enough time at home. His wife, Katie, was sliding into her third bout of serious depression, soaking up what money they had on psychiatrist visits. He had drifted into that affair with Camille, which then blew sky high. He came home from a conference in Chicago to find Katie gone and "FUCK YOU MARTIN" written in bright red lipstick on every available surface. The divorce hit just as the department was going out for letters, and Katie's lawyer kept the flames burning throughout the fall. By the time he heard from Fitzgerald that his promotion had made it through, he had lost twenty pounds and was having occasional three-day bouts of diarrhea, tentatively diagnosed as irritable bowel syndrome aggravated by stress.

The only bright spot in the divorce mess was that his lawyer was able to convince the judge, over Katie's objections, to accept his proposal for partitioning of assets. Martin would buy out Katie's share of the house with ten years of $3000 per month alimony payments and grant her half of his accrued pension rights.

That amount, $3000 per month, was a huge chunk of his take-home pay, but with the promotion in hand and free of a depressed wife, he gradually pulled himself together. He created and kept to a miserly budget, became a functional if not exquisite cook, cleaned his house once a week, ironed his own shirts, gave up alcohol, started regular exercise at the CTI athletic center, gradually calmed his irritable bowel, and, best of all, figured out what had been wrong with their attempts to make the surface modification work. Within one year, he had confirmed a real breakthrough and become famous in the semiconductor materials world. Three companies took out licenses on the technology and one of them, Semiconductor Tools Corporation, hired him as a regular consultant. He could ease off on the penury. He put his inventor's share of CTI's patent royalties into a separate account, planning eventually to buy out Katie's remaining alimony rights with a lump sum. He resumed moderate consumption of alcohol. He bought a treadmill and a decent Schimmel upright piano, one with excellent key action and a graceful sound. He unpacked his music and began practicing *The English Suites,* not every night, but often. As he liked to tell himself, "Just thirty minutes of Bach is better than any therapy imaginable." He told Sumner and Horatio that it was finally time to reconvene their trio and make some music.

The one thing he didn't do was date. Not until that ski trip where he met Jenny, perhaps the best thing that had ever happened to him. When he arrived home, he was flushed with gratitude for her being there, in his life, as his partner. Best of all, he told her so, with a big hug and kiss.

- - -

Kat lived in the lower floor of a Brookline two-family, with off-street parking, a detail she would occasionally mention to Martin in jest. But there was no jesting now. On the way home that evening, she stopped at the market and picked up a small roasting chicken, some poblanos and several onions. She mixed yogurt, garlic, cilantro, canned chipotle peppers and some chili powder to make a paste, pressed part of it under the chicken's skin, put the remainder on the outside, coated the onions and poblanos in oil, salted them, and put everything in the oven to roast. While it was cooking, with the aromas permeating the apartment, first of the onion, then the poblanos, and finally the chicken, she got onto Skype to talk to her mother. She needed some encouragement. But instead of her mother, it was her uncle Alejandro at her home taking the call, saying he was about to call her. The news wasn't good. Anita, he said, had found a lump in her right breast and was having a mastectomy and possibly more extensive surgery depending on what the surgeon found. Alejandro looked drawn on the tiny Skype screen, and his voice was subdued. Kat promised to call again every day until her mother was home again.

The comfort she had hoped to get from the chipotle-roasted chicken proved elusive. Yes, it tasted good, and, yes, she did eat at least a little, but her mind kept racing around the fact of her mother's illness. What if this was it? Would her mother die? Could she even think about staying at CTI if her mother needed her?

Furthermore, Martin's visit had rubbed her nose in her own loneliness. Before he joined the PC and became one of her judges, he had been her buddy, the only male member of the faculty with whom she could really talk about her hopes, her ever-present fears of failure, and her observation, made wistfully over coffee one day, that there must be a lot of unhappy marriages at CTI. Unlike in graduate school, where there was a natural cadre of friends, at least acquaintances with whom one could go through the forms of friendship, at CTI she was adrift. Put simply, her colleagues were not her friends. Several of her male counterparts found her attractive, and said so, but most of them had wives. The two brief affairs she had, one with a divorcee and one with an about-to-be, didn't develop into anything worth crowing about.

CTI had only a smattering of women faculty, and most of them were as driven and self-centered as the men. The one bright spot was Amanda Finley, who taught Spanish literature. They met through a Provost's Committee on Women at CTI to which Kat got appointed in her second year. With Amanda she could talk. About everything, including Kat's penchant for taking up with unsuitable men. Amanda didn't take up with men. She had other preferences.

Kat picked up the phone and called her, just to talk.

- - -

Martin and Jenny were getting undressed at bedtime. "How's the new project?" he asked.

"We had a really good meeting today. It was just my client and the general contractor, the guy who's doing her kitchen and bathroom rehabs. I have the rest of the house: four bedrooms, front and back parlors, study, sunroom, dining room. She liked my drawings and now wants a preliminary concept. Deadline is in two weeks. Then we get down to the business of selection — basic décor for each room, wall coverings, floors, furniture, the works. She's serious about a New York shopping trip."

"Wow. Can you get the basics done in two weeks? That's awful quick."

"That depends in part on you, my darling," said with a hint of lemony tartness. "It really helps when you get home by five-thirty like tonight instead of at seven. And if you could cook once in a while…"

"Hey! Slow down. I've got my own messy deadline. A week from Friday — the big DARPA grant. Once that's in, I'll cook, clean and sew, and keep JJ entertained all that next weekend. Will that help?"

Jenny brightened. "Yes. It'll help a lot. And could we maybe split JJ this weekend? One day for each of us?"

"Sure. Will do. Now I've got some news." Martin came up behind Jenny, who was in her underwear. He unclasped her bra, which fell off her shoulders as he reached around to hug her, one hand cupping each breast. "I got an invitation to give the plenary at the ESM meeting in Istanbul in July. Want to go to Turkey? All of us? Probably a one-week trip, or maybe longer if we want to do some touring. I want to go to Troy, at least."

Jenny leaned back to enjoy the embrace. "Yikes. If I'm not pregnant by then it might be fun."

"So can I accept the invitation? They need to send out the call for papers pretty soon."

Jenny freed herself and turned to face Martin. "Could I cancel if I'm too pregnant to travel? I mean, with everything we've been through…"

"I'm sure we can manage."

"Then, okay, go ahead and accept. It might be fun. A real adventure."

"And there's more." Jenny looked up, eyebrows arched. "I forgot to tell you yesterday, what with getting ready for our rehearsal. Morris has put me on the Personnel Committee."

"You mean the tenure committee? So soon? I thought that was just for graybeards."

"It is. Apparently now I am one."

"So am I supposed to say congratulations?"

"Absolutely. It's the only committee worth serving on. I'm just, I don't know, I feel so pumped. We start reviewing promotions in a couple of weeks and he put me in charge of Kat Rodriguez's case."

"Martin, Martin, Martin. Sometimes you just baffle me. I'm glad that Morris wants you for such an important job. It's a wonderful compliment. But why should you even think about taking on more stuff with all the stress you have? What if I get pregnant again? You might need to pick up more of the home jobs."

"Don't get started on the stress thing. I really want to do this right, and I can handle it."

"Okay, so you say. But I hardly see enough of you as it is. This has to make it worse."

"I don't think so. They meet every Wednesday afternoon. I'll have stuff to read, of course, but Wednesday's the only time commitment."

Jenny sighed. "Okay, I give up. You just can't say no. Maybe you'll be worn out enough from the meetings to come home right after."

Martin wrapped Jenny into his arms. "It's a promise. Scout's honor. Home right after, every Wednesday. You have any interest in a shower tonight?"

* **9** *

Martin's Thursday lecture in C&E, the first one with serious technical content, was well-received, and his section instructors and TAs had no problems to report at the staff meeting. He wrote the Abstract for his Istanbul lecture and attached it to an email to Carl Urquhart, accepting the invitation and asking once again about the chance of visiting Troy. On Friday, he received reviewer reports on two papers he had submitted to *JSMT*, one with Khalil and one with Natasha. Both reviews were positive, with only minor revision required before publication. On Saturday, a bright but cold day, he took JJ ice skating on the Frog Pond at the Boston Common and then went across Tremont Street to McDonalds for lunch, where JJ could stuff his face with fries. That afternoon, with Jenny in charge of JJ, Martin finished and sent to his co-investigators the draft text for the White Paper, now with only the budget section remaining. His reward was a serious plunge into Clark, thrilled to discover his analysis of conversations as having two simultaneous threads, content and signals. It mapped perfectly onto his notion of the two components of education: intellectual and social. On Sunday, he gave Jenny a whole day for her project, taking JJ to the Children's Museum and bringing Chinese take-out for dinner. On Monday, Khalil's and Yu-Chong's SMSC abstracts were finished and submitted, with only Christina's to go, giving him the rest of the week for finishing the White Paper budgets and whatever final corrections his colleagues sent him. A normal week.

-    -   -

Martin got up early on Wednesday and headed to CTI. Christina's redraft of the SMSC abstract was in his email. He checked it over, made two small tweaks, and sent it on to the conference, turning again to the DARPA budget. Each university has its own rules on how to figure the indirect costs, the part of a research grant that pays the university for keeping the lights on, the building in repair, and the accounting system fully functional. Reconciling seven budgets from three universities into one coherent whole required quiet, concentration, and meticulous attention to detail. He was making decent progress when his computer beeped with a reminder to go to lunch with Kat.

At the faculty lunch room, Martin went through the buffet line and picked out a table for two in the one quiet corner. As he waited, he thought back to how Ken had handled his own tenure case. He had already become familiar with the details of Martin's work while managing his Associate promotion, so he needed only a brief update on student progress, new projects, and publications. Maybe it was Ken's confidence that Martin's tenure was assured, but when it came to the letter writers, Ken was pretty casual, just asking Martin for a list of ten outside names and five inside names to serve as references. No strategizing. No concerns about a speaking tour. According to Ken, Morris would pick some names from Martin's list and some not on the list. Trust the process. Excellence and impact. However, given Martin's worry about Kat's situation, he felt he needed to be more structured and strategic. He had a plan.

Martin waved to Kat coming out of the lunch line. As she sat down he asked, "So how was class?"

"Pretty good, considering." She was not smiling. "I've got twenty-four students this term, so six lab teams. Should be okay. I got a lot of good questions today. They seem awake." Suddenly more subdued, she said, "And I made your list, but I have a question."

Martin looked up, waiting as Kat paused. "Is this list the people that you will write to for tenure? I don't even know all of them. Last time, for the Associate, Ken asked me to put in my own list. Nothing about the top ten."

"You're right. You will create your own list, but later. In a month or so. I will turn it in on your behalf. But tenure is a do-or-die thing. Morris will be picking the letter writers, and some of them will not be on your list. That's always the way it works. But when he picks somebody who isn't on your list, chances are it will be from the top ten. I want to use the top ten to scope out your field. Get you visible to as many of the world leaders as possible before letter-writing time. We've got six months before the requests go out."

"Do I send them publications and stuff?"

"No, don't do that. Getting an unsolicited package from a junior faculty person screams 'I'm up for tenure.' The one thing Ken told me was not to alert prospective letter writers. Better to do what he called proactive inviting."

"What's that?"

"We pick out the people you need to visit. You write to the prof and say something like, 'I'm going to be in your area on such and such a date, and I'm wondering if you would let me visit your lab and see your work.' Ninety-percent of the time you get a yes and you also get an invitation to give an informal seminar to the prof's group. Bingo. That person now knows of you and knows you're up for tenure. It isn't as tacky as sending a pack of stuff."

"But I'm not sure how much traveling I'll be able to do, because…" Tears trickled down her cheeks.

"Kat, what's wrong? Did I say something?"

"It's not you. It's my mother." She broke down for a moment, but continued through her tears. "We just found out she has breast cancer. Stage 4. Mastectomy. Metastasized to her spine. She's not out of the hospital. She has to do chemo and then radiation. I may be needed at home."

"My God, you should go home today, at least for a few days. I'll take your classes. Just tell me what you plan to cover and give me your PowerPoints. Go home. We can continue this when you get back."

"I don't know what to say."

"Say yes, for Christ's sake. Go home."

"I guess I will. I really want to. Thanks, Martin. You're a godsend."

"But before you disappear, let me at least see your list. I might have some suggestions."

"Here it is. Four of them aren't even in the U.S. There's Fujita at Hitachi, Urquhart at Southampton, Asahi at Kyoto, and Burgomeister at Zurich. When it comes to that, whatever you called it, creative inviting, do I contact them? That seems a little extreme."

"No, but listen. ESM is going to be in Istanbul in July. If you can get an oral paper accepted there, I expect most of your top ten and most of your list of favorites will be there. They'll be sure to hear your talk because it's a single-session meeting. It's the perfect time to get some world-wide exposure."

"Istanbul in July? Maybe by then my mother will be finished with treatments." The tears stopped. "And I actually might have something. When's the submission deadline?"

As Martin looked at her list, he mumbled, "The call for papers goes out pretty soon, so I'm guessing about a month." He continued to scan Kat's list. "Your U.S. ones are Andersen at UCLA, of course, Koppin at Cal tech, yes, right, myself, okay, but I'm an inside letter, Paderewski at Berkeley, sort of I guess, Blaha at Georgia Tech, maybe, and Covington at Cornell. Yes. Terrific list. Well done. So which of them don't you know?"

"I don't know Blaha or Covington and I don't think Koppin knows my recent stuff. I did give a talk at Berkeley last year, so I think Paderewski will remember me. As for Istanbul, as I said, I might have something. But travel money? Ye gods."

"If you get a paper accepted, I'll find the money to pay your expenses. Go home. Deal with what your mother needs. Email me once you know. But the paper for ESM, that's important. It needs to be accepted. You can contact the U.S. folks on your list once you get back from your mother's. Okay?"

"Yes, Martin. As I said, you're a godsend."

-    -   -

When he got back to his office, he found three messages from Felice. She had set up a meeting with a student, Gina Farrell, for three-thirty today, a meeting with Emmanuel Encarnacion for next Tuesday at four, and his sister had called and left a number, saying it was urgent. He didn't recognize the number on the slip, but when he dialed, Helen answered.

"Is that Poochie? Where are you? What's this number?"

"I'm at the Mid-Coast Medical Center. In Dad's room. He's come down with pneumonia."

"That's awful. How's he doing?"

"He's on oxygen and antibiotics. The docs think he'll do fine, but is there any chance you could come down this weekend? I need some relief. Carlo's coming down with a cold too. And work is…"

Martin cut in. "Sure. I'll manage. I'll try to come Friday after work. Can Dad talk on the phone? Can I say hello?"

"He's sound asleep now, but I'll tell him you're coming. It will cheer him up. And me too. And the kids."

As the call ended, Martin remembered that he had promised Jenny a free weekend to work. He tried to reach Jenny, leaving messages both at home and on her cell. Now, with less time than ever, he turned to the merger of the seven separate White Paper budgets.

A little after three, the phone rang. It was Jenny. "I'm really sorry about your dad," she said, "but I need this weekend. I can't go with you. In fact, I want you to take JJ."

Martin had guessed that this would be the outcome, so he chirped, "Of course. We'll make an excursion out of it. I'll call Helen and tell her."

-    -   -

He was making real budgetary progress when, at three-forty-five, he was interrupted by a knock on his door. He bounced up to open it and found the auburn-haired student from his C&E lecture. She turned out to be nearly half a head taller than Martin's five-foot eleven. She blushed, saying, "Oh! Sorry I'm late, Professor Quint. Class ran over... It was... Sorry."

Martin pulled the door fully open and gestured her in.

"Gina Farrell?" he asked, extending a hand.

She nodded, shook his hand, put her backpack on the floor and started to remove her coat. Martin helped her unwrap, catching a whiff of jasmine, hung the coat on his gray Steelcase coatrack, and pointed toward the sofa. Gina sat as Martin slouched into his chair, reflexively noting her athletic body, well sheathed in a forest green sweater that complemented her shoulder-length hair glistening with highlights that reminded Martin of sugar maples in the fall.

"You're in my class this term, right?"

"Omigosh," she answered. "Do you recognize all those hundreds of faces? After just three classes?"

Martin smiled. "A few stand out. Aren't you the one who had the courage to ask that question on the first day? Anyway, what can I do for you?"

Gina blushed, leaned forward, flipped her hair back, and, in a breathless rush, said, "I'm in your, yeah, you already know that, but you maybe don't know that I sat in on one of your lectures during my campus visit last spring, and, anyway, you are, I mean, the kind of teacher, like the best I've ever seen. Your lectures, I mean about how to use solved cases and stuff, they get me so totally pumped, and, so y'know, I want to be one too so I want to figure out what I can, y'know, what I should do, to be a teacher like you so I came to ask you, especially if there's some job or something I could do to learn."

Whatever irritation Martin might have felt at her lateness sublimed away amid echoes from some quarter-century earlier when, as a freshman at Harvard, he had entered the office of Professor Henderson

Crawley, that legendary teacher of elementary chemistry, and gave a speech much like the one he had just listened to. Just as breathless, just as immature, just as enthusiastic, just as adoring. *Déjà vu*.

Leaning back, his hands together with fingers pointing up just to touch his chin, he replied, "I'm glad you enjoy the class. Frankly, I enjoy teaching it, and it pleases me that you want to become a teacher. It is, truly, the greatest profession on earth. So tell me, Gina, you must be a freshman, right?"

"Yes, sir," she replied. "I'll be majoring in EE."

"Have you done any teaching before?"

She squirmed in her seat. "Not really," she said, "unless you count tutoring in the dorm. I did a lot of that last term."

"Great," said Martin, leaning forward. "The best way to start. That's how I started." He paused, remembering, then continued. "Yes. I was a tutor at the Harvard Bureau of Study Counsel. They would schedule one-on-one sessions with students needing help, and we would occasionally record them. Once a month, the tutors would meet with the director and we would listen to and then critique one of the sessions for the benefit of all of us. It was an amazing experience. I learned a lot."

"Is there a program like that at CTI?" asked Gina.

"Regrettably, no," said Martin. "At least not one where the tutors record and discuss sessions. And in the CTI program, you have to be at least a sophomore to be a tutor." He sat upright. "But I can tell you the most important lesson I learned there. Maybe it will help you."

"Oh, please," said Gina.

"When you're tutoring, besides just knowing your subject, you need to create in your own head a model of what the student knows or doesn't know and exactly how that particular student thinks about things. Only then can you construct the best pathways to learning for that student. If you create that model, and it's accurate, you will succeed. If you can't, you will fail."

"Wow," said Gina. "That sounds so simple."

"It's not simple. It's a serious craft. Takes lots of practice. But it's the most important single thing a teacher can do: listen to and understand your students. Be able to think like them. Teaching is like a conversation and you and the student need to speak the same language. Then you can communicate."

Gina got up, smiling, once again tossed her hair back, and said, "That's really helpful. But can I ask are there any other jobs or stuff I can do to get experience? Besides the dorm tutoring, I mean."

Martin paused and took a slow, careful look at his visitor. "Let's assume you really have this as a goal," he said. Gina smiled and nodded. "In that case, what I recommend is that you do lots of tutoring in the dorm this term, and, assuming you get a solid grade in C&E, we can talk next fall about your becoming a homework grader. Grading homework is a fabulous way to learn what students do and do not understand."

"Oh, that would be terrific. And thanks, y'know, thanks so much for seeing me. I know how busy you are. I'm going to try that idea about a model and see if I can do it. I mean, I appreciate getting help like this. Y'know, it's important. A model. Okay, I'll try that."

She extended a hand. Martin got up, shook hands, helped her into her coat while enjoying a jasmine encore and ushered her out the door, wishing her good luck while thinking that she must be a volleyball player.

-     -   -

JJ was inconsolable when he was told at dinner that he and daddy would be going to visit cousins Carlo and Angela for the weekend. "I hate Carlo," he wailed. "He's too big and too loud, and he hits me alla time. And Angela is a pest." Jenny tended to agree with JJ's diagnosis, but she needed him out from under her feet for a few days, and a trip to visit family was as good a plan as any.

Martin asked Jenny if she would put JJ to bed. "I've got another complication besides DARPA. I'm taking Kat Rodriguez's class on Friday because her mother is seriously ill and she went home, so I've just gotta work on DARPA tonight."

Jenny wondered why Martin would take on yet another task in the midst of the DARPA deadline, but since she was getting a free weekend, she took care of JJ and left Martin to his budgetary misery.

Unlike many things in life, deadlines for government proposal submission are absolute — ten seconds late and the proposal is rejected. With more than five million dollars on the line and six colleagues at three universities depending on him, there was no margin for error. So Martin worked late into the night, then rose Thursday at six to continue. He would have preferred to do it all from home, but he was committed to teaching his class and running the staff meeting, so he trundled himself to CTI and got to work, putting a note for Felice on her desk saying 'no disturbances for any reason.' The rest of his collaborators had submitted their final editorial changes, so except for the break for his lecture and staff meeting, he spent the day re-assembling what was now a final draft of the text. Exhausted, he called it quits, leaving the final ugly part, double-checking the budget, for deadline day.

His Friday started early, departing for CTI before Jenny and JJ were up. He was two-thirds of the way through the final budget, checking each line, when his computer reminded him to go teach Kat's class. After, he returned to his office, sandwich in hand, and by three o'clock, he was done. He submitted the White Paper to the DARPA website and sent copies to his co-investigators, hoping that they wouldn't find any mistakes.

He took a taxi home. Jenny had collected JJ from school, packed bags for both of them and prepared sandwiches for dinner. Martin clipped JJ into his child seat, and off they went, just in time to hit the rush-hour traffic heading north. With the traffic slowed to a 15 mph crawl, Martin helped JJ play the alphabet game, first finding an A, then a B, and so on. They were stuck on the letter Q when JJ said he was hungry. Martin pulled off into a McDonalds and bought him some French fries, the universal kid-quieter, and eased the car back into the procession of snails.

It took almost two hours to get to the New Hampshire rest stop.

Martin ate his sandwich accompanied by a large cup of coffee but JJ, now stuffed on fries, just wanted some chocolate ice cream. Cleaning up JJ after his bout with the ice cream took some aggressive face, hand and clothing wiping, but finally, after calling Helen with a new guess at an arrival time, they again headed north. As they crossed from New Hampshire into Maine, the weather turned unfriendly — a kind of freezing drizzle. The traffic density had eased at Portsmouth, but just past the entrance onto the Maine Turnpike, with no possible escape for ten miles, the lines of cars and trucks oozed to a halt. Nothing moved.

Martin turned on the radio. He fiddled with the dial until he found a Portsmouth station, which reported that two tractor-trailers, one with a hazardous cargo, had skidded into each other and jackknifed just south of the next exit. Emergency vehicles were on the way from the north side of the interchange, but the state police estimated it would take about two hours to clear the road enough to allow traffic to move. In the meantime, people were advised to turn off their engines and wait.

It didn't take long for JJ to start complaining. He was getting cold, so Martin got him an extra sweater from his bag and even put on his snow pants. Then he got JJ to sing some of his favorite songs with him. But after about ten minutes, JJ said no more. Jenny had tucked a few of JJ's favorite books into the luggage. Martin picked out *Winnie the Pooh,* and this worked for nearly forty minutes, until JJ suddenly said, "I need to go peepee." Martin did too. The coffee from the rest stop was taking effect.

Realizing that there was naught to be done, he and JJ got out of the car and walked just to the edge of the gravel shoulder. Martin pulled down JJ's pants and said "Okay buddy, you get to make peepee right here." But JJ wouldn't, saying he needed a bathroom. "What if we make peepee together? Can you do it then?" JJ giggled and nodded. So Martin unzipped and let loose a stream, at which point JJ did the same. Suddenly, there were sounds of car doors opening all around them. Five, six, eight men came to the roadside and helped water the gravel, with shouts of thanks to Martin and JJ for getting things started. Then a woman came out from an SUV with two young children, a boy and a girl. She told them that it was okay, so first, the boy, then the girl, unmasked and let loose. The woman looked all around, finally deciding, in a what-the-hell manner, that she was as entitled as the men. She walked a bit out onto the weedy verge, squatted, and added her contribution to the general irrigation process. Horns were honking while she did, but then three more women came from stuck cars and did the same thing. Everyone was laughing — men and women alike. It was the silliest party Martin had ever been part of.

About this time, the headlights up in the distance were being turned on. Martin called Helen with another ETA as everyone returned to their cars, bladders now relieved. Thirty minutes later, they passed the accident scene, with wreckers still at work on the two trucks, but with one moved far enough aside to allow one lane of traffic to trickle through. Finally, they were on the move, slowed somewhat by the drizzly conditions, but rolling north.

As the signs for the Kennebunk rest area came into view, JJ suddenly vomited. Martin quickly changed lanes and almost made it onto the rest-area exit road. His car did a graceful 180 on a slippery patch and came to rest facing backwards, the two right wheels sunk into the soft shoulder. With cars exiting toward the rest area right in front of him, he didn't dare try to drive out. One of the exiting cars stopped and offered to get someone from the service station to come over. Fifteen minutes later, with JJ screaming the whole time and totally unresponsive to anything Martin said, they got pulled out of the muck, turned around and drove into the rest area. Cleanup of the car and JJ followed, with a change of clothes and the destruction of many wet paper towels. The smell in the car was hideous, but JJ had stopped crying. He took a few sips of water and got buckled back into his slightly damp but vomit-free car seat.

The rest of the trip was uneventful. JJ drifted off to sleep and the roads remained passable. In the quiet and the dark, Martin thought about his on-demand morning depositions, wondering with what kind of exponent a second child might expand the potential chaos level. If this trip was the one-kid baseline, how would it grow with two? Like a quadratic? Cubic? Worse?

* **10** *

Jeremiah Quint, Professor of Classics and Philosophy, Emeritus, at Bottlesworth College, remarried after Martin had started college. Karen, twelve years younger than Jeremiah, had died of pancreatic cancer in September, after which Helen and her two children moved into the rambling gray house on Columbia Avenue, a quarter-mile southwest of the campus. It helped ameliorate Jeremiah's loss, and it offered benefits all around. Jeremiah enjoyed the liveliness of his some-times wonderful, sometimes awful grandchildren, and was a grateful recipient of Helen's taking on house management, shopping, cleaning, and cooking. Helen, for her part, was delighted to unload the rent and utilities for the tiny house she and the kids had been living in, and the evenings were a bonus, talking with her dad about books and life in general. It also gave her a baby-sitter when she would, in a tentative way, explore meeting new men, something Jeremiah encouraged in just so many words.

Martin and JJ arrived at ten-thirty. Helen, her black hair in a long French braid, was holding back tears as he climbed out of the car. "This is the first time he's been in a hospital since I can remember," she sobbed, "and it frightens me." Martin carried JJ into the house and after tugging off his coat and snow pants, deposited him, fully dressed, on the cot that had been set up next to the sleep sofa in the first-floor sunroom. Martin and JJ would bunk down there since five-year-old Carlo and three-year-old Angela now shared Martin's old room.

Over hot cocoa, Helen and Martin talked well into the night, not just about their father's health, but about mortality and its implications, the reality that their father would die, and possibly soon, and what this would mean to each of them. At one point, Helen said, "Y'know Martin, it's at times like this I appreciate that children is a plural word. I'm really glad Dad had two kids, and I'm really glad you're my big brother. Thank you for being."

Amid echoes of her teen-aged shrieking of 'phony, phony,' Martin said, "Yeah, thanks, Poochie. I'm glad I have you too," wondering when it was that she had finally started seeing some worth in him. At two in the morning, totally drained, Martin settled in for the night.

The next morning dawned slowly, a mix of grisly gray and weak sunlight. Helen's kids galumphed down the stairs, waking Martin. Carlo was tall and heavy for his five years, with jet black hair like his mother, while Angela was a curly-headed, blondish kewpie doll. They barged into the sunroom with shouts of joy at seeing their uncle, jumping on his bed. The ruckus roused JJ, who looked suspiciously at his cousins. Helen was already up, making pancakes, so the three children went to the kitchen for breakfast while Martin called Jenny to report on their wonderful trip north.

After breakfast, Martin used the upstairs facilities to give JJ a bath, take a shower, shave, and dress the two of them while Helen stuffed the smelly laundry in the washing machine, pulled out JJ's car seat for a proper cleaning and gave the rear seat area of Martin's car a thorough wipe-down and spray of air freshener applied to the seats and the backseat rug. When he came down with JJ, he not only thanked her, he joked that practice seems to make perfect. Helen said that it sure did, and she had had enough practice to be a professional.

JJ got hysterical when Martin tried to leave for the medical center. It took ten minutes to assure him that Aunt Helen would be there and would make sure that Carlo played nice, and maybe they could all go ice skating later. After finally getting JJ calm, Martin shivered his way to the car and drove to see his father.

In his prime, Jeremiah was ten times as fit as Martin, at least when it came to portaging a canoe with a full backpack. His normally bronzed skin now looked like pale leather, and his feathery brown hair had turned mostly white. He was awake and brightened when he saw his son, if brightening is possible in such an ashen face. Martin was shocked at how thin he looked. The IV stand and oxygen tube in his nose suggested a level of frailty totally foreign to the senior Quint.

"Good to see you, boy," said Jeremiah, with something of a croak. "Can't wait to get outta here. How's Jenny? And that boy of hers?"

"We're all fine, Dad. I brought JJ with me. Don't know if he's allowed to visit, but I'll find out. The thing is, how are you?"

"Doc says everything's gonna be okay. We owe a cock to Asclepius. They put me on this drip, and I started feeling better within a day. Maybe another three days or so in here, then home again."

"Helen wants to get a day nurse for when you get out."

"That's nonsense," said Jeremiah. "I'll be just fine. Can take care of myself."

"Actually, Dad, she and I agree on that, and we're not taking no for an answer. She needs to work and manage the kids in and out of school and day care, and you're going to be weaker than you think. So we're hiring someone, period. You don't get a vote."

"With what money? My insurance won't cover that."

"I'm staying over to talk to the Bottlesworth people on Monday morning. If we can't collect, I'll pay. Think of it as a benefit of the successful raising of your son — I actually make a good living now."

"Did you forget, boy, that Monday is a holiday? Presidents Day? I think the Bottlesworth office is closed until Tuesday."

"Oh, right. I forgot. Okay. I'll stay until Tuesday morning, but I've gotta send some emails. Just a sec." He got out his iPhone and fired off an email to Steve Campbell asking him to take the Tuesday lecture, saying he would email him the notes later today, and a second one to Khalil asking him to run the Tuesday group meeting if he didn't make it back in time. Turning back to his father, he said, "Okay, done. But you are getting a day nurse, period."

It was a sign of just how frail Jeremiah was that he didn't protest further. Martin described his trip north with JJ, and his father howled with laughter as Martin described the pee-in. "What are ya gonna do, in a case like that? Wet your pants in your car? So the women did it too? Good for them. Shows they got backbone. Not getting shy just because some men were around. When I used to take Karen camping with Cabel and Sandra, she would usually be modest about it, but when you're on a narrow trail in a swamp and ya gotta go, ya go right there by the trail. And she would."

Martin also told him that he would be going to Turkey in the summer, and that got Jeremiah fired up. "You will visit Troy, won't ya? You've just gotta visit Troy. I used to tell you the Iliad stories, and the Odyssey..."

"I remember, Dad. Helen remembers too. I've asked the Program Chairman if there's a tour or something."

"Yeah. You go that far, you've gotta visit Troy. Any chance you'll get to Greece too?"

"Probably not."

"Pity," said Jeremiah. "A pity."

- - -

Since Martin was staying over until Tuesday, he had time on Sunday to take the kids on an excursion to Jeremiah's cottage on Sagahadoc Point, a rocky spit of land extending south into the ocean just past the mouth of the Kennebec. The cottage itself was closed up for the winter, but the ocean-side beach on the point could be fun as long as the road wasn't too icy. The sun was out, so it looked promising. They took Helen's van since it had room for all three car seats.

The beach is not large, but it is dramatic, bounded by two huge outcrops of vertically folded schist into which granite seams have intruded, remnants of processes deep in the earth from long ago. The tide was nearly high and the waves were crashing over the edges of the promontories. Carlo and JJ scrambled up to the top of the biggest one while Martin hoisted little Angela. As they looked over the ocean, with occasional splashes hitting only ten feet away, Carlo asked Uncle

Martin which way was Portugal. "You mean where your father was from?" said Martin.

"Not my father, silly. My grandfather. He was from Portugal."

Since the beach faced nearly east, Martin guessed the correct direction would be over the water toward the right, and he pointed. "Can anybody swim from there?" asked Carlo.

"Oh no," said Martin. "It's way too far. Your grandfather probably came on an airplane."

"He told me he swum. He's dead now."

They inched their way back down the rocks to the beach, where the kids ran back and forth, kicking up the sand, JJ scrambling to keep up with his larger cousin. Angela toddled along, looking at what had washed up from the last storm. After a sand-throwing episode, when Martin had to separate Carlo and JJ, Martin shepherded them to the van and drove up the road to Route 1, stopping for lunch at the Dairy Queen. A climb on some rocks, a run on the beach, and a hot dog with fries. Maybe two kids really could be more fun than one, even if they might fight from time to time.

He asked his father about that during his afternoon visit.

"Hell, yes," said Jeremiah. "As I've told Helen maybe a thousand times, 'children' is a plural word. Kids need kids, not just as playmates but later, too, as grown-up siblings, family support to face the world. And kids are different. You're a pusher, a plugger, and Helen is gentle, caring. We need all kinds."

Raising his eyebrows at Jeremiah's casual categorization of his two children, Martin continued, "Well, Jenny and I are trying for a child, but she's had trouble getting past ten weeks."

"Don't give up, boy. JJ's a nice kid, and all that, but something special happens to you when you have a child of your own."

-   -   -

During his Monday visit to the hospital, Jeremiah and Martin talked about choices in life. Martin wondered how his life might have turned out if he had gone to Bottlesworth instead of Harvard.

Jeremiah was blunt. "Harvard opened doors for you that never would have been opened if you'd gone to Bottlesworth. That's why I wanted you to go there. Hell, boy, I knew Bottlesworth inside and out — the good, the bad, and the ugly. You needed a bigger place."

"But why didn't you encourage Poochie to go to Brown? Or Penn?"

"She's different from you. She's quiet. Not so ambitious. And maybe she didn't tell you, but she was really nervous about the competition at a place like Brown. Afraid of getting run over by smarter kids."

"But she's plenty smart. Didn't you tell her? I thought you were encouraging her to stay, not to go."

"That's right. Unlike you, she was a perfect fit for Bottlesworth. I'm glad she went there."

"Is she glad?"

"You'll have to ask her about that."

They parted with a promise from Martin to try to visit during his spring break at the end of March. In the meantime, he was to get well, follow the instructions of the home nurse, and take care of himself.

That evening, after getting the children bedded down, Martin asked Helen about her choice of college, whether it was free choice.

"Well," she said, "Dad sort of bullied me on that one. He really didn't want me to leave. He made up a bunch of stories about how I would get a better education if I stayed here, but at some level I never believed him. I think he just wanted me to stay."

"And are you sorry? That you stayed?"

"Not really. I like it here. The college has plenty of activities — theater, music, a good library, some interesting people on the staff. And I'm not good at cities, actually. I like the fact that I can comprehend the totality of my town."

"Good God, Poochie. Such a literary remark. Comprehend the totality."

"But I mean it. There's something about this place that I just get. I understand it. It makes me comfortable. Unlike you, I don't care what the world at large thinks of me. I've got some good friends here, and my father. We eat well, we enjoy the cottage, and we enjoy each other."

"And are you looking to marry again?"

"I'm looking, but with caution. I don't want another drinker, and most of the men around here tend in that direction, but the college gets some good ones in from time to time. So I keep an eye out."

"What does Dad think?"

"He pushes me, like always, although he admits he has no magic formula that will produce a suitable candidate. He says his second marriage saved his life, and I could be as lucky as him, if I looked. So I look. But like I said, with caution."

The drive back from Brimfield Junction, following a successful meeting on Tuesday morning with the Bottlesworth Benefits Office, was blessedly calm. JJ dropped off to sleep just north of Portland and stayed that way until they reached home. Jenny welcomed the travelers with hugs and whispered thanks to Martin for letting her get her work done. Martin disappeared into the study for email catch-up, finding messages of thanks from his DARPA collaborators for a job well done. After a quick lunch, he walked to CTI for his meeting with Emmanuel Encarnacion.

That evening, Jenny honored him with a spectacular dinner of green goddess chicken, marinated in a basil-lemon-yogurt sauce and roasted in a very hot oven to a deep brown crisp. JJ ate enough dinner to justify a frozen-lemonade popsicle for dessert and went happily with his mother for his bath, story, and bed. After JJ was asleep, Martin and Jenny had decaf in the living room, where he reported in full on the visit, including his shock at how frail his father had become. They talked about the two-children issue and how supportive Jeremiah was about continuing to try. Jenny said, "So let's try some more tonight, the fun way. How about I wash your back?"

"And other parts too?"

"Absolutely. Other parts too."

* **11** *

The next morning, an email from Kat reported that her mother was out of the hospital and that she was returning to Boston on Wednesday, but not in time for class. There was also a note from Felice that Koppin's review of the Schultz paper was in.

Martin, trying to imagine the stress Kat was under, opened the shared directory containing *JSMT* correspondence. Koppin's review said, in effect, that the paper was not hugely important in terms of impact, but the theoretical formulation captured in Equations (3) and (7) looked pretty interesting and would make the paper worthy of publication if a few minor revisions were made, which he listed. No mention of the Chang paper. Useless! Martin immediately sent an email to Andris Andersen:

```
Andris - I know we sent you the Schultz article JSMT
2012-48 only a few days ago, but it's kind of a
touchy re-review, and I was hoping you could do me a
big favor and get to it fairly quickly. A question
has been raised about the originality of the formula-
tion. Schultz is hot for an answer, so I would really
like your take on that. Don't worry about commas and
periods. We already have reviews on that stuff in
hand. Thanks in advance, and best regards. /M
```

Within minutes, Martin had a reply:

```
In dc, flying home this pm. Pls give greetings to
Kat. /A
```

Martin leaned back in his desk chair, thinking about Harry's request for help and how that might connect to his passion for the role of conversation in education. Thrilled with the support Clark's writings gave to his ideas, Martin could now visualize *Education as Conversation* as a completed book, out in print and being favorably reviewed in the *New York Times* and *The Chronicle of Higher Education*. It was now fully alive *in utero* and simply needed a bit more gestation before birthing.

But what about Harry and his MOOC? How could he possibly get calibrated on the student-experience issue or on what the students actually learn in these damned things? He didn't have time to take the course he was also teaching. The image of an auburn-haired freshman who wanted to be a teacher popped into his head.

```
To Gina Farrell:

I was impressed with your interest in, and commitment
to, becoming a teacher, and this has stimulated an
idea for an RP that might suit you.

Would you please make another appointment to talk
about it?
```

Martin taught Kat's eleven-o'clock class, and after lunch, returned to his office to find Gina Farrell waiting. "Hello, volleyballgina@cti," said Martin with a twinkle. "That's a cute logon ID. I had guessed you were a volleyball player. How's the team?"

"It's fun," said Gina, curling herself into the sofa, "but it takes, like, a lot of time. I'm not sure I can handle that and the studies too."

"And what's that on your shirt?" Gina was wearing a gray sweatshirt blazoned with an odd array of symbols. She smoothed it out and pushed her chest forward so Martin could read it.

$$\sqrt{\frac{E}{m}}\;\frac{PV}{nR}\;\sqrt{-1}$$

"Very clever," said Martin, who, not wishing to prolong his chestward stare, relaxed back into his chair.

"Yeah, well, the girls all wear them when our team is warming up, and it freaks out the other team 'cause they can't understand it."

"Good. I like it. The nerds will inherit the earth. Well, team or no team, I'm going to make a suggestion that will add to your load, if you agree to do it. I'm impressed that you already know you want to be a teacher. Not many students have that inclination as freshmen. You know that the MOOC version of C&E started this week?" Gina nodded. "And did you see that piece in *The Widgit,* about credit for MOOCs?" Gina nodded again. "Well I want to find out what's what with these online classes. You're already in my class, so you're already doing the work and learning the stuff, at least I assume you are." Martin chuckled and Gina blushed. "What I would like is that in addition to my class, you register for the MOOC. You don't have to do all the work, but just enough so you can do a comparison for me of what it's like as a student in the two versions. I already signed myself up, but I don't have the time to look at everything, and besides, I need a student's point of view. I would like to set up a research project on the MOOC. Short weekly reports on what they're doing right, and what they're failing at. I'm especially interested in the student support and interaction that's available in the two versions. Does this sound interesting?"

"Omigosh," said Gina. "You mean, like, I look at lectures and the homework and ask questions and see what happens? And write down notes for you? Stuff like that?"

"Exactly."

"How much time would this take?"

"I'm really not sure. I have enough budget for ten hours per week, but I suspect it will be more like six. And, of course, you can do it on your own schedule."

"So this is a paid RP? Not a credit one?"

"Exactly. At the usual undergrad RP rate, something like $10.50 per hour, or whatever the standard rate is now. What I really want is your judgment as someone who is interested in how to teach. I want to know whether students can really learn in the MOOC environment compared to a live class. Not only will this help me, but I think you'll learn a lot about teaching by comparing the two modes of pedagogy."

"Omigosh, Professor Quint. This sounds so, y'know, exciting. I'm worried about time, but I've just gotta say yes. Working with you, I mean, like, it's just exactly what I want. So yes, I'll do it. For sure."

After Gina left, Martin puzzled over what it would take to convince him that MOOCs could work as well as a live teacher. It would be fun to get Gina's point of view. She seemed smart and was certainly enthusiastic, just the kind of student he enjoyed mentoring. He picked up the copy of Clark and continued his reading, dreaming of the day when he would have enough time to start writing *Education as Conversation*.

-    -   -

The next morning, Martin found a message from Andris:

```
Martin — Finally looked at the Schultz article. Funny
you asked about it. I recall something very like this
from a young guy at a conference a few years ago.
Don't remember his name. Do you know about this?
```

Martin responded, suggesting that it might be SMSC 2009. Andris promised to check the abstracts from that meeting once he could retrieve the conference book from the student who had borrowed it.

-    -   -

Dinner that evening was with Seamus and Colleen Kelly, who lived next door to the Quints. Seamus taught mathematics at Bunker Hill Community College and Colleen was a nurse, now retired. Their two children were grown, married, and moved away, so they clung to their much younger neighbors as if they were family. Martin would occasionally help Seamus with home-maintenance issues and Colleen was a treasure for Jenny, stepping in as acting grandma for JJ from time to time.

Jenny had roasted sockeye filets on a bed of leeks and shallots, served with green beans — the only vegetable JJ would eat. Everyone was chuckling over the fact that JJ loved the salmon. He was eating up a storm, pushing fistfuls of the pink fish into his mouth and then playing with each green bean as he sucked it up, straw-like, one bite at a time.

Martin, still stimulated by the buzz around the MOOCs, asked Seamus what he thought of the new online educational craze.

Seamus answered, "I just love FIE. They're putting stuff up I can actually use. My students can study at home, and they do. I can tell which ones take advantage. They have better skills and they ask better questions."

"But is it really education?" asked Martin. "Or is it the training part — learning to do algebra, or whatever."

"It's mostly what you would call training, but that's a lot of what we do at Bunker Hill. Our students were not the ones at the top of their class in high school — more like middle third — and often their experiences were so dreadful they graduated without basic math skills."

"Yeah," said Martin. "I sorta see that."

"But listen," said Seamus. "It's such a joy to see these kids, the motivated ones, now that they've been out in the work force for a few years. They realize how much they need to understand basic math, and they really dig in and learn. Our most popular course is statistics. But they can't do that without algebra, so some of them have been skipping our algebra class by taking the FIE version."

Martin interrupted, "How do you know they learn it? Really learn it, I mean."

"All you have to do is see the questions they ask in class. It's clear that they can think with symbols. Frankly, what I would really like is to use the FIE materials directly for our courses — have the students view the lectures as homework and spend our classroom time on discussion and examples. But we can't count on everyone having computer access at home, so we can't do that yet. But our new President is hot for this kind of thing, so it may happen."

"Can anyone take these courses, or just college students?" asked Colleen.

"Anyone at all," said Seamus. "No cost. Just log in and sign up. Hey, why don't we go look at the web page? Maybe Jenny will want to take a course in antiques. Whaddya think?"

Jenny smiled. "I don't know. Maybe. I don't know how much time I'll have. Just landed a big new client, and, of course, we keep trying for another child."

Colleen and Seamus cooed over the news while Martin blushed. When you say you're 'trying for a child,' it's basically saying 'we fuck a lot.' So which is stranger? Telling your friends you fuck a lot or not saying anything until you're sure? Jenny, as usual, was comfortable with the 'we fuck a lot,' but it made Martin uneasy, as if his friends were peeking into their bedroom. What do friends think of the sex they know their friends must be having? Do they imagine him in the midst of an orgasm and then smile?

Colleen asked whether there were online courses in history or literature.

"A bit of everything," said Seamus, "and more coming every day. Can we go take a look?"

They trooped up the stairs to the study, where Seamus used Martin's computer to log in to FIE. Jenny just took a quick look and packed JJ off to bath and bed, but Martin scanned the entire list of offerings. He had to confess that the breadth was pretty amazing, especially considering how new the program was. Seamus's enthusiasm was a jog to his views.

They returned to the kitchen to do dish cleanup. Seamus asked Martin whether he still found his classroom teaching satisfying, now that he had become such a hotshot in research.

After a deep breath and a long exhale, Martin said, "It's really strange, Seamus. Sometimes I think the research I do is the most exciting, most important thing in the world. But, like now, when I'm putting together a really complicated seven-person program from three different schools, I ask myself why I'm bothering. What made you ask?"

"Well, you seem to be under stress all the time. I'm wondering if it's good for your health."

"Stress? Yes, there's plenty of that. But if I'm going to work with grad students, I need money, so I've got to write grants, get them funded, and keep attending the sponsor meetings and conferences. But when you do have the money to support students, the kind of one-on-one education you do is truly exhilarating. So it's a mix, I guess."

Seamus teased, "Is everybody at CTI driven like you?"

Colleen laughed. "Martin, driven? Surely, you're joking, Mr. Kelly."

Martin smiled. "Yeah, I might be considered a bit driven. After all, CTI only promotes type-A's, and once we get tenure, like the Energizer Bunny, we just keep running. If we didn't do that, the whole set of assumptions behind the award of tenure would break down."

"Well, I'm glad I don't have to do what you do," said Seamus. "My job is just to teach, and I love it."

"And at some level I envy you. But, listen to this. A few days ago, I had a grad student do a critical measurement but she forgot to run the standards correctly, so the data weren't properly calibrated. When I called her on it, she almost broke into tears, but the fact is she will remember that, especially the embarrassment, and never make that mistake again. I encouraged her to keep going, and a day later she popped in with everything done right. That kind of education can't be done in the usual classroom, and I really get a charge from it."

Colleen asked, "So when you get a new baby in the house, are you planning to slow down at all?"

"Yes, Martin, how about that?" asked Jenny, who had just come into the kitchen.

"We'll just have to see, I guess. Slowing down doesn't sound all that bad just now."

- - -

On the following Wednesday morning, Martin turned with interest to the front-page article in this week's *Widgit*.

PROFESSOR SKEPTICAL ABOUT MOOCS
By Emmanuel Encarnacion

Professor Martin Quint, lecturer in the very popular Circuits and Electronics course in EECS, has expressed significant concern about the possibility that CTI might offer full credit for MOOCs, such as the FIE version of his own course currently being taught by Prof. Hoo-Min Huang. *The Widgit* sought out Profs. Quint and Huang to get their views.

"What concerns me most of all," said Prof. Quint, "is that the grasp of the concepts I try to get across in my course is enhanced enormously by person-to-person interaction, by direct conversation. Whether it's in a lecture, a section, a tutorial, or a laboratory, the personal interaction is, in my view, essential. It might be student-to-student rather than teacher-to-student. What matters is the personal exchange of ideas. MOOCs lack the capability for that kind of interaction, partly because of their massive scale, so I'm not convinced that the educational experience can be of appropriate quality to merit credit at CTI."

Prof. Huang was somewhat supportive of Prof. Quint's view that the student-interaction portion of the MOOC is, at present, a weakness. "In fact," he said, "I have asked for Prof. Quint's help in trying to improve that aspect of what we are doing. He represents an important resource as we move ahead. I am more optimistic than he about the ultimate merit of this form of teaching, but we are both agreed that student interaction must be of high quality."

Martin was happy with *The Widgit's* piece and wondered what the reactions would be, if any. He knew that the students would support the idea of credit for MOOCs and was counting on Gina's project to help him assess the merits of their case. As for the faculty, he had no idea what they thought. Perhaps the Chairman of the Educational Policy Committee would invite him to a meeting to discuss the issue.

He turned to his email and found the hoped-for message from Andris:

```
A guy named S. J. Chang gave a paper with an appro-
priate title. I happened to hear it but I can't
remember details. Is that the one in question? If so,
can you send me a copy? /Andris
```

Martin sent Chang's article to Andris. He then dove into his

Personnel Committee notebook, studying each CV line by line. He grabbed a sandwich for lunch and ate at his desk, notebook open. At 2:55, he headed for Department Headquarters. Rebecca advised him to make a cup of coffee if he wanted one, since refreshments were not provided. Martin was hyper enough without, so he entered to find most of the seats at the long table already taken by his more senior colleagues.

"Hi Martin," said Arnold Grand, an expert on organic semiconductors. "That was Ken's seat in the middle there. It's now yours. Welcome aboard." There followed general greetings and welcomes from around the table.

Promptly at 3:00, Morris entered with the two Associate Department Heads, Bill Burke on the EE side, who worked on laser physics, and Ellen Zefrim on the CS side, in computer networks. They took their seats, and the meeting began.

"You all know Martin, I assume," said Morris. "He's Ken's replacement. And Martin, you know everyone?" Martin nodded.

"For Martin's benefit, I want to lay out our plan. What we do each spring, Martin, is review CVs and the status for everyone who is not a Full Professor, starting with the non-tenured faculty, first Assistants, then Associates. Some of the Assistants are ready for promotion, and we'll spend real time on them. For the others, they either need reappointment or, perhaps, discussion to see if any mid-course counseling is needed. Three of the Associates are mandatory for tenure this year, Kat Rodriguez, Pierre DeMaitre, and Phillip Van Rijks. As we discussed, you will take over from Ken as Case Manager for Kat, and to give you enough time to prepare, we'll discuss her last in this group, I'm guessing early April, after spring break. After the non-tenured Associates, we'll look at the tenured Associates to see who is ready for promotion to Full. Any questions before we plunge in?"

And plunge they did. For each faculty member that came up for discussion, someone on the PC was in charge of presenting the CV, summarizing the subject of the research, the status with students and publications and a brief review of what teaching had been done. The depth was impressive, the tone respectful. While listening and learning, Martin recalled what Ken had told him at tenure time: "The EECS Personnel Committee is the best organization I have ever belonged to. The integrity with which it operates is unmatched. The privacy of the letters is honored by everyone, and the discussions of promotion cases are completely free of the kind of political nonsense and infighting that satirists of university life like to invent." Based on what he heard so far today, Martin would agree.

-    -   -

After the meeting, Martin checked his email before heading home. He found a pearl from Andris, to which he replied with thanks:

```
I sent in the review to the journal web site. Schultz
was there that year. I know, because we were both
trying to recruit the same PhD candidate for a job,
and he was very aggressive (he won). I'm pretty sure
he would have been at Chang's talk, although I don't
remember. Anyway, in light of Chang, the Schultz
paper has nothing new, but it's a bit awkward since
apparently Chang hasn't published his stuff in a
journal. /Andris
```

That night at dinner Jenny reported that her period was late. Martin said how excited he was, that maybe this time it would work. He asked if was she feeling okay (yes, she said) while inwardly wondering how excited he really was — unless nervousness counts as excitement, of which he had plenty, enough to create a tingle in the small hairs on the back of Jenny's neck.

* 12 *

"What is this bullshit?" Wolfgang Schultz's telephonic explosion forced Martin to move the receiver away from his ear. "Not original? That's bullshit. Chang didn't do that stuff. I cited what he did as background and then presented the new stuff."

"Actually, Wolfgang, it doesn't appear to be bullshit. As you saw from the reviews, one of the reviewers was at SMSC 2009 where Chang presented virtually exactly what you have in this paper."

"Did he ever publish it? How the fuck am I supposed to know about a conference paper?"

"Look, Wolfgang, here's the problem. It's not a question of whether you knew about the conference paper when you submitted the manuscript. No one is accusing you of anything like that, so please calm down. But the fact is that Chang presented virtually identical work at SMSC 2009, and at a minimum, you have to cite him. But what the reviewer said was that if you do revise the manuscript and include a proper cite to Chang, there isn't enough original stuff left in your manuscript to warrant publication."

"Who is this guy Chang, anyway? Is it the Texas A&M guy?"

"Actually, no. When the reviewer raised the question and cited Chang's SMSC paper, we looked him up on the web. He's at Minnesota. I contacted him and asked him for a copy of the paper, which he sent so we could compare. It seemed important to do that, given the review."

"My God," said Wolfgang. "So why didn't you send me a copy of the paper along with the review? You owed me that, at least."

"You're right," said Martin, abashed. "I'm sorry. I should have. I'll send it to you right away."

"I can't believe you would go to this kind of trouble to shoot me down? Why?"

"Jesus, Wolfgang, you think I'm trying to shoot you down? That's nuts. I don't shoot people down. But when a reviewer raises questions I have to figure out what to do. It seemed that finding Chang and getting his paper was required by circumstances. What else could I do? What would you have done in my shoes?"

"Well, if you put it that way," said Wolfgang, somewhat chastened, "I guess you did the right thing. But it feels strange. Was Chang the reviewer?"

"Absolutely not," said Martin. They ended the call. Martin turned to his email and sent Wolfgang a copy of Chang's paper, at which point he found a message from Miles Callaghan, Editor-in-Chief:

```
Martin – Wolfgang Schultz has kicked up quite a fuss
about your second rejection of his paper. It now
seems I have to get involved. Please send me the
paper, the reviews, and copies of all related corre-
spondence. I'm sorry to have to do this, but Schultz
wants his day in my court, and I'm obligated to give
it to him.

Thanks, Miles
```

Martin called Miles and was surprised to find him available and ready to talk. "I need your assurance that this conversation is confidential," said Martin. "You could do real damage to an innocent player if this leaks."

Miles agreed, so Martin continued. "When you asked me to do a re-review, I was a bit short on prospects, so I took S. J. Chang's name from the list of cited references and sent Schultz's paper to him. Chang wouldn't do the review, but he did alert me to his 2009 SMSC paper that had the same stuff as in Schultz, and he even added that Schultz was in the room when he presented. He said he wouldn't do the review because he was afraid of Schultz."

"Afraid?" asked Miles. "Why?"

"He's not yet tenured at Minnesota, and Schultz is a likely letter-writer in his field. If he revealed the conference paper, then Schultz would know he was the reviewer. I agree with Chang on this. It's a problem."

"So where did you get the paper?"

"I asked Chang to send it to me, and I guaranteed that I would not reveal anything that would lead Schultz to identify him as a reviewer."

"But he was a reviewer, in effect," said Miles. "I mean, he read the paper and pointed out the flaw."

"Yes, but if Wolfgang thinks Chang is the culprit, and then Chang doesn't get tenure because Schultz writes a negative letter, our dear journal could be complicit in wrecking the career of a totally innocent man. So when I told Wolfgang about it, I reordered the sequence a little. I said a reviewer mentioned the conference, I contacted Chang and got the paper, sent it to the reviewer, and the reviewer concluded that there was nothing new."

"Who was this reviewer?"

"Do you need to know? Aren't we better off keeping that confidential?"

"Under the circumstances, I think it best if I know."

"Okay. Andris Andersen. He was at SMSC 2009 and heard Chang give the paper. My only prompting to him was to say that a question had been raised about the originality of Schultz. It was Andersen who remembered the SMSC paper and he asked me for a copy. I sent it to him, and he then wrote the do-not-publish review. Satisfied now?"

"Okay. I think I get it," said Miles. "Given the circumstances, I think you handled it correctly. Ask Felice to send me copies of the correspondence. And you should probably send me the Chang paper too, just for completeness. Let me review everything, and then I'll send you a draft of what I will write back to Wolfgang."

-    -   -

The Ides of March had arrived. Martin was enjoying his once-a-week chat with Gina. "Have you ever designed a survey?"

"You mean, like, a questionnaire?"

"Yes, exactly. I've been thinking about the low attendance in my lectures compared to the sections. I would like us to do an anonymous survey of all the students in C&E this term. I have a bunch of questions like, how many are signed up for the MOOC? Do they regularly attend lecture? Sections? What's helpful? What's not? Stuff like that. Do you think you could draft up a good list of questions, now that you've seen how both courses run?"

"Wow, Professor, this is pretty new for me, y'know, but maybe, sure. I'll try it. Will you help with it?"

"Of course, but I want you to learn while doing, so give it a try. Think about what would be good to ask."

"And can you actually be anonymous? People won't answer if you know who they are."

"We'll use one of those online survey tools. They can be completely anonymous. In fact, CTI may already have one installed for community use. I'll find out from Ahmed how many CTI students are signed up for the MOOC, so we can cross-check with survey results."

"Do you want this from everyone, or just the ones signed up for the MOOC?"

"Everyone. We need some real data. Are you going somewhere for spring break?"

"Yeah, well, the volleyball team is going to North Carolina for a Div 3 tournament. But I'll have my laptop. I can work on it. Is that okay?"

"Sure. Try to put together a list of ideas we can talk about next time, so maybe we can have a rough draft before you head for the sunshine."

Gina left and Martin turned to his email, finding a note from Miles with a draft of what he would send to Schultz. It contained a review of the facts followed by a succinct final paragraph:

```
Please be assured, Dr. Schultz, that no one is
questioning your integrity here. These things happen.
```

It's impossible to keep up with everything that is
going on. On the other hand, JMST should not be
publishing as original work that was presented elsewhere, albeit by others. My decision on this matter
is final. The paper stands rejected.

Sincerely,
Miles Callaghan
Editor-in-Chief
Journal of Semiconductor Materials Technology

Martin sent a huge thank-you to Callaghan. Case closed.

- - -

That night at dinner, Martin said, "I really want to spend some time
with Dad over the spring break, week after next." Jenny looked up,
expressionless. "I have to go to the Integrated Electronics Conference
in Denver for that Monday through Wednesday," he continued, "but
do you think we could go down there for a few days after that? Dad
would be thrilled to learn you're pregnant."

Jenny harrumphed. "First of all, it's way too soon to tell anyone that
I'm pregnant. I want to wait a full thirteen weeks this time. As for going
to Maine, I have mixed feelings. Helen's kids are kind of rough, and JJ
gets caught between the two of them. It's different when we can go
to the cottage, but in that Brimfield Junction house, it's just not that
much fun."

"Yeah," said Martin, nodding. "I guess you're right. That Carlo especially is a handful. What if I go down by myself for a few days and get
back during the weekend. Would that work?"

"You mean leave me alone with JJ when you don't absolutely have
to travel?"

"Hey, take it easy. I'm not trying to start a fight. My dad is getting
old and he's been sick. I don't know how much longer before…"

The two sat in silence. Finally, Jenny said, "Yeah. I'm sorry. You're
right. I tend to forget how much older your father is, compared to my

parents I mean. You need to go. How about three days? Is that enough?"

"I'll make it enough. Thanks. Yes, thanks."

-    -   -

Kat, Amanda, and her partner, Felicity, were nursing TGIF beers at The Brewer's Friend, a tiny boutique brewery between Central and Harvard Squares. While of similar height, the two women could not have been more different. Amanda was slender, brown-haired, with narrow, light brown nose and chin. She had just introduced Kat to Felicity, who was somewhat plump with black, tightly braided hair, chocolate skin and a broad smile. Kat was talking about the rigors of the tenure process. "It's like getting undressed," said Kat. "All of a sudden Martin needs to know everything, every student, every problem, every failure, every wart. It's driving me nuts."

"Actually," said Amanda, "you're lucky. That will help get you through. Details. When my tenure came up two years ago, my Department Chairman barely talked to me about it. Wanted a list of names for possible letters and had just one meeting with me over my CV. That was it. I was scared. In languages, as you can guess, there are dozens of people in the area who will teach for a lot less money than a professor's salary. Like Felicity, here. You would love to teach at CTI, isn't that so?"

Felicity laughed. "Stop with the bullshit, already. I'm quite happy at Rindge. None of this tenure crap anymore. Just the kids."

"Anyway," continued Amanda, "I was scared shitless that they would toss me out and hire an Adjunct in my place. I must have lost ten pounds that year, maybe more. But because I teach literature as well as language and got onto one of the program subcommittees at the Modern Language Association meeting, I had enough buddies out there, and apparently my letters were okay. Anyway, I made it. Oh. Here's Carly."

Carly Finch, who worked at Cambridge City Hall as Deputy Assistant City Manager, was approaching their table. The tall, slender, close-cropped blonde, beer in hand, reached them just as Kat muttered, "Scared shitless, yeah. That's exactly how I feel."

"Scared of me?" asked Carly. "Hi. I'm Carly. " She reached out her hand.

Kat blushed and laughed, accepting the hand. "No, not you. I'm Kat, Kat Rodriguez. We were just talking about the meat-grinder at CTI, getting tenure."

"Yeah, Amanda's told me all about you," said Carly. "A real Hispanic woman doing engineering at CTI. A pioneer. Mentor to the Hispanic Student Club. So is this your tenure year?"

"Well, we start now. My year, as you put it, is next year, and I'm scared shitless."

"Enough shitless, already. Let's change the subject to something snowy white. Don't you get a spring break?"

Amanda said, "Week after next. Why? You have plans?"

"You know how impulsive I am. I rented a condo near Killington for that week, and the friends I was going with have backed out. So I'm offering a free one-week end-of-season ski holiday. They still have snow. Wanna come?"

Felicity said, "My breaks don't match yours, so I'm here teaching, but as for Mandy..."

Amanda said, "I'd love to come, but I'd have to get home by Tuesday night. Would that be okay? Felicity's parents are coming to town on Wednesday, and I need to be here for that. You know, meeting the parents? It's a big deal for us. They're still struggling a bit with reality."

"Of course. A few days is fine." Carly turned to Kat. "Do you ski?"

"Sort of. I learned in grad school. Our whole group did stuff together, and that included teaching me to ski. I'm just past the baby slopes, at least I was. I haven't skied once since coming to CTI. Too damned busy."

"You should come. Not just for the weekend. Too long a drive for that. Come for the whole week. By the end, you'll be on black diamond trails."

"Do they rent equipment?"

"Yup, no problem. You'll love it."

Kat was intrigued. "Sounds like fun and I could really use a break. Very tempting. But first, let me check on my mother."

"Your mom?" said Carly, a wry smile crossing her lips. "You live with your mom?"

"No, she's at home. In Merida. But she's in chemo now, and I want to be sure she doesn't need me to fly home that week. My uncle is there. I just want to check."

"Breast cancer?" asked Amanda with a grimace.

"'Fraid so," said Kat.

* **13** *

Feeling guilty that he would be abandoning Jenny for the week of spring break, Martin arranged a weekend in New York for the two of them, with operas Friday night and Saturday afternoon, dinner at a multi-star restaurant Saturday night and two nights in the privacy of the New York Hilton, thanks to frequent-traveler points.

Jenny picked up JJ at school on Friday, drove to CTI to pick up Martin, and off they went, Martin now at the wheel. Jenny began singing, "Over the river and through the woods, to grandmother's house we go…"

JJ did his best to sing along, but he didn't really know the words, so Jenny and he played the alphabet game. JJ immediately saw an A and shortly after that, a B. It wasn't long, though, before JJ needed some coaching on which letter came next. It was odd; he could sing the alphabet song perfectly, but as Martin put it, he couldn't do random access into the middle of the sequence. That would come in time, they felt.

Grace and Harvey were happy to see their darling grandson. Harvey owned one of the more popular furniture stores in Worcester; he was featured in the TV ads and was something of a local celebrity, with his trim white beard and twinkling eyes. In person, though, he was reserved and left most of the talking to his wife. Grace, now retired, had been the acquisitions manager of the Worcester Public Library. She resembled Jenny in many ways, or perhaps it was the other way around. Both women were of medium height and shared a softness, a roundness, with wavy brown hair and big cheeks. Martin liked Grace, especially that she liked books.

Grace invited everyone in for some refreshment, but Martin said that Friday traffic in New York being what it was, they preferred to keep going. With hugs all around and a promise to call JJ in the morning, they launched themselves back into the gradually thickening parade of cars.

Out of the blue, Jenny asked, "What does she do?"

"Who?"

"Kat Rodriguez. The woman who has become the focus of your life, who gets you to take her classes when you are already overloaded. Is she an atom tickler like you?"

"Hey, that's not fair. I offered. Her mother has cancer. Anyone would have done that. And anyway, it's her tenure that's the issue, not the woman part. You're the only woman woman I care about."

"So what does she do?"

"Well, it's like this. If transistors can work faster, computers can work faster, and that's a good thing. Kat has an idea about how to make transistors work faster. She guides impurity atoms into a special arrangement that is created by something called a quantum-interference effect. I'm not going to try to explain how that works, at least not while driving. But she has a theory that if she can get the impurity atoms into the right arrangement, one of the mechanisms that slows down electrons will be suppressed. Transistors made with this method would work faster."

"So could this be important?"

"If it works, maybe. It's risky, though. Especially for a tenure promotion. If it doesn't work, she'll probably get fired."

"Fired?"

"Well, if she doesn't get tenure, she has to leave. But she's making good progress, and there's still time."

"Were you worried about tenure?"

"Sure, everyone worries. But my situation was different. My big breakthrough had already been proved and reproduced. Kat's stuff hasn't worked yet."

- - -

Because of delays on the West Side Highway, they didn't have time to go to their hotel before the seven PM curtain for *Siegfried*. They parked in the Lincoln Center garage, ate hot pastrami sandwiches from a pushcart three blocks north on Broadway, then hustled back to the Met with just minutes to spare.

They sat in the back row of the Dress Circle, a place Martin preferred because the overhang helped bring in the sound even though it felt like they were three miles from the stage. The chandeliers went up, the orchestra tuned, the house lights went down, and Wagner's music drew them into the dragon-filled domain of the Niebelungen. In the final act, Siegfried braves the ring of fire and climbs the crag on which Brunhilda lies sleeping. After he wakes her and persuades her that he is rightfully destined to be her husband, she comes around. By the end, the pair sings of their love.

After the opera, Martin collected the car and they drove to the Hilton, where they were happy to turn the vehicle over to the valet. After checking in, they went to the coffee shop for a late-night snack — fresh fruit for Jenny and a club sandwich with a beer for Martin. While munching, Martin said, "You were a bit like Siegfried, y'know. You braved my ring of fire, woke me up and helped me fall in love."

Jenny smiled. "I guess I did. A good image, the ring of fire. I woke the sleeping goofus. And I'm guessing that you are now awake. I want to play a tune on your flute, so finish up. I haven't felt this randy in months."

- - -

They opted for breakfast from room service, eating in their pajamas amid the aroma of crisp bacon and dark-roast coffee. A joint shower, always fun in its own right, led them back to bed with the need afterwards for a second shower. By the time they were dressed, there was just enough time to walk to Lincoln Center before the 1 PM curtain. Jenny loved to walk in New York. It wasn't just the shop windows, especially those offering antique furnishings. It was the people, every skin shade, body type and language imaginable, the energy, the smells, the fruits stands, the crazy cyclists, the African peddlers quick to pack up when a policeman was spotted, the bustle of the taxis, even the panhandlers.

Today's opera was *Cosi fan tutte*. The plot is, at one level, stupid, and at another, deeply disturbing. Two young men, each with a fiancé, get taunted into a bet by an old cynic, saying that if the two disguise themselves and court the other man's loved one, the women would give in and be unfaithful. The two women do fall for the disguised men, but everything is forgiven at the end.

Over dinner, Jenny said, "I hated the idea that a man, supposedly in love with a woman, would do such a thing, not only to his own girlfriend to but his friend's girlfriend too. It may make for humor, but it's a pretty disgusting trick. What's the point of the opera?"

"Well," said Martin. "The title means something like 'women are always like that.'"

"But they're not! I bet women are more faithful than men."

"How can you say that? If one man fucks one woman, it seems the numbers come out even."

"That's not the point," Jenny argued. "A woman makes a pledge to a man, a loving pledge, and then gets tricked by a conspiracy set up by the man she loves. Would you do that? Would you egg on one of your friends, somebody I don't know, to try to seduce me so you could win a bet? Jesus, Martin. That's just sick."

"No, the point of the opera is that all humans have weaknesses, both men and women, and forgiveness and love triumph."

"Then why is the title just about women? It's the men who set it all up."

"Yes, that's true, but the women do succumb. The point is, they do."

"And then they forgive the men for playing the trick? Ridiculous. If you ever did that to me, regardless of whether I succumbed or not, you would have no balls left when I was done with you."

"You wouldn't succumb, would you?"

"Would I? How the hell would I know? How does anyone know ahead of time what they would do? I mean you succumbed, with that Camille woman. Was she leading you on? Like in the opera, in disguise?"

"Wow. How did we end up here, with Camillle? I'm really sorry. For the record, I can't remember who seduced whom, but she sure had an active role in it. It happened in her house. And it's a dead issue anyway. Please leave that alone."

"This opera just stirs all that up and it frightens me. Especially now that I'm pregnant — with your child, a child I know you're nervous about. What would happen to me if you panicked, turned tail and ran? I've had bad dreams." Jenny was fighting to retain her composure. "Like nightmares." The tears came.

"Oh, God, Jenny. Don't say that. And don't cry. I'm not going anywhere. Listen, why don't we go upstairs so I can give you a massage? I would never play that kind of trick, and I will never succumb to anyone else, no matter what."

The massage helped Jenny's anxiety, but she wasn't up for any activity that would require extra showers.

-   -   -

A night's sleep improved Jenny's mood, and they cuddled together for a long while, in silence, enjoying the touch and smell of each other and the sound of gentle breathing. Amid the peace of their bed, Martin wondered about Jenny's fear, with all that talk about succumbing. There was nobody around tempting him to succumb to anything. Yet Jenny's pregnancy seemed to ignite a vulnerability he didn't know she had.

Martin got up and ordered breakfast. The simple act of pouring Jenny's tea and buttering her toast seemed to bring things back into the sphere of normalcy. They called JJ, got up, dressed and headed for the Metropolitan Museum, where they spent an hour in the Egyptian and Greek sections before driving home. They didn't talk much along the way, but a barb had been planted in Martin's flesh, and while it didn't hurt at the moment, the notion that it might hurt in the future was palpable. How on earth, without starting a fight, could he convince Jenny that there was absolutely nothing sexual with Kat looming anywhere on the horizon? That his devotion to her promotion was required by his job? That Jenny's fear of abandonment might be a reliving of the horror of George's sudden death rather than a response to anything Martin had done?

The miles rolled by. After a brief stop in Worcester to collect JJ, life in the putty-colored house resumed, but the demon remained unexorcised.

* 14 *

On the Monday morning of spring break, Martin signed in at the registration desk for the Integrated Electronics Conference, just off the lobby of the Denver Marriott. As he was picking up his badge and program book, he bumped into Ryszard Pulaski, Chairman of Materials Science at Minnesota. "I'm really glad to catch you, Ryszard. I'm a little surprised actually. Integrated electronics isn't exactly your thing, is it? I thought you were a fracture guy."

"All materials fracture, Martin," said Ryszard with a chuckle, "even semiconductors. Actually, I'm recruiting. We have a new tenure-track slot in electronic materials, and where better than here? I have three interviews coming up today and tomorrow. I was surprised there was no candidate from your group."

"Yeah, well, my new PhD this year isn't faculty material. Can't write English. He's going to Intel."

Ryszard started to move on but Martin stopped him.

"Can we chat a minute?" said Martin. "I have a nagging worry about one of your junior faculty, S. J. Chang."

"He's a super guy," said Ryszard. "We're delighted to have him. What's the issue?"

"Well, you may know I'm one of the editors on *JSMT*, and I had a run-in on a paper with Wolfgang Schultz. You know who he is?"

"I've heard the name. Isn't he an industry guy? ChipsOnDemand? Or is it that other one, Semiconductor Something-or-other?"

"No, right the first time. He's at COD. Well, anyway, Schultz submitted a paper that I had to reject because Chang had presented the same stuff at a conference several years ago. I had asked Chang to do a review, but he wouldn't do it because he was afraid of calling out Schultz. He sent me the backup materials, but he was not the reviewer who rejected the paper. Schultz raised a huge stink and probably blames Chang for the trouble, even though Chang did exactly the right thing. It's not like it was an earth-shaking paper, but Wolfgang hates to lose. It's an ego thing, and when he's fired up, he's a bit unpredictable."

"So what can I do about this? You want to talk to Chang, by the way? I think he's here this week."

"I might like to meet him, but that's not the main thing. When does Chang come up for tenure?"

"We go out for letters this fall. He's a shoo-in, based on everything I hear."

"Let me just ask that you not write to Schultz. It might cause trouble for Chang. I would feel terrible if something I did as editor ends up kicking Chang in the teeth."

Ryszard laughed. "I guess we do things a bit differently at Minnesota. We always ask a candidate if there are individuals we should avoid writing to. My guess is that Chang will mention Schultz, and we will honor that. So don't worry."

Martin thanked Ryszard and they parted. "Good idea," thought Martin. "Something to add to Kat's lists."

- - -

Home from Denver Wednesday evening, Martin and Jenny shared a gentle reunion in their bed, with no hints of the angst of the previous weekend. The next morning, Jenny delighted in showing Martin the details of her new project: the drawings, plans, the furniture pieces that had been selected so far. Martin was impressed. This was going to be a showcase job. After a departure embrace that reminded Martin of the best of their courting days, he left for Maine.

Helen was shoveling a dusting of snow off the walk when Martin drove up. She dropped the shovel, ran to his car and gave him a tight, desperate hug when he climbed out.

Martin said, "Hey, Poochie. What's wrong?"

"I'm so glad you're here. Thanks for coming."

"How's Dad?"

"He's weak. You'll see. Let's get your stuff and c'mon in."

Jeremiah, looking even older than when he had been in the hospital, was in his easy chair, a blanket over his knees. Angela and Carlo came running in and hung onto Martin's legs while he bent down to give his father an awkward hug. He asked, "So how's it going? Ready to go snow-shoeing?"

"Nice try," rasped Jeremiah. "That goddam pneumonia just wiped me out. Haven't been able to exercise much and that just makes me slower. I hope we can do some walks while you're here. When I go out with those two little devils, they run off and I can't keep up anymore."

Carlo shouted, "Hey Uncle Martin. Come see my new train set. Come see."

Martin, still in Carlo's grip said, "In a minute, okay?" Wriggling out of the child's grasp, he turned back to his father. "Well, Dad. We've got three days. We'll start off with a ten-miler tomorrow, okay? Build you up."

"Boy, if I could get to a mile without running out of breath, I'd call it a victory."

Helen interrupted. "C'mon, Martin, let's get your stuff settled. Then I have a Shaw's list for you."

Martin collected his bag, took it to the sunroom, used the upstairs facilities to freshen up from the drive and came back downstairs. He was immediately commandeered by Carlo, with Angela in tow, and dragged into the front parlor to see Carlo's new train set and Angela's doll house, both gifts purchased with money Martin had sent to Helen.

"Will you help me set it up?" asked Carlo.

"Sure, little buddy," said Martin, "but I need to go grocery shopping for your mom. When I get back, okay?"

-    -   -

That night, with the train set assembled and working, the doll house all organized, the children asleep and Jeremiah helped upstairs to bed, Helen and Martin finally sat down in the parlor. Martin flopped back in his father's easy chair, Helen sitting upright on the sofa, rigid.

"You okay, Poochie? You seem tense."

Helen stared straight ahead. "I'm about to lose my job. At least I think so, and I'm scared."

"Why? What's happening?"

"One of the copy-print chains opened a big new center out at Clements Corner, and it took away too much business. Elmer says he may have to cut back, and I don't think he would have mentioned it if he planned to keep me on."

"But if he doesn't, aren't there other jobs?"

"There are, but it's a slow time. There's lotsa folks looking for jobs right now. Elmer'll give me a good reference and all, but I'm just plain scared."

"Have you talked to Dad? About money, I mean?"

"Our dad is the most close-lipped person about money I ever met. I don't know anything about his finances. True, I'm not paying rent or utilities here, and that's a help, a big help, and I guess I'll get some unemployment, but feeding us all, and gas, and doctors. It's frightening."

"So you haven't tried to talk to him?"

"I've tried, but he won't talk about money. He pushes it aside. No need to worry, he says. We're fine."

"That's odd. When we hired that day nurse, he was all worried about the insurance. He was anything but fine. Pissing all over the place about the waste. He didn't seem to know that between Medicare and his Bottlesworth plan, it would be covered."

"That's just what's worrying me. One day we're fine, and one day he yells at me for spending too much. I'm not sure he's thinking clearly these days, at least not about money."

"So you want me to beard the lion, right? In his den?"

"Yes. Please. I need to know."

-   -   -

The next day dawned as one of those bright, clear mornings, crisp as an apple, that keep Maine folks from moving away. Martin got Jeremiah bundled up and they went walking around the neighborhood, up toward the campus and the pines. There were snowy places underfoot, but they inched their way along, father and son.

"Dad, I need to ask you some stuff," said Martin.

"Sure, boy. About what?"

"Money."

"Oh, we're fine with money. Why do you ask?"

"Has Poochie told you she might lose her job?"

"Really? No. She hasn't said a word. The poor kid. Why?"

"Apparently a chain store came into Clements Corner and is killing their business. I'm sure she can find something, but it may take a while. She's worried sick, and you keep pushing her off. So we need to talk about money."

"I can pick up the slack," said Jeremiah. "Not to worry."

"Dad, now you're pushing me off. You're not hearing me. I need to know about your finances. Your savings. Your pension. Debts. Whatever. If you should get sick again, I mean, what if you get really sick? Do you have a medical proxy? Is your stuff organized? Is your will up to date? "

Jeremiah stopped walking and stared at Martin. "You're getting ready for me to die, aren't you. That's what this is about. Well, I have no intention of dying any time soon."

"Nonsense. It's not about dying, it's about living. We want you to live for thirty more years, but we also want to be sure there's enough money around to feed you and Helen and the kids for those years. So we need to talk. This week."

"I'm ready to head back."

And in silence, that's what they did.

-   -   -

After dinner, Jeremiah took Martin into his study, opened a file drawer, and took out three folders. "Here," he said, "my assets, my bank records, and my health proxy, which lists Helen first and you second. I've tried to keep you kids from worrying about all that, but I guess you're right. I'm getting a bit long in the tooth, and it wasn't fun in that hospital. So okay, I'm stripped naked in my tent. Take a look, and ask me anything you want."

It was a great relief for Martin to see that things were organized. The Bottlesworth monthly pension was adequate not only for him, but was also enough to keep Helen and the kids in food, clothing and gasoline if needed. As for assets, besides the pension, there was a $400,000 fully paid-up life insurance policy with the two of them named as joint beneficiaries, the Brimfield Junction house, the cabin on Sagadahoc Point, and a Schwab account with nearly $120,000 in large-cap stocks. There were no mortgages and no debts beyond the monthly credit card, paid off in full each month. There was even the contact information for the lawyer who had prepared Jeremiah's will.

Later that evening, Martin brought Helen up to date. She stopped fretting, which made the remainder of the visit much more fun. He and Jeremiah took walks together, all the way to the campus on the last one. Helen even hosted a dinner party on Saturday night with two of Jeremiah's best friends from the college: Fred Walsh, the President, and Win Henderson, Dean of Faculty.

After dinner, Helen and the two wives retired to the kitchen, not just to do dishes, but to compare notes on raising children in Brimfield Junction. Both women had teenagers and told sobering tales of what Helen could expect in the future.

The men, meanwhile, retired to the parlor with coffee and brandy. Martin, never one to pass up a podium, expounded on his views of education and the MOOCs, how disturbed he was by the trend, and how it ran contrary to his theory of education as conversation. Jeremiah said that it all started with Plato, of course, using conversation for education, and Win probed with questions about Clark, asking

Martin to send him the book reference. When Jeremiah's fatigue finally imposed a nine o'clock end to the evening, Jeremiah joked that maybe Martin should get a job at Bottlesworth so he could teach the way he wanted. Return to Maine, live close to his family. "After all," said Jeremiah, "you're a direct descendant, through your mother, of the original Josiah Bottlesworth."

* **15** *

The Flame Thrower is a community blog for CTI. Its home page has a column on the right with the "Rules of the Game" and a set of boxes on the left with the heading "Topics." Topics are selected by the monitors, and discussion from the community can be posted as "Comments."

Ethel McKinsey, a junior in Political Science and co-monitor for the blog, returned from spring break to find two requests for new topics. The first one dealt with Adjunct Professors, who were unionizing at several area colleges. The second one was more ominous. A student with the logon 'qwibble' had just heard that Sharon Gillespie, the much-beloved teacher of robotics in Mechanical Engineering, had been denied tenure, and qwibble wanted *TFT* to set up a place for student comments.

The first one was easy. Ethel clicked on the "New Topic" button and wrote:

ADJUNCTS
Have you ever been in a class taught by an Adjunct
Professor? Are Adjuncts a step up or a step down in
teaching quality compared with the regular faculty?

On the second request, she was nervous about posting something that would name Prof. Gillespie. She knew Gillespie was a fabulous and exciting teacher, so she guessed that the issue might be her research record. She posted the following:

TEACHING v RESEARCH
Do you think teaching is important when CTI evaluates
faculty for promotion and tenure?

Ethel's first topic lived for a few days and then died a quiet death, but the one about teaching and promotion ignited the kind of firestorm that *The Flame Thrower* loves.

On the question of Adjuncts, the first few postings churned the topic, but it was clear that the students lacked basic information. Someone emailed Bill Burke, asking for help with facts and definitions. Burke responded, clarifying in a long post the difference between Adjuncts, Instructors, Lecturers and the regular professorial ranks.

By the time Burke visited the Adjunct topic to post that comment, there had been many postings on the Teaching v Research topic, many laced with misinformation, weakly disguised obscenities, and painful complaints about the now public decision to deny tenure to Sharon Gillespie. Burke scanned the vitriol and couldn't resist the urge:

```
There has been a flurry of postings on the subject
of whether teaching is considered in promotion and
tenure. I am the Associate Department Head of EECS,
and I wish to assure everyone that teaching perfor-
mance is an important component of every promotion,
including the award of tenure.
wjburke
```

Much later, when asked why this might have set off such a con-flagration, Burke said that perhaps it was an issue of tone. But like so many things that happen on the internet, once that 'Submit' button is clicked, retractions or editorial changes are no longer options. The reaction was instantaneous.

```
Such bullsh*t. All that matters is research. Publish
or perish. Everybody knows that. Prof Gillespie is
probably the best teacher at CTI, and she just got
canned. Isn't that proof enough?
truth46

It's all about research. I should know. I got booted
a few years ago. Not enough research, they said.
trojanhorse
```

It's all done in secret. Burke can say anything he
wants about it, because its secret. Why is Prof
Gillespie given a walk?
qwibble

qwibble's right. Thers so many profs who can't teach
worth piss. And they got tenure. Somebody like
Gilespie, she doesn't? How does that happen? they
should let us see.
rogerrabbit

It has to be secret. At least I think so. Do you
think they can have, like, a public vote? Of course
not. It would tear the place apart.
notforprofit

So who decides? Is it really a vote?
rtmartin

It starts in the department. The department decides.
notforprofit

Doesn't the dean decide?
orogeny

Why does it matter who decides if the decisions hurt
the best teachers? It goes department head, dean,
provost. Take your pick. Any of them can say no. And
all they care about is research.
trojanhorse

The denial of tenure to Sharon Gillespie was too much for Julian
Kesselbaum. It was one thing for CTI to let him go, but Sharon? He
knew he was competent, but he never thought of himself as legendary.
Sharon, now she was legendary, inspirational. To turn her away felt
criminal. It was time to open the belly of the horse. But how?

That night, he set up automated search criteria on the various CTI
computers that he had already invaded, looking for keystrokes with
any reference to Gillespie. He also decided on a second search with
keyword 'tenure' to see what that brought in.

- - -

That Wednesday morning, Martin went to Kat's office for an update and found her on crutches with her ankle in a walking cast. Kat was sheepish. "It happened on the last run of the last day," she said. "I was doing so great."

"Skiing? I didn't know you skied."

"Apparently I don't, at least not very well. I was at Killington, with a friend of Amanda Finley's. You know Amanda, don't you?"

Martin shook his head. "Don't know her. Is she at CTI?"

"Yeah. She teaches Spanish."

"Does it hurt?"

"A bit. The crutches should be gone in a day or so and the walking cast comes off in two weeks. At least that's what the Vermont doctor said. I don't know what the guy at CTI Medical will say. I see him tomorrow. I have the X-rays and everything."

"And news from home?"

"My mother's in chemo. My uncle says it's pretty hard on her, but he said everything is going as well as possible, whatever that means. I offered to go home over spring break, but he and Carmen told me to take a holiday instead, so I did. And ended up on crutches."

"Can you manage okay at home?"

"It's not easy, especially shopping, but Carly is helping out." Kat blushed.

"Carly?"

"The friend of Amanda's… my host. She's… uh… feeling guilty about my injury."

"Oh, okay. And is there any news on the research front?"

The blush faded. "Leah's taken a short break from thesis writing to draft something for *JSMT*. That's about the only thing since we talked last. Oh yes, and my Master's student, Susan Zeltzer, will definitely finish in May and will stay with me for a PhD. Her thesis will be to go after the transistor speed. I'm hoping to have preliminary results by the end of the summer so we can plan out her research program in detail.

So was your break good?"

"Lots of travel. The Integrated Electronics Conference in Denver and then a quick trip to my father in Maine. He's getting old, so I go when I can."

"You're lucky to have your family so close."

"I hadn't thought of Maine as close, but I guess you're right. Compared to Merida, Maine is close."

-   -   -

Later that day, Martin's presentation of Kat's case to the PC went well. He explained the basics of her idea: how if the processing is done just right, the speed and power efficiency of transistors would increase. There were questions about the pace of progress, but Martin was able to recount Kat's newest results showing experimental demonstrations of the requisite profile, and he mentioned that her next student was starting on the transistor measurements this summer. Rachel Pless, who did high-frequency circuit design, said that if Kat was right, the result could have immense significance for high-speed electronics, but the risks for a tenure case looked enormous. Dieter Tannhauser, in quantum computing, asked about her teaching. Martin was happy, even proud, to cite the most recent student polls which showed that Kat had developed into a highly-rated classroom and laboratory instructor, at least in small specialty classes. Bill Burke asked whether Martin thought her stuff was well enough known, especially these new results, to have a decent chance of getting good letters. Martin reported on the upcoming speaking tour and on the plan for her to submit a paper to the summer ESM where the hundred-or-so leaders in the field, at least from the US and Europe, would be meeting.

At the end of the discussion, Morris both thanked and congratulated Martin on the thoroughness of his preparation and mentoring. "Pretty good for a rookie," he said. The consensus around the table was that Kat's case would go forward in the fall as planned, and that the prospects were reasonable.

* **16** *

The first week of April, when the weather in Boston occasionally starts to resemble what the rest of the country experiences as spring, students come out of their dorms, their fraternities, their apartments, and want to join together in some kind of communal activity. Usually, it would take the form of a huge open-air rock concert in the student center courtyard with the aroma of weed permeating the air. But this year, the activity of choice was the protest in support of tenure for Sharon Gillespie. The news had first showed up in qwibble's *TFT* post, but when asked directly, Professor Gillespie freely told *The Widgit* that, yes, her tenure had been denied. As for an appeal, she said that there was such a process and that she had requested a Provost-level review, but that would probably take months. In the meantime, she had no option but to look for another position.

The robotics lab that Prof. Gillespie ran was the most popular course in Mechanical Engineering, and the January-term contest that she organized, attended by hundreds of cheering fans for one team or another, regularly made the national news. The denial of tenure to someone so prominent and beloved by students was taken by the early-April liberated as a slap in the face. Once *The Widgit* published the interview with Professor Gillespie, a protest boiled up. More than a hundred students, some with placards saying "Gillespie, Yes" and others, "Has CTI lost its mind?" marched up and down the main corridor of the interconnected skeleton of buildings, shouting "Heigh-ho, heigh-ho, we want Gillespie, so don't say no."

Being indoors, it was an all-weather protest, and with students ducking in and out of classes and replacing one another, it could be maintained at a fever pitch from early morning until dinnertime without anyone falling behind in their studies. Any classroom that was close enough to the main corridor periodically got overwhelmed by the shouts. On the second floor, above the main corridor, another group mounted a sit-in outside the Provost's office. No doors were broken down, no windows were shattered, no walls got spray painted (although a few bulletin boards did get trashed), and no one called for a boycott of classes. The post-2008 job market loomed too large in students' minds to allow themselves that degree of self-destruction.

While *The Widgit* faithfully reported on the protests, the numbers, the slogans, the calmness of the campus police, and the general civility of the whole thing, Manny Encarnacion was hoping for a higher-level discussion. He penned a column for the April 6 edition of *The Widgit*:

TRANSPARENCY IN TEACHING EVALUATION
by Emmanuel Encarnacion

At the end of every semester, thousands of teaching evaluations are collected by the various departments. Summaries prepared by student committees get published in *The Course Guide*, but, as *The Flame Thrower* is now asking, how do departments really weigh teaching in their evaluation of faculty for promotions and tenure? Are the departments pro-active in developing teaching excellence? Do they use the student evaluations, and if so, how? Will they promote an excellent teacher who is not a world-famous researcher? We, the CTI student community, want answers to these questions.

We suspect that the higher one goes up the promotion ladder, from Department Head to Dean to the Provost, the incentives shift from teaching to research. After all, the Provost and the Deans want CTI to be number one in the world, and the usual metric for that ranking is research superiority. Top researchers bring both prestige and grant money to CTI. What does a good teacher bring?

Unlike *TFT*, which functions more as a pressure valve than as an information medium, *The Widgit* is read by most students, some faculty, and by everyone in the upper academic ranks: Department Heads, Associate Department Heads, Deans, Associate Deans, Assistant Deans, Counseling Deans, the Provost, Associate Provosts, and Assistants to the Provost. Even Phillipa Prendergast, the CTI President, takes time out from her fundraising when a hot enough topic comes up. She asked the Provost to write to all concerned.

```
To: all-institute-council
Subject: Widgit article on role of teaching
in promotions

The article in today's Widgit about the use of
teaching in the evaluation of promotions raises
some important questions, especially regarding the
issue of different incentives at the various levels.
It is not something we discuss explicitly, but it
merits attention.

Those of us involved in the promotion process know
how heavily we weigh teaching in promotions deci-
sions, but the denial of tenure to Professor Sharon
Gillespie and the article in The Widgit have posed
for us a serious challenge: How can we document the
seriousness with which we take teaching without vio-
lating the confidentiality of the promotion process?

As you know, Associate Provost Marsha Collins is
in the process of convening a review panel on the
Gillespie case, and with this email, I now wish to
expand the charge of this panel to consider both
the incentives issue and how best to communicate our
seriousness around education. She will be asking some
of you to serve. She has my full support in asking,
so be prepared to say yes.

Alberto Ricci
Provost
```

Julian Kesselbaum, reading this message relayed to him by the infected computer belonging to Marsha Collins' assistant, muttered, "Okay, let's see what the emperor thinks he is wearing."

- -   -   -

The following day, Martin got some good news and some bad news. The good news was that DARPA selected Martin's White Paper for the full proposal phase, allowing sixty days to get it done, after which there would be a site visit at CTI during the last week of June. If they could win this grant, it would mean three more years of funding for one third of Martin's research group. The bad news was that until the submission deadline, Martin's life would be hell. It wasn't the CTI part. Peter Dempsey and his other CTI collaborator, Tony Fiorello, were usually prompt and reliable, getting their stuff in on time and in a reasonable state of accuracy. And Phelps from Purdue was too, although his junior colleague, Eamon McNair had been late on his pre-proposal section and screwed up his budget. It was the two Berkeley guys, Paderewski and Benson. Their ideas were good and greatly strengthened the potential impact of the program, but their concept of meeting a deadline was to send everything a week late, and their budgets had been hopelessly muddled the first time around.

Martin downloaded the instructions for the required format, created a page limit for each of the seven project descriptions, sketched out a timeline that would enable the full proposal to be completed two weeks before the deadline — including three days for the mandatory budgetary review — and then buffered it by an additional week in honor of Paderewski and Benson. Based on that highly compressed schedule, he sent emails to his colleagues telling them what they needed to send him in terms of project descriptions, biographies, publications lists, and budgets, and by when.

- -   -   -

Associate Provost Marsha Collins, generally considered to be Provost Ricci's best trouble-shooter, had convened her Tenure Review Panel. Including herself, the members were William Burke, now notorious as the author of the *TFT* post, Edwina Gamble, Associate Dean of

Engineering, Phil Galsworthy, Chairman of Chemical Engineering, and Carleton Hepplewhite, Dean of the School of Humanities. They drifted into the Provost's conference room, exchanged greetings, and took their seats.

"Thanks to everyone for agreeing to help," said Collins. "How many of you have served on a Tenure Review Panel before? I know Carleton has. Anyone else?"

Phil raised his hand and said, "I served on one at Harvard three years ago, but none here at CTI."

"In the past, we would have waited to do our tenure review until after all the spring tenure cases are complete. Then we would look at the cases that made it through and see if the challenge case, Professor Gillespie in this instance, was or was not comparable to the successful cases. But this year is different, given what the Provost wants us to do."

Marsha looked around the room at four attentive faces before continuing. "Alberto, possibly driven by the noise surrounding the Gillespie case and that highly thoughtful piece in *The Widgit*, really does want us to address how we can demonstrate to the community at large that we value teaching performance in promotions and tenure. And second, are there really incentives that drive us to devalue teaching? I would like hear from each of you, briefly please, on your initial takes on these two questions. Let's start with Bill, who, after all, we have to thank for Alberto's additional tasks." Laughter rippled around the table.

Burke blushed, smiled, and began. "Except maybe for mathematics, I think we teach the largest number of undergraduate course units at CTI, and we have far and away the most majors, so we must be doing something right. When we hire a new faculty member, we assign a senior faculty to be their teaching buddy — someone to talk to them about teaching, perhaps sit in on a class or two, and help each person get comfortable with a roomful of students. At promotion time we assign a member of our Personnel Committee to read all the student evaluations on that candidate and prepare a summary report to the committee. We get at least one inside letter from someone who has taught with that person and we have episodic input from members of the committee. We really do invest faculty time in developing good teachers, and we pay attention to teaching at promotion time."

Phil broke in. "But Bill, isn't the question whether you would promote in the face of a poor teaching record? I mean, what do you do with the brilliant superstar who is a disaster in a classroom? I know we have two or three of them in ChemE."

Burke said, "We do, from time to time, run into that. We'll have an Associate case next fall with exactly that problem. Well, not exactly, because he refuses to teach undergrads, period. A different problem, but a problem still. We don't want to lose him to Stanford, so I predict we'll want to promote. But for most of our faculty, the teaching needs to be at or above par to justify going forward."

Marsha asked, "Edwina, could you comment on that in the School of Engineering, overall?"

"We don't try to keep statistics, but I would say that more than eighty percent of our promotions have a strong teaching component."

Phil said, "But again, the question is whether you promote in the face of a poor teaching record. I've only been on Engineering Council for one year, but I've seen several cases go by like that."

"Yes," said Edwina, "but not anything like half."

"Carleton, you want to chime in?" asked Marsha.

"We live in a different world from you engineering types. If we didn't teach well, CTI would burn us into cinders and commit us to the ashcan. Look, we have MacArthur Fellows on our faculty, and they teach. It's true, by tenure time, everyone must have made some kind of scholarly contribution, and it needs to be pretty good, supported by outside letters. But I would say that we rank at top of the CTI spectrum in terms of valuing teaching."

"So I'm wondering," mused Marsha. "Thinking out loud. Suppose we, as a group, take a look at every tenure case from the past, say, three years, including this year of course, and do some kind of scoring on the extent to which teaching figured in the promotion. And then report the result back at our next meeting? Would that be useful?"

"That would be fantastic," said Phil, "but to be an honest review, it needs to include the unsuccessful cases as well as the ones that got through. Can we do that?"

Marsha said, "If a department sent a case forward to the School level, we can get it, but probably not for those that were turned down at the department level. Would that help?"

Phil responded. "Absolutely. I wonder why that information isn't already part of what the Provost's office compiles. Maybe it's related to incentives."

"Okay," said Marsha, "Incentives. I, for one, was offended by the *Widgit* editorial suggesting that the incentives did not match up and down the line. Do any of you agree with the statement that the incentives shift as cases move to the School and then to the Institute Council?"

"Of course I agree," said Carleton. "I've been on the Institute Council for three years, and my impression has been that teaching gets a check-mark. If it's okay, the case passes, but I can recall only one case in three years in which someone in engineering or science got tenure with a mediocre research record and exceptional teaching. It's pretty clear to me that at the Institute level, it's research, research, research."

Bill Burke said, "But we pay a lot of attention to teaching. It's really important."

"Bill," said Phil, "can you recall a single successful tenure case of a teaching superstar with only a mediocre research record?"

Burke hesitated. "Actually, no. No I can't. Well, maybe one. In CS, maybe five years ago."

"What about my suggestion?" asked Marsha. "We're going to have to review this year's cases no matter what. Isn't it also worth looking at the older cases? Right now, we're dealing with episodic memories. This is CTI. Shouldn't we look at some real data?"

Everyone agreed, and the task was parsed out. There had been twenty-eight tenure cases that made it at least to the School level over the past three years. Each member of the Task Force agreed to read and score a set of cases distributed over different years and departments so that each case would get two independent reads. The scoring scale was to be coarse: 'A' for either something innovative and important or a hugely popular teacher evidenced by growth in enrollment; 'B' for acceptably good but no real highlights; 'C' for a case with weakness on the teaching side. They would give a similar grade to the research component. Marsha said that her assistant would prepare the files for distribution later that week, and that the next meeting would be in a month to compile and compare results.

-    -   -

Kat was smiling when Martin arrived, the mid-afternoon sun brightening her office. "It's working, just like you said. I've got invitations to speak in June at Georgia Tech, Columbia, Cal Tech, Berkeley, and, just for good measure, Purdue, where Phelps is. I might want him on my own list, so I decided…"

"That's terrific," said Martin. "So now we're really ready to work on…"

"There's more. We got our final confirmation of actual diffraction-pattern implant arrays, and I already put that in to ESM for July."

"Wow, excellent. So let's get to the next…"

"And Leah, bless her heart, has just about finished a short paper for the Letters section of *JMST*. It should be ready to go in by the end of next week."

Martin beamed. "That's great. So before we get to my stuff, is there any more good news?"

"Yes. Frank Carillo's revised paper has been accepted for *JSMT* and I updated my CV. Here's a copy. I already sent it to Rebecca." She handed Martin a multi-page printout. "It has everything up to date, including Frank's paper and the anticipation of Leah's submission."

"You're a star. This is all great. Now let me tell you what I've come up with about names. By the time we're done with this, I will want to get three lists from you. The first one is what you already expected, the list of ten outside and five inside people that you think would be good letter writers. But we're going to need to work on that together because — here's my idea — we make a little chart. Each column is a student project, and each row is the name of a potential letter writer. We check off the boxes so that I know which letter writers know about which projects. Then when I give it to Morris, he'll be able to make sure there's at least one person who knows about each project."

Kat was already sketching a chart on the pad in her lap. "I like that. Very sensible. You want this chart now, or should I work on it a bit?"

"Take your time. I won't need it for at about a month, but it's worth doing well. And there's two more I want."

Kat looked up.

"I want you to make a list of your peers. Everyone in your field, broadly considered, that is within, say, three or four years of your academic age."

"Why do you need that?"

"Burke told me to get it. When we go out for letters, we ask for comparisons with peers. Burke tells me that sometimes, when a letter-writer makes a comparison, we don't know anything about the other person. At that point, it's too late to ask you because the contents of those letters are held in absolute silence. What I need to do is get educated about your peers before any letters come in. I probably know most of them, but I want you to think about it carefully. I'll want to know which ones are your direct competitors, and where exactly you think their stuff might be stronger or weaker than your stuff."

"Do you turn that list in too?"

"Actually, yes. I'm not sure how much annotation goes with the names. I'll find out, but I need to know about them, regardless of what detail goes to Morris."

"And there's one more?" asked Kat.

"Yes," said Martin. "Just in case. Anyone that you definitely don't want us to write to."

"I'll have to think about that one. I don't think there's anyone like that. Anyway, come see the results." Kat went to her computer screen and pulled up the graphic that demonstrated the diffraction-pattern implant arrays. Martin was impressed. Things were looking up.

* **17** *

Patriot's Day in Boston is full of celebrations. There are reenactments of the April 18th rides of William Dawes and Paul Revere, a mock battle on Lexington Green between the Redcoats and the Militias, and the Red Sox play their Monday home game at 11 AM so patrons can exit into Kenmore Square in time to enjoy the best event of all: the running of the Boston Marathon. From Hopkinton through Wellesley, Newton, Brookline, past Kenmore Square and into the Back Bay area of Boston, the streets are lined with cheering supporters as thousands of runners, some elite, others not, make their way to the finish line on Boylston Street.

Many CTI students, at least many of those not still marching up and down the main corridor, headed across the river to join the crowd. But this Patriot's Day was not typical. At just before three o'clock, two bombs went off in the midst of the crowd gathered near the finish line, killing three and maiming many, including several CTI students. There were body parts and rivers of blood on the street. Police, EMTs, people from the crowd, even doctors and nurses who were running in the marathon — everyone pitched in to help the injured. The medical tents already set up near the finish line to help exhausted runners became field hospitals to triage and treat.

The shock of the bombing put an immediate end to the Sharon Gillespie protest. As word spread up and down the corridor, the march and the sit-in disbanded. Everyone was too stunned to do anything resembling normality. Many tried to call those who went to the race, but the cell phone network was saturated. Masses of people streamed over the Mass Ave bridge from Boston, many crying, reporting to others what they had seen. The Dean of Students ordered the large campus theater opened and had TV news coverage piped in. It filled to overflowing within an hour.

In the absence of any understanding of the degree of threat that might still be around, President Prendergast ordered cancellation of regular classes on Tuesday, urging instead that professors use their class time for discussion with students, for counseling, and for comforting. Her formal statement of condolence urged the CTI community to pull together and volunteer to help in whatever form made sense.

It took until Thursday, but the FBI identified a pair of suspects from the videos, and they broadcast the pictures. Within hours, they had names, and the manhunt was on. The city was ordered into lockdown. No public transit, taxis, or train service. The airport stayed open, but under martial-law type security.

Martin, as distressed as anyone over the carnage and the terror lurking in the streets, stayed home on Friday with Jenny and JJ, glued to the television.

JJ asked, "Did they catch the bad guys yet, Daddy?"

"They caught one, but not the second," said Martin. "Those are very bad guys. They hurt lots of people."

"Did people die?"

"Yes, JJ. Some people died, and lots of people were hurt. It's very sad."

At around four o'clock, the phone rang. "There you are. I got no answer at your office. You've gotta come." Helen's voice was quavering over the phone. "He's had a stroke."

"When?" he asked.

"At lunchtime. He was coming down the stairs and he suddenly fell. We got the EMTs here quick, but they… I mean. Just come. He's in the hospital. I've got the kids at home."

"Is he awake?"

"Yes, but he can't talk and his left side is limp. Please come right away."

"Did you tell the hospital about his proxy?"

"No, but I'll call the nurse now. When can you get here?"

"Cambridge is in lockdown right now. I may need a permit to be out on the road, maybe not. I'll do whatever… You stay tight. Once I know my arrival time, I'll give you a call. I may even be there by tonight."

Martin called Steve Campbell at his home, asking him to take over lecturing whenever classes restarted. Jenny agreed that she and JJ would stay home and indoors until there was an arrest — no school, no shopping, nothing — and to call the police if anything suspicious turned up in the neighborhood. He called Seamus and Colleen and asked them to please keep an eye out for Jenny. Throwing a few things into an overnight bag, he got in the car and headed north, zigzagging across Somerville to the interstate, hoping not to hit police roadblocks, not knowing that the 'shelter-in-place' order had been lifted just about the time he left. The suspect had not been found in the cordoned search area.

As Martin hit the Maine border, the radio reported that a local resident outside the search area had found blood on the canvas cover on his boat parked in his backyard. Police were called in and the wounded suspect was found hiding in the boat. Boston's nightmare, if not over, was at least entering a new phase.

-     -   -

Martin went directly to the Mid-Coast Medical Center. The duty nurse said that Jeremiah was very weak. In addition to the damage from the stroke, he had congestive heart failure, so it was touch and go. She led Martin to a double room. Jeremiah was in the bed nearest to the door, a tangle of tubes, IV drips, electrodes, and oxygen monitors. A screen showed his heartbeat with all sorts of numbers Martin couldn't interpret. "You can stay if you wish," said the nurse. To Martin's raised eyebrows about the other patient in the room, she responded, "He's on heavy sedation. It's okay."

Martin sat next to Jeremiah's bed and picked up his right hand, squeezing it. A faint squeeze came back. Martin began talking to his father, telling him how much he valued the stories of the classics, rambling on about the expeditions into the wilds of Maine, the lessons about intellectual integrity and the importance of family, and Jenny's pregnancy. He took a brief break to get some coffee in the hospital canteen, anticipating a long night's vigil. When he returned and squeezed Jeremiah's hand, there was no response. The heartbeat screen suddenly went flat. Alarms started beeping and the nurse rushed in. "Oh, dear. Looks like... But his daughter said we were not to..."

"That's right," said Martin. "It's what he wanted. No heroics. It's over." Martin wept.

- - -

The funeral reception was winding down. Martin was seated in Jeremiah's study as Helen came in. "Ready?" he asked.

"I guess so," she said. "It was nice of Fred, President Walsh I mean, to come. That was pretty special. He and Dad were friends. And the Dean too. Anyway, Jenny's putting the kids to bed and the food's been stowed. The dishes can wait. Jenny said we should listen, just the two of us. Turn it on. Let's see what it was he... "

"Okay. Here goes." Martin pressed the switch, and that familiar raspy voice, but with uncharacteristic halting and pauses, filled the room.

> "I meant to do this sooner, kids... talking straight... but I kept putting it off. After Martin shook me up about the money thing, I've been meaning to tell you. The need... I mean the wish... the urge... whatever... I started to feel it the year I turned seventy. All of a sudden I was in the third act... of a three-act play, except... except... I didn't know when the curtain... And how... But I could see that damned curtain, suspended over the stage, just hanging there... hanging... waiting to drop. And I

felt I owed you. They say the show must go on... And it did. Even though foreign trips no longer seemed interesting. Even though I saw no point in going to a party to meet people whose names I wouldn't remember and who I wouldn't see again 'til the same party next year. Even though the medicine I take so that I can pee diluted whatever enjoyment I used to get from sex to the point where I wondered if it was worth the bother... Yes, kids, Karen and I had regular sex right up until she got sick. I hope you have the same good fortune... Anyway, the show must go on. Even though the arthritis was eating at my hands and God-knows-what might be growing in my brain. That's what killed my mother — a brain tumor. Age 72. Malignant. And my uncle Mike. Same thing. Same age. I was 35 when my mother died. It just felt like the end of an act. Act one. I guess that made turning seventy into one of those weird anniversaries shrinks talk about... At age seventy, act two, also 35 years long, was over. Or maybe it was retiring. Talk about a milestone. For the first time since I was a teenager, I didn't have a job. Karen used to tease me that way. She was always after me to travel abroad. Egypt, Greece, Vietnam, Cambodia. 'Travel in your seventies,' she would say, 'while you still can.' But something had already died in me, and even though we did go places, I almost always wished we had either stayed home, or gone where I wanted — to the woods up north, with a canoe and a tent. I'd seen enough goddam temples. Maybe that's a lame excuse. Maybe I was frightened... And ashamed of it... The world is less friendly to Americans than when we were young, and that gave me pause. And speaking of shame, I'm still ashamed about the time I slapped Helen. You were maybe five or six, and something you said around bedtime blew my fuse. Of course, it wasn't you... It was your mother... You took the brunt of my fury at her, and I never apologized. I should have. I do now. It wasn't until after the divorce that I got some perspective on all that. Your mother was really unhappy about life — depressed. She couldn't sell her crazy paintings and she didn't want to take care of children... And she had started drinking. I didn't understand what that does to people, although after seeing what Helen went through with Felipe, I do now. All I knew at the time is that she would drink, pick fights, go to bed, and wake up the next morning with no memory of the night before. I couldn't get her to stop drinking, even after I stopped altogether, and she wouldn't go to any kind of counseling. Then one day she just up and went to New York, leaving me with the two of you. I never really found out why."

Martin paused the tape. "What is it about us Quints that our first wives turn out to be depressed?

Helen sighed. "You just don't realize how full of yourselves you are."

"Really?"

"Really. After Mom left, Dad seemed to wake up. He had to care for us on his own, so he wasn't first in line anymore. You don't remember? And you, with your incredible fuck-up. Katie did you a favor by blowing things sky high. You've actually become sort of a nice person, cut down to size, especially since you've been with Jenny. She's amazing. So is there more?"

Martin, with a quiet harrumph, restarted the recording:

"Anyway, I did the best I could with you two. It was Evelyn who straightened me out. Yes, yes, I know.

She was only a year older than Martin, but she was wise beyond her years. She helped me heal. We had no future, of course. She wanted kids and I didn't want any more. You two were more than enough for me. I'm assuming you're together, by the way, listening to this. If not, whoever has it should copy it for the other. One of the things I've taken pleasure from is the way the two of you have finally become friends. Sometimes it really does take thirty years or so for sibs to recognize the worth in each other. I've gotta go now. I'll finish this later. I still need to tell you about Karen and how she saved my life."

Helen, dabbing at her eyes with a tissue, looked to her brother. "Is that it?"

"I guess so. I could only find this one cassette."

-    -   -

Jenny stayed at the house to mind the children while Helen and Martin went to the lawyer's office on Maine Street for a reading of the will. It was simple. Martin was named executor. Helen got the Brimfield Junction house, mortgage-free, and the survivor rights on the portion of the Bottlesworth pension that was in a 401(k), worth just over two hundred thousand, but not something Helen could draw on until her own retirement. Martin got the Sagadahoc Point cottage and the Schwab account. No other bequest and no instructions about furnishings or possessions. The lawyer set up Martin with instructions for establishing the appropriate estate accounts and notifications and how to claim the life insurance, and their meeting was adjourned.

Martin was happy to have the cottage, but he was concerned that his father had not provided Helen with access to some cash. When they sat together that evening, Martin wrote her a check for two-thousand dollars to tide her over until they could get into his father's bank account and collect the insurance. He said it was a loan, but they both knew that it wasn't.

-    -   -

Martin, dressed in his concert threads — a black turtle neck, black slacks and his black dress shoes — was at the piano in the Little Theater, warming up an hour before the 2:30 concert. Vladimir and Sumner, similarly attired, arrived with the programs, followed shortly by black-clad Horatio. They headed for the cramped green room to the right of the stage to unpack and warm up. After a few minutes, Horatio came out with his electronic tuner which he adjusted to match the A on the piano, returning to the green room to allow full tuning before coming onstage.

Martin finished his warm-up and arranged the music stands for the Beethoven, set up his audio recorder on the tripod and put the programs on a music stand just outside the entrance to the hall. He waited until Jenny and JJ arrived with Seamus and Colleen. JJ had on a little blue suit, complete with a red clip-on bow tie. His job was to hand everyone a program and the sheet of program notes. This was his first ever ushering at one of Martin's concerts, and he kept asking, "Mommy, Mommy. When are the people coming? When, Mommy?"

By the time 2:30 rolled around, the hall was half full, mostly CTI people with a mix of family and friends of Horatio and Sumner. Martin surveyed the audience before retreating to the green room. Kat was there, seated to the left with a taller blond woman. So was Charlotte Papadopoulos, seated well to the right. She was Alex's ex-wife and the person who had introduced Martin to Jenny. Tamara Eliot, who Martin knew was on the Educational Policy Committee, was there with a man too young to be a husband, and Morris's shock of white hair was visible toward the back. Even Marsha Collins was perched in the third row with her husband and two teenaged girls.

Martin, Vladimir, and Horatio emerged from the green room, took a bow, and went to their seats. JJ shouted, "There's Daddy," and was immediately shushed by Jenny. Before starting the concert, Martin got up and asked everyone to stand for a moment of silence to honor the victims of the Marathon bombing. After a full minute, he said, "With the event so fresh, with the wounds still raw, not just to bodies, which is horrible enough, but to our communal sense of safety, in our own homes, in our own streets, we commend those who stood strong and continue to stand strong. Boston Strong. We dedicate this concert to everyone involved: the victims, their families, the police and emergency personnel, the helpers of all kinds, and to our city, our people, and our spirit." After another short pause, he took his seat at the piano, and with the launch of the *Archduke* trio, the concert began.

The music was mostly well played, but with those occasional hiccups performers always want back. Horatio missed the rhythm of the ending of the Beethoven, Martin played a wayward C-sharp in the Brahms, and Vladimir's intonation in the schmaltzy Bruch trio was a bit off. But the audience was happy. The final cadence of the *Opus 114* trio brought down as much thunderous applause as one could muster from an audience of fifty.

Vladimir, who didn't play in the Brahms, brought out cider, cookies and a fruit plate, and the audience stayed around for the refreshments. Charlotte sought out Jenny just as Kat was introducing Martin to Carly, who bubbled over about the music before the two of them drifted off together. Martin introduced Horatio to Tamara, telling her that he had been enormously helpful as Martin developed his ideas about education as a conversation, ideas that he planned to bring up with the Educational Policy Committee in the fall. Tamara asked, "So tell me. Isn't there someone at CTI who does this kind of research?"

Horatio smiled. "Well, linguistics at CTI is kind of held captive to a particular theory of grammar, and the guys I've been telling Martin about are not in that camp. So I guess the answer is no. You have to cross the river to be able to hear the sounds of a different drummer."

"So be it, I guess. I'm looking forward to learning more about Martin's point of view."

* **18** *

Marsha Collins' Tenure Review Panel met to discuss the results of the study of the twenty-eight tenure cases that had been approved by the various departments, seven of which got turned down at either the School or Institute levels. Since each case got two reads, there were fifty-six scores for each topic. Marsha was at the white board writing out a chart from the notes that her assistant had compiled:

Teaching	A	B	C
Tenured	7	27	8
Denied	4	6	4

Research	A	B	C
Tenured	38	4	0
Denied	0	12	2

When Marsha finished, the room went silent. There couldn't be a cleaner result. After what felt like an interminable silence, Phil Galsworthy said, "Well, no need even to do a chi-squared test on these data. Research grade predicts tenure. Teaching grade doesn't."

Carleton said, "Looks like there were only two cases with 'B' grades in research that got tenure, accounting for the score of four. These were probably Humanities cases. Is this right?"

Marsha, Phil Galsworthy, Bill Burke, and Edwina confirmed that they had each scored one tenured Humanities case with a 'B' in research.

Carleton continued, "As I said last time, Humanities values teaching first, research second. But for CTI as a whole, my theory is confirmed.

Education performance is a check-mark. You need an 'A' in research but you can get tenure even with a 'C' in teaching. So how on earth can we go out with a straight face, like Bill did, and tell the community that teaching is highly valued in our promotion process? What kind of liars are we prepared to be?"

Bill protested. "But Carleton, we really do value teaching, and we invest money and effort and time to make sure our teaching is good. Our cover letters always spell out the teaching record along with the research record."

"Maybe so," said Carleton, "but by the time your cases get to the Engineering School, or further up the line to the Institute Council, the 'A' filter gets applied to research and, with only two exceptions in the past three years, without that 'A', no tenure. So whoever wrote that *Widgit* article about incentives may be right. No matter what departments do, the upper-level filters go only for research."

Phil asked, "Who are the denied cases with an 'A' in teaching? Is one of them Gillespie?"

"Yes," said Marsha. "The Gillespie case is one of them. The other, I think, is Kesselbaum, yes?" Edwina and Bill nodded. "I had to review Gillespie right after she filed her appeal. Her research was probably a 'C' at best, although our group seems to have given it a 'B', and while the department put the case forward, it was in full recognition that it might fail. Isn't that right, Edwina?"

"Yes, it's true," she responded. "Mechanical warned us that it was bringing forward a strong teaching case with a questionable research record. The Engineering School just couldn't buy it, but that was partly because the department itself was ambivalent. So in the brouhaha that resulted, the official word was 'lack of department commitment' to the case."

"So CTI lied about that one too?" Carleton was getting agitated. "Why the hell not tell the truth, that it was turned down at the ES level? Why push the blame on the department?"

"Because the department waffled," said Edwina. "They didn't come to ES pounding the table. They sort of tiptoed into the room hoping she would pass. Didn't want the stigma of turning down a woman. If they really wanted her to succeed, they went about it the wrong way. They should have demanded she be approved, and when it wasn't, gone public and made a stink, showing full department support for her case. But that's not what they did. They went through the right motions, telling her they had passed the case up, but then wouldn't fight for her when ES wasn't happy."

Carleton asked, "But why wasn't ES happy? As I recall, she had an absolutely stellar teaching record, design labs and the robotics bake-off, with teams from all over the Institute. What was ES worried about?"

Edwina said, "It's the Dean's decision, and he can tell you better than me. But tenure is like a thirty-year commitment, and he was worried that there wasn't enough substance to last for thirty years. So he signaled back to the department that he wasn't satisfied, and the department simply didn't fight back. They let her be thrown under the bus."

"So are we going to pull the bus off her?" asked Marsha. "We still need to do a specific review of this year's successful cases after the Corporation approves them. I'll circulate instructions when we're ready."

-    -   -

Manny Encarnacion was puzzled.

```
To: e.encarnacion@cti.edu
From: mark.felt@cti.edu

You might be interested in the fact that the
Provost's Tenure Review Panel on the Gillespie case
has gone back to look at three years of tenure cases
and the results prove, beyond a shadow of a doubt,
that only research determines tenure. Teaching just
doesn't matter.

I've got the data. If you want to publish it, let me
know right away.
```

Manny scanned the CTI on-line directory to see who Mark Felt was, but there was no such person listed. He tried Google and discovered that a person named Mark Felt was none other than Deep Throat of Watergate fame. He called the office of Associate Provost Marsha Collins who, he knew, was the likeliest candidate to chair the Review Panel. Good journalists verify. He got an appointment.

\- \- \-

Marsha grew more and more furious as she read and reread the printed copy of the email that Manny had just given her. "Listen," she said, "I think you have done the responsible thing here. To alert me, I mean, to what looks like some kind of leak. This is a serious problem. Can we talk off the record?"

Manny took his recorder out of his pocket and put it on the table, showing Marsha that it was off.

"It is true," said Marsha, "that we're doing a review. Your editorial in *The Widgit* was the stimulus for a lot of thinking within the academic administration, and the Provost asked us to do a policy review. But the fact of it as well as the content of it is confidential. Of course, everyone knows that Professor Gillespie has appealed her negative tenure decision, and that appeal is part of our responsibility. But on the larger questions, we don't intend to issue a report until the fall. Can I ask that you not publish on this until our report is ready?"

"Will I be able to interview you about the report in the fall?"

"Of course, Manny. We're happy to talk when we've done our work properly."

"Okay. I can wait. It's the end of term anyway, and everyone will scatter as soon as exams are over. But who is this Mark Felt person? And if what he got is real, how did he get it?"

"My top priority," said Marsha, shaking hands with Manny and ushering him to the office door.

There was no Mark Felt at CTI. There was an account in that name, but the home address was bogus, the telephone number was disconnected, and the CTI ID number was not one that had ever been issued by either the Registrar or by Human Resources. What now?

- - -

Marsha passed around copies of the smoking email at an emergency meeting of her Review Panel, convened within the hour after Manny left her office. "Okay, you see what I see. I met with Mr. Encarnacion and he has agreed not to publish anything, but the fact is, I'm very troubled that there's been a leak. This email is too specific, and it came out right after we drew that chart of results. Anyone have an idea as to how it happened?"

A grim silence descended on the table, heads shaken in disbelief.

"Well, did anyone actually write the chart down and take it from the meeting?"

They all had, but consistent with standard CTI policies, everyone had put their notes into a locked file after the last meeting. Did anyone else have keys to that file? Of course — everyone's assistant had access.

"So do I get campus police? To interrogate your assistants?"

Carleton said, "Marsha, perhaps you're overreacting. After all, there has been a lot of chatter on *The Flame Thrower* about this issue, and maybe some student is just being cute."

"But there is no such student," said Marsha. "Mark Felt is the name of Deep Throat."

"You mean the sender is a ghost account?" asked Bill Burke.

"That's what I mean," said Marsha.

"Sounds like somebody's computer has been hacked," said Bill. "If the account is bogus, it means the author of the email is a skilled hacker. Maybe we should be checking computers. Who compiled the results?"

"It was my assistant," said Marsha.

"So get IT to check her computer. Much more likely than one of our assistants."

"And," said Carleton, "you should probably tell *TFT* not to accept posts from Mark Felt."

"Good point," said Marsha. "Will do."

But it was too late. As soon as the meeting was over, Marsha called Ethel McKinsey, who agreed to delist the mark.felt logon ID, but Ethel said that there had been one post from that ID under the Teaching v Research thread. Marsha went to *TFT* and saw their chart, exactly as it had been drawn on her white board, posted with this explanation:

> The Provost's Tenure Review Panel has examined all the tenure cases from 2011 through 2013, two review-ers for each case, giving grades of A, B, or C to both the research and teaching records. Here are the results. Can anyone look at these results and say teaching matters in the award of tenure? Only research predicts tenure. Just look.
>
> mark.felt

Marsha immediately sent an email to the *TFT* team to get the post taken down, knowing full well that it had probably been copied by students and would appear in Twitter feeds and on Facebook pages, but she had to get that post off of a CTI-sponsored website. She also sent a message to her Review Panel, with a cc to Alberto Ricci, notifying them of the post and telling them that, in the event that any questions come to them about the Review Panel, they should be referred to her office. She told her assistant that she was to answer no questions at all about the Review Panel. It was stonewall time, Deep Throat or no Deep Throat.

She then called in CTI IT Security, the Campus Police, and, on the advice of IT Security, the FBI, since it was always a possibility that cyber break-ins like this violated a federal law. The FBI asked IT to keep the Felt account in the system while they did their forensic work. Meanwhile, the IT team called in their most sophisticated consultant, Julian Kesselbaum.

After a few days, Julian did a Julian. He identified a subtle bit of malware code they had never seen before. It had been installed on the assistant's machine, permitting reading of every keystroke and every file by an external agent. While Julian did not manage to identify who the external agent was, he did write a memo documenting what he had learned. The security team then worked furiously to develop a patch that would prevent other machines at CTI from becoming infected.

After discussing the entire incident with the Provost and several of the Deans, Marsha sent an email.

```
To: cti-academic-deans; cti-department-heads
Subject: Highly Important Computer Security Issue

There has been a serious computer break-in within the
Provost's office complex by an unknown individual who
appears to be targeting sensitive information specific
to the subject of promotions and tenure.

We have no idea whether the upcoming fall promotion
sequence will encounter similar problems, but to
reduce the risk of electronic compromise of sensitive
information, we ask that you put into your promotion-
solicitation letters an explicit request that the
letters be sent to you via fax or in hard copy, not
in email.

Marsha Collins
Associate Provost
```

When Julian got home that evening, he found a copy of Marsha's email on his computer, having been snarfed up by his keyword search. He had to give the Provost credit for recognizing the threat. But, as he liked to say, the weakest link in any network is the people who use it. He went to the list of Personnel Committee members that he had extracted from Rebecca's computer, wondering how best to get hold of a set of letters once the time was ripe.

* **19** *

Mark Felt's posting on *TFT* produced what might be called standard outrage from the small fraction of students who were still reading *TFT* in the midst of preparation for final exams. Calls for statements from the Provost got no reply, and once exams started in earnest, things quieted down.

For Martin, the end of term had finally arrived. Only a few loose ends to clean up before the summer break. As he left for CTI, Martin thought back to that poem he had to memorize in high school. "And what is so rare as a day in June? Then, if ever, come perfect days." It wasn't June yet, but it was that kind of day, a bluebird day, warm, no clouds, no wind. Martin took the long way, taking in the fragrance of the feathery lilacs behind Loeb House, diagonally through the Yard to the Square, then down to the river through the undergraduate Harvard houses, with their blazing patches of red azaleas in odd corners and the occasional blossoming dogwood. Flurries of students, some hurrying toward the Yard, others packing up to make room for the various class reunions. The chaos of May. He loved it.

Gina and Ahmed were waiting in the outer office when Martin arrived, ready for their final report. Martin ushered them in, directing them to the sofa, and looked from one to the other, asking, "Okay, who goes first?"

Ahmed glanced at Gina, then said, "I guess I'll start. I found that one hundred and forty of your students from this term were also signed up for the MOOC. We segregated their surveys by a code so we could look at the two groups. No names, just groups. The results are really interesting."

Gina took over. "We got a 72% response, I mean, survey returns, from the ones registered for the MOOC. For the ones taking only the class, it was, like, 54%. And it's pretty clear that the, y'know, convenience, I mean flexibility, of watching the lectures at home on their own schedule is, like, the most important thing. The students in the MOOC basically no longer came to lecture. A lot of them didn't even come to section. And here's the most incredible thing. The MOOC version has an online circuit simulator, and, like, the people in the regular class were using it to solve your homework problems."

Martin sat silent for several minutes. "Ahmed, tell me about your interactions with students."

Ahmed looked sideways at Gina. "Uh, pardon the blunt language, but it sucked. They have this online discussion forum, and students can type in questions, and other students can comment, but it's horribly inefficient. I would spend hours responding to things that had already been answered, but the students couldn't find the answers in the clutter on the website. It's pretty hopeless. "

Gina added, "But they liked the little online tutorials. The videos with Prof. Huang working out examples by hand. The MOOC people said, like, it was as good as they would get in section."

Martin asked Ahmed, "Do you think those tutorials replace section?"

"They certainly help, but no, not really. I'm pretty fed up with this teaching style. When I was your TA, we could really talk to the students, and they could ask questions in real time. The forums are just typed text — no eye contact and no way to judge comprehension."

"Meaning no real conversation," said Martin.

"Exactly," said Ahmed. "It's all one way, or at least one way at a time."

"What about the final exam?"

"Ahmed did the statistical analysis," said Gina. "The students who signed up for the MOOC scored twelve percent lower on the final than the students who didn't."

"Yes," said Ahmed, "and it's statistically significant. The p-value is .02. A clean result."

"Wow. But let me ask," said Martin, "how many of the MOOC students were CS instead of EE. Is there any way to tell that? I mean it's possible that this result just says that the EE students did better than the CS students, and that's not so interesting."

Ahmed shrugged. "It's the spring term," he said. "Most of the students are freshman, and they don't have majors identified yet. There weren't enough sophomores in the sample, so we just can't answer that. Does it mean this was all useless?"

"Not at all," said Martin. "The reason to do research is to learn not just the answers, but the next set of questions."

Gina asked, "So what should we put in our final report?"

"Tell it like it is," said Martin. "Report the results. Ahmed will help you to get the statistical language right, for that part, but you also have the survey results about class attendance and the circuit simulator as well as your own impressions. I think both of you did a bang-up job. Thank you, thank you. This will be immensely helpful when I raise my concerns with the Educational Policy Committee."

As they rose to go, Martin asked, "I know Ahmed is going one hundred percent into thesis-writing mode, but Gina, what's on tap for you?"

"Oh, I have an internship with HP in Portland."

"Maine?" asked Martin.

"No, Oregon. That's where my boyfriend lives."

"Well, be sure to check in with me when you get back. I'm sure I can use your help again next term."

-    -   -

Kat's walking cast was gone but she still needed the occasional support of a cane. She was looking over her lists while she waited for Martin, who was uncharacteristically late. First, the outside letters, organized as Martin had asked. Each name had a two-sentence descriptor of their field and her relationship with them, and Kat had constructed Martin's suggested matrix, one column for each student project, one row for each name, and a checkmark in the box if that person knew about that project. Next, five inside letters covering research, teaching, and service. Finally, the peers, a rambling list of eight, none of whom, in her opinion, were doing any better work than she was.

Martin rushed in, apologizing for his tardiness, but eager to share his new result. "Did you know that the students from my course who also signed up for Harry's MOOC did worse than the ones who didn't sign up?"

"You mean C&E students did both? At the same time?"

"Yes. More than a hundred. Most of them stopped coming to lecture, and a lot of them also skipped sections. And they did worse. Exactly what I predicted."

Kat smiled. "No conversation, right?"

"In fairness," Martin said, "we don't know whether the ones who did worse were from CS, but the results give me some ammunition. I hate the whole idea of these MOOCs."

Kat giggled. "You mean your mind is made up, so you need to find some facts to support it?"

"Hey, that's not fair. I told you we don't know their majors. Anyway, are we ready for the final lists? But before that, what's the news from home?"

"She's in radiation now. But my uncle is worried. She's very weak, apparently. Feels bad all the time. I'm going home for ten days right after the end of term. I can squeeze that in before my lecture circuit. But the good news is that I got an email this morning from Carl Urquhart. My ESM paper is accepted for oral presentation. On Wednesday morning."

"Fantastic. So we'll go together. I'll get Felice to make arrangements, and, remember, the travel expense for this one is on me, on my slush fund, that is. For today, though, it's time for a final run-through on your names. I want to take some notes."

When they had finished going through the names for outside letters and the peers, Martin said, "Before we move to the insiders, I need to know whether there's anyone out there you feel would be an unfair or hostile writer. Anyone you had a run-in with who might bear a grudge. Something like that."

"I thought about it as you suggested, but I couldn't think of anyone. I mean, mostly, people are nice to me. Even Phelps. He can be cranky, but he's always been completely supportive, as far as I can tell."

"So you've never had a professional fight with anyone? Problems with reviewers, things like that?"

"Not really. My problems with reviewers have been that the papers really weren't that good until they got revised. So no, if there's somebody out there with a grudge, I don't know about it."

"Okay, let's move to the insiders." Kat handed him her list.

Martin commented as he read. "One from me, Ken another, and certainly Milton. But wouldn't Dan Cranagh be a better teaching reference than Andy Ulster?"

"Uh… Dan? That term wasn't as good for me as I wanted. I did a term of E&M with Andy, and that went pretty well."

"Okay, he'll do, but Gabrielle Visconti? Humanities? Who's she?"

"She chaired the Committee on Women at CTI that I was on a few years ago. We really hit it off, and I think I had some good input."

"But I'm curious, why not Peter Dempsey? I mean, with his expertise he would be an important advocate."

"Well," said Kat, now blushing, "he was… um… kind of aggressive, socially, when I first joined the faculty, and I'm just not sure what he thinks about me now."

"Aggressive socially? What is that code for?"

"Martin. What do you think it means?"

-    -   -

Talking with Martin about the lists had worn Kat out. She picked up the phone and called Carly. They agreed on dinner at Sandrine's in Harvard Square, and then to Carly's condo on Trowbridge Street to watch a movie.

Since that ski trip to Killington, Kat had made gradual peace with the shocking discovery that Carly, both as friend and as sexual partner, was better than any man she had ever been with. She had been so gentle. Getting Kat to talk about life at CTI, her life back in Merida, grad school, the men she had enjoyed, or not enjoyed, Carly wondering why Kat only went with unsuitable men, wondering on the fourth night whether she had been choosing the unsuitables for a reason, perhaps wondering what it would be like for her to be with a woman, how attractive Carly found her, and wanted to kiss her, and how she did, and how it led to the rapture she had imagined as a teenager, but taking a form she had never anticipated.

They skied only half days after that, discovering each other in ways that made Kat blush to think about, but also made her eager for more. She was looking forward to the day, post tenure, when she and Carly could declare themselves in public.

- - -

"When I asked Kat who out in the world should be avoided, she didn't mention anybody, so I'm assuming you have a pretty free hand. How many do you want to take from her lists?"

Morris, in the black leather chair facing Bill Burke and Martin on the sofa, replied, "Her list of insiders looks fine, at least at first glance. On the external letters, I think the best thing is for you to talk through her list with us, one by one, so we know the territory. Normally, I would want to take something like seven from her list, trying to get decent topic coverage. But beyond that, I prefer that Bill and I make a final decision in private. It will be easier for you in your interactions with Kat if you don't know the exact list of names until the letters come in."

"You're probably right. We're going together to the European Workshop on Semiconductor Materials. It's in Istanbul in July. She'll have a chance to meet the top international players there. She's giving a paper on her newest results, the interference patterns. But you're right. If I don't know who will be asked to write, I won't accidentally fuck things up."

"Yeah, that's the idea," said Morris. "You've done a super job getting her ready. She told me the other day that she has a big speaking tour in June, through all the major US centers. And this European deal will help a lot. You've done amazing things with her. For her. I'm really hoping that the letters give us the support we need to get her through. She would be a fantastic role model for both our women and our Hispanic students. And it would be a gold star for CTI's mentoring of women and minorities, especially after that catastrophe with Gillespie. We need a win this time."

PART II: Summer, 2013

* 20 *

Martin and Jenny were celebrating her thirty-first birthday and her having passed the thirteen-week milestone with a picnic lunch at the Arnold Arboretum, amidst the riotous reds and pinks of the azaleas and the wafting perfumes from the lilacs. JJ was riding his bicycle up and down the nearby path, rocking on the training wheels, screaming, "Mommy, Mommy. Look at me. Look at me!"

"He's so cute," said Jenny. "Isn't he ready to try without the training wheels?"

"He's getting really close. Certainly this summer. It means I'm going to have to get a bicycle so we can go out together."

"Hey. Why just you, goofus? I know how to ride."

"You too, of course. But not until our little creature has emerged."

"Foo," said Jenny. "I can probably ride until August, anyway. So let's go bicycle shopping, okay? Two bicycles."

"Okay. Two bicycles. It'll be fun."

"Speaking of going places, I think it's time we talked about travel this summer, with or without bicycles. I'm a bit edgy about the baby, so I'm hoping you can minimize the time you're away. I'd like to spend as much time at the cottage as possible. Yes?"

"Let's see. The DARPA site review for the new proposal is here in Cambridge, so unless another sponsor summons me to a review I can't fob off on someone else, I have only the Device Research Conference next month. I guess I could skip that, actually. Maybe one or two short consulting gigs — just two nights each, and the Istanbul thing in July. I really can't cancel that."

"Why not? I thought you said we could work it out if I got pregnant?"

"Well, the stakes are higher now."

"Why? What stakes? You're already king of that world, aren't you?"

"Yes, maybe, but Kat isn't, and this is her only chance to meet the international big shots before we go out for letters."

"Kat? She's going with you? Why can't she go alone?"

"Look, Jenny, it's my job. Do you remember the campus riots over Sharon Gillespie? The department needs to get her through, and I'm responsible. It's important."

"Important? Your family is not important? You want to take off for a week in a foreign country with a seductive woman while your pregnant wife takes care of your house?"

"Jesus, Jenny. Where did that come from? Seductive? You sound jealous. Where the hell did that come from?"

"Ever since you joined that committee, it's been Kat this and Kat that and oh, goody, Kat got a speaking engagement, and how neat, Kat got a paper accepted. She has cast some kind of spell on you, and she's had plenty of practice."

"Now that's just not fair. It's my job, my assignment, to get her through tenure. Istanbul is her best shot between now and the fall."

"Is she worth it? Really? Are you sure she deserves tenure?"

Martin paused. "I've never heard you like this. That's what we're trying to find out. She deserves an honest shot at it, and my responsibility is to see that she gets it."

"You mean that she gets what she deserves?"

"Yes. Exactly."

"Well, based on… I mean, I suspect that CTI would be better off without her."

"My God, Jenny. What are you saying?"

"Martin, wake up. Don't you know what she's done?"

"I don't know what you're talking about."

"She sleeps around. With her faculty colleagues."

Martin's mouth hung open. "I just can't believe…"

"Tell me," said Jenny, brushing some ants off their picnic blanket.

"What exactly has Kat told you about her relationships at CTI?"

"She doesn't tell me much. She did say that she and a friend, a woman friend, by the way, went off skiing over spring break and how nice it was to finally have a close friend outside of CTI. We met her, or at least I did, at the concert. Her name was Carla something-or-other. You might have noticed her. Tall blonde. Short hair."

"That's it? Nothing else?"

"There was something, a long time ago. Kind of odd, actually, so maybe that's why I remember it. During her first year or maybe second, she said that there must be a lot of unhappy marriages at CTI. Oh yes, and she did mention Peter Dempsey when we were talking about letter writers. She said he was socially aggressive toward her when she first joined the faculty. But she never indicated that she had… "

"But she has. At least twice."

"How do you know?"

"Charlotte. Charlotte Papadopolous. She knows everything about everybody. Real estate is like that. You gossip."

"And you think she actually knows about this stuff? It's not just malicious twaddle?"

"Oh, yes. She even told me about your fling way back, right away, at the inn where we met."

"You mean she told you before I did?"

Jenny nodded.

"And you never let on?"

"No. You told me about it yourself. That's what mattered."

"But that was later. Why did you even go out with me?"

"I'm not sure. Maybe it was because Charlotte thought you had gotten a raw deal in your first marriage. As I said, she knew everything about everybody. She liked you, in spite of... Told me to be careful, but her intuition said you might be worth it."

Jenny paused to remember, so Martin, with a teasing lilt in his voice, asked, "So was I? Worth it?"

Jenny cracked a smile. "Well," she said, with a dramatic pause, "you were kinda cute, sexy, and I guess I was curious and maybe a bit lonely. It had been more than a year since George…"

"I'm sorry. I know you still miss him."

"Yes and no. He was wonderful, but he's been dead long enough for me to find some peace with it. The fact is, when I saw you at the inn, I missed the smell and touch of a man. I was, to use a man's term, horny. I went slow with you because I was afraid of mixing you up with George. But not as slow as you did. Yikes. You were turtle slow." Jenny giggled. "At least I knew you weren't taking me out just to get laid."

Martin reddened. "Well I'm glad you... But tell me. I really need to know. Who has Kat been with?"

"How about Charlotte's ex-husband."

"Ohmigod. No wonder she knew. And he's on the PC."

"So stand back and take a look. You have a pregnant wife for whom sex has become slightly uncomfortable, and you want to take a seductress to God knows where? So you see why? Why I'm upset?"

Martin nodded. "I'm sorry. Yes. I get it. But you've gotta realize, she has never come on to me. At all. Nothing. Nada. We're buddies, partners. That's it. I promise you, there will be no nonsense with Kat. I'll sign it in blood. I'll stay strapped to the mast."

Jenny looked puzzled. "It's from the Odyssey," he said. "To keep himself from falling prey to the Sirens, Odysseus put wax in the ears of his sailors so they couldn't hear and had them strap him to the mast of his ship as he sailed past their island. It worked."

"Well, I think we still need to talk about this." But Martin barely heard her. How could Alex Papadopoulos possibly act on Kat's tenure? Wouldn't he have to recuse himself? And wouldn't that blow things open?

-     -   -

The week before the Memorial Day weekend, Jenny and her client went off to New York to do serious antique shopping. Jenny had found most of what they wanted through Boston dealers, but her client had fallen in love with the work of David Roentgen and there was a game table coming up for auction in early June that she wanted to see in person before authorizing what might be, at a minimum, a $150,000 purchase. Since there were six other New York dealers who had responded with interesting proposals to Jenny's inquiries, they decided to make a week of it.

Martin, still sweating the DARPA proposal, had asked Jenny's mother to come to Cambridge that week, but she and Harvey had already booked a Caribbean cruise out of Miami. Luckily, Colleen volunteered. She would cover JJ's day shift, including taking him to the Montessori and picking him up, as long as Martin could get home by four each day.

With only a little over two weeks before the deadline, Martin was still missing three of the seven proposal sections, but he did have the required boilerplate parts — bios, previous grants, and publication lists. While at CTI, he could work almost full time on assembly, editing, checking page counts, negotiating with those who submitted too much, and nagging those who hadn't submitted anything. By the time he would get home at four, he was burned out, but JJ was armed and ready for his daddy.

The playground, or bicycle practice, or setting up the sprinkler in the back yard, or, on the two days it rained, playing a board game, or doing a jigsaw puzzle, or reading together, or encouraging JJ to practice the piano. As much as Martin wanted to cook the kind of healthy food Jenny would have preferred, they would end up at McDonalds or with pizza, or Martin would grill hot dogs served with fruit. The one vegetable JJ really liked was green beans, and Martin cooked up a batch early in the week and parceled them out over the five nights of Jenny's absence.

After getting JJ bedded down each night, instead of picking up the DARPA grind, Martin would play the piano, some nights for two hours straight. He hoped to perform one of the Schubert *Impromptus* at their fall concert as a solo, and his group had made enough progress on the

Menotti to include it as well, so there was plenty to practice along with his favorite *English Suites.*

Lying in bed each night, missing the familiar warmth of Jenny's body, he had time to think about his marriage and the impending arrival of a second child. His only up-close child-rearing experience had been with JJ, who was three when he and Jenny married. What would it be like with a newborn, his own? Would he be able to love it, whatever that meant? His father said something wonderful happens when you have a child. Would it happen to him, that wonderful something? Would Jenny have to quit working? Would they need a nanny? Could they afford one? Would Jenny even want one?

Jenny had often complained, and Martin agreed, that he tended to put his schedule ahead of hers, but he wondered what he could really do to fix that in the coming months. The looming DARPA submission deadline was bad enough, but the planning for the site visit promised to be just as bad. The format was a morning session with seven project presentations by the faculty, a catered lunch, an afternoon session with poster papers put up by graduate students from each of the seven research groups, a room reserved for the visit team for an evening executive session, and another meeting the following morning with the seven investigators providing opportunity for each member of the visit team to ask additional questions about the proposal.

And then there was Istanbul, something to which Jenny remained firmly opposed and to which he remained equally firmly committed.

If they could just get past DARPA and Istanbul, he could take some time off. They could spend maybe a full month at the cottage.

-    -   -

It happened exactly as Martin had predicted. On that Friday, one week after the buffered deadline Martin had sent to his co-workers, the final three sections of the proposal arrived. With Jenny coming home that night, he looked forward to the entire Memorial Day weekend to put everything together and start on the budget reconciliation. What he hadn't figured on was that he and Jenny would spend a good part of the weekend having their first scary fight. Over Istanbul.

Jenny's client dropped her off Friday afternoon, a little after four, and JJ went berserk seeing his Mommy after such a long absence. She was too exhausted to talk much and went upstairs to unpack, shower, and rest before dinner. Martin grilled hamburgers for dinner, served with what was left of the green beans and a fresh arugula and avocado salad, one of Jenny's favorites. He cracked a bottle of Rioja and offered a toast in honor of Jenny's return, to which Jenny raised her water glass.

Over dinner, Jenny recounted a week of frenetic shopping, uptown, midtown, downtown, the village and Brooklyn Heights. She made a few very good purchases, with several new pieces coming up for auction, and lots of contacts that could be followed up over the internet over the coming weeks. The Roentgen piece, in particular, was perfect, so Jenny introduced her client to a New York associate who agreed to serve as straw bidder, with an agreed limit price for the Roentgen and for each of the new target pieces. It had been a good week but Jenny was worn out.

Jenny asked JJ whether he had a good time while she was gone, and he enthused over the park, the puzzles, the sprinkler, and, especially, the McDonalds. But then he asked, "Can you read to me tonight, Mommy?" Jenny said yes, then turned to Martin asking about his week.

"It's all about DARPA, at least at work. Colleen was a huge help, and JJ and I had fun. Right buddy?" JJ grinned. "But the DARPA thing. Just two weeks left and the final pieces only arrived today. I'm going to need the weekend to work, so I'm hoping that's okay with you."

"Once I get a good night's sleep, I'll take over on the home front. But for now, I need to put JJ to bed and then me."

- - -

It wasn't until Saturday night that Jenny pulled the pin. Martin had spent the entire day at his computer, making huge strides toward the final proposal. It now looked like the deadline could be met. Jenny cooked an apricot glazed pork roast for dinner and had bought Martin's favorite fruit tart for dessert. She volunteered for JJ's bedtime while Martin did the dishes, after which he practiced piano for an hour.

By the time he got upstairs to his study, Jenny was at her computer, organizing her notes from the trip and linking them to the specific places in the house where pieces were intended to go. Martin found a red card on his chair.

"Red?" he asked. "Really? After covering the home front for a week?"

"It's not red for last week. It's red because you seem to insist on that trip to Istanbul, and I need you here, at home. It was haunting me the whole time I was in New York. I got so exhausted, it was just crazy. You simply have to cancel that trip."

"You really want to talk about this now, when you're still so tired? Maybe you're measuring your tiredness against New York instead of Cambridge. Can't it wait a day or so?"

"No. You need to hear me, and I'm just not getting through." And with big spaces between each word, she said, "I ... do ... not ... want ... to ... be ... left ... alone ... while ... you ... go ... to ... Turkey ... with ... that ... woman. Do you get it?"

"No. I don't. I just covered for you, a whole week."

"But you're not pregnant."

"That's true, but I've got other pressures. DARPA. And even with that, me and JJ, we did fine, and he's healthy and happy."

"And my client was not a seductress."

"Jesus. There you go again. Kat is not a seductress, at least not as far as I'm concerned. She's a colleague who needs a boost to get a fair shot at her tenure. Would it be different if she were male? Is that what this is about?"

Jenny burst into tears. "I don't know why it upsets me so much. But yes, the fact that she's a woman and that you have a history — I just can't let go of that."

"But I don't have a history with her, for God's sake. And there hasn't been any history, as you put it, for years. I've been helping Kat for more than five years, and there has been absolutely nothing going on but business. Nothing."

"C'mon, Martin," said Jenny, still blubbering. "You covered her classes when her mother got sick. Is that normal business?"

"Actually, it is. Steve Campbell covered my classes when I had to stay over with my father. We always cover for each other."

"Well, I need you here at home, not gallivanting around the world. She doesn't need you there. She should go by herself."

"And I think you're just plain wrong. If I'm there, she'll get the kind of introductions that lead to good letters. That's what I care about."

"And what about preening in front of the conference as lead speaker? Don't you care about that too? Isn't that part of this? Being the star?"

"Look, I asked if I could accept this before I did, and…"

"And you said if I got pregnant we could manage. You call this managing? Such bullshit."

"But when I said that, I didn't know that Kat's situation would be so critical. If I don't help to the max, she might not make it."

"And that wouldn't bother me one bit. If she deserves tenure, she'll get it. If not, she's a grown-up. Let her deal with it."

"You're just being spiteful. That's not like you. I suggest you get some rest, and we can talk about this again."

"Very well. We'll talk again tomorrow, and the day after that, and the day after that, until you change your mind."

With that Jenny stalked out of the study, and, no surprise, she did not shower before going to bed.

-    -   -

While life at home had turned to hell on earth, what with Jenny's nightly insistence on raising the Istanbul trip, Martin did get the proposal in on time, meeting every detail of the format requirements, budget approval, page limits on each section, boilerplate, the works.

He was justifiably proud of the outcome, especially considering the hundreds of hours he had spent since early February getting to this point. Now it was time for show-and-tell.

Felice managed all the reservations for conference rooms, the blocks of hotel rooms for the team members and their students and the catering plan for both the coffee breaks and the lunch, chuckling over the fact that the DARPA people could have coffee and donuts but had to pay for their own lunches. It made no sense, she said.

Martin, meanwhile, with an infinitude of emails flying back and forth among his cohort, worked out an agenda for the morning presentations, the list of student poster papers for the afternoon, and a dinner plan for his team to discuss the first day's events in preparation for the next morning's question session. Khalil, Yu-Chong and Christina would put up posters from his group, three among a total of eighteen.

The day before the site visit, a series of violent thunderstorms, one of which spawned a small tornado in Worcester, closed Logan Airport for six hours, making everyone's incoming planes late. Amazingly, everyone still made it.

A complete but tired crew showed up at CTI the next morning, ready to go. Martin led off with an overview of the program, selling hard. It was this unique grouping of expertise — from deposition methods, to characterization, to defect control, even to process scaling for manufacture — that made this team worthy of DARPA support. This was followed by the seven individual proposal presentations, each team member representing his work as one-of-a-kind and world-leading, the kind of objective reporting that the DARPA visitors were used to hearing. They interrupted with questions, some sensible, some not, but kept the harassment level to a minimum.

The atmosphere eased up at lunch. While the investigators did not know the DARPA team, they all knew each other, at least the senior ones did. And the DARPA people mixed with the proposers at the lunch tables, talking about yesterday's incredible weather, swapping competitive travel stories, and generally behaving like professional colleagues — interacting civilly with those whom they would judge.

The afternoon poster session went well. It never hurts to trot out students in situations like this. Their eagerness presents a refreshing foil to the grinding aspect of program reviews. They dress up, they have laser pointers, and they gush through their work with each visitor to the poster-board. Even Christina, in contrast to her usual provocative dress, wore a knee-length blue skirt and a modest white blouse, and she got many compliments from both the DARPA team and the other investigators over the surface images from her SMSC paper.

When they broke for dinner, the DARPA people went off for their executive session, and the eighteen students, led by the CTI cohort, went as a group to a beer-and-pizza joint up toward Central Square. The seven investigators removed a few blocks to a private room in the Marriott to chew over the day's events and prepare for tomorrow.

The next morning was harassment time. The DARPA team came prepared with highly detailed questions for each of the seven investigators, and each spent their allotted time on the hot seat, doing their best to remain upbeat even when one of the DARPA queries struck home. By noon, everyone was worn out, and with an exchange of handshakes, thank yous, and taxi requests, the site visit ended. Martin had no idea how they did. He wouldn't find out until late July at the earliest, after Istanbul.

Speaking of Istanbul, he knew that when he got home, there would be yet another battle, but he was determined to find a solution that Jenny would accept. Maybe if they went bicycle shopping, the air would clear a bit.

* **21** *

Jenny's mother saved the day for Martin. She had heard Jenny's daily complaints about the upcoming trip, so she volunteered to stay with her and JJ while Martin was away. It didn't calm Jenny's simmering rage over Kat, but it did answer to the 'I'm pregnant' part. Martin would drive the three of them to Brimfield Junction on Wednesday, say hello to Helen and the kids on the way, and then install them in the cottage. The neighbors on both sides would also be there for the whole week in case Grace or Jenny needed help with anything. Martin would stay at the cottage until Friday, when he would take the bus back to Boston, meeting up with Kat at Logan for their Friday night departure. He would send emails every day and have his cell phone in case of emergency.

Jenny loved the cottage. It had been built as a simple structure, but Jeremiah had enlarged and modernized it over the years, putting in insulated windows, drilling a well and installing electric heat. It now had two bedrooms plus a sleeping loft and a combined living-kitchen-dining space with picture windows looking west onto Sagadahoc Bay, which twice a day would empty to mostly mud flats, then refill to varying depths, depending on the season. When the tide was out, she and JJ could go clamming on the mud flats. During the high tides, they could take the canoe up into the marsh, their nostrils filled with the corky smell of the black mud on the banks. JJ delighted in surprising herons and egrets as they turned each bend of the narrow reed-lined channels. And when the ebb started, just past high tide, the water flowing from the sun-drenched marshes at the end of the bay was warm enough for real swimming. It was especially wonderful at sunset, with the pinks and reds reflected off the clouds, but even when there was fog, it was mysterious, cooling, enticing, and restful.

AT&T had built a new cell-phone tower just across the bay, so the wireless reception was excellent. Jenny could be in touch with her clients in Boston, especially with her big project, now in the floor-sanding, papering and painting phase, all overseen by the project's general contractor. Martin and Kat would be gone for a week, with three days at ESM and then a two-day trip to Troy, about which Martin had been adamant. As a tribute to his father, he had to visit Troy and touch the stones that had housed Paris and Helen and witnessed the wrath of Achilles and the forewarnings of Cassandra. On the bus to Boston, Martin thought about Cassandra. The oracle of doom. He hoped it wasn't a metaphor for this trip. Cassandra had certainly been right. Was Jenny right?

Martin arrived at the Lufthansa check-in, finding Kat in deep conversation with her friend Carly, the one he had met at the concert. He was struck by the intensity of their departure hug as she and Martin reached the security gate, glad to know that Kat seemed to have a close friend. As they climbed out of Logan Airport, Kat asked that Martin give her the run-down on who she would meet at the conference. Martin pulled out the program and talked his way through the speakers, many of whom Kat already knew about: her thesis advisor, Andris Andersen, Koppin from Cal Tech, Phelps from Purdue. For the ones she didn't know, Martin provided some background. Carl Urquhart had left Cambridge and gone to Southampton to build a semiconductors materials program. Very clever, a 'climber,' sucking up to the world leaders in order to get the plum of Program Chairman for ESM. A nice enough fellow, but always looking out for number one. Hans Burgomeister, from ETH Zurich, had developed several new atomic-beam sources for deposition experiments; he liked German beer and had a belly to prove it. Fujita would probably be there. Quiet. Hard to get to know. On through the names he went, one factoid at a time.

As the flight attendants brought cocktails, Martin got preachy. He reminded Kat that this meeting was the best shot she had at international exposure and if she wanted to do the best for herself, it wasn't just that she needed to deliver her paper well. She needed to ask good questions.

"Ask questions?" said Kat. "You mean to get known? Does it really work that way?"

"Actually, it does," said Martin. "You will hear people joking about me. It's become something of a tradition. I always ask the first question at the first talk. It's now called the Quintessential Question, and it's a kind of opening for the conference. The session chairman always looks for me first, and everyone laughs. But then I do ask a question, and it has to be a good question. It won't happen this time since I'm giving the plenary talk, but you get the idea. Watch what happens after the second talk. I'll ask the first question and I expect you to be in line, right behind me, to ask the second one."

After dinner, Martin and Kat unfolded their blankets and drifted off to sleep, woke at what felt like the middle of the night to make their connection in Frankfurt, and dozed off again before landing in Istanbul.

Carl Urquhart, breezy and cheery, collected them upon arrival and escorted them in the conference van (with a Turkish driver, thank goodness) as they plowed through Istanbul insanity, with taxis dodging at high speed and even higher recklessness around everything that moved. They reached the Conrad with a severe adrenaline rush.

Carl helped them get checked in, suggested that there was a good fish restaurant just down the hill at the Bosphorus, and left them to get settled. He offered to take them sightseeing in the morning with a group from the conference.

After a short rest, during which Martin took a shower, shaved and sent Jenny an email, he and Kat walked down the hill from the hotel to the waterfront, staring across the narrow waters of the Bosphorus, the water barrier between Europe and Asia. Martin took several photos as Jeremiah's stories echoed in his ears: Xerxes, Alexander the Great, Constantine, Suleiman the Magnificent, the Ottoman Empire, the Silk

Road, the end of the Orient Express. Martin stood in awe. "The cross-roads of the world," said Martin. "So many civilizations have been here, fought here. Hittites. Persians. Greeks. Mongols."

"Yeah. My father would sometimes talk about Turkey that way, the crossroads of the world. He only visited once. Just before he died. So how did all these invaders get their armies across? Were there bridges?"

"The best crossing, the most creative one I know of, was a bridge made of boats," said Martin. "It wasn't here exactly. Farther south, at the Dardanelles, close to where this channel reaches the Mediterranean. Not so far from Troy, actually. Xerxes, the Persian general, in something like 480 B.C., used a whole bunch of boats, all anchored together, to allow his armies to cross from the Asian side. He actually made two bridges, one for troops and one for supplies. It was an engineering marvel. And a big problem for the Greeks."

They strolled along the waterfront until they found the restaurant Carl had recommended where they had a standard Turkish waterfront dinner of grilled fish with butter, a boiled potato and half an onion, with baklava for dessert. Needing sleep, they passed up the offer of Turkish coffee, walked slowly up the hill to the hotel as twilight set in, said their goodnights, and went off to their rooms. An email from Jenny said that the fog was thick and lovely, but that JJ had developed a bad cold. She closed with, "Don't forget the rope."

At nine the next morning, Martin, Kat, Andris Andersen, Hans Burgomeister and his wife Heidi, and Akira Fujita from Hitachi gathered in the lobby to wait for Carl. Martin thanked his lucky stars for the chance to introduce Kat personally to Hans and to Fujita, the kind of connection that can make or break a tenure case.

Carl finally showed up, bubbling with enthusiasm. He introduced Mustafa Mörkiç, the Local Arrangements Chairman for the conference, who would lead them on a walking tour. "Best way to beat jet lag," bubbled Carl. "Get out in daylight and walk your legs off. Better bring a sweater or a jacket, though. Wind off the Bosphorus can chill your bones."

They set off on foot, down the hill from the Conrad, south along the water to the Galata Bridge leading to the city center. Martin, realizing that in the brain fog of jet lag he had left his camera at the hotel, pulled out his cell phone to take a photo looking along the length of the bridge with three graceful minarets in the background. He leaned out over the rail for a better perspective just as a group of schoolboys came rushing up the sidewalk. His elbow got jostled and his phone took flight. He and the rest of the group watched it splash and settle into the deep of the Golden Horn.

Mustafa said, "That's too bad. Is that your only phone?"

"I'm afraid so," said Martin. "And my wife is pregnant. She needs to be able to reach me. Can I buy a new phone here?"

"Yes, for sure, but I don't know if it would work in the U.S. Do you want to do that? I think there's a phone store not far from here."

Martin turned to the group and started to apologize for having to make a detour, when Kat said, "Listen, Martin, why don't you just give Jenny my number? If she calls, I can always get you."

Martin knew that Jenny wouldn't like having Kat as intermediary, but swept up in the embarrassment of the moment, he said, "That would work, I guess. Can we find an internet place so I can send a message home?" Mustafa thought for a moment, then led to group to a wifi-equipped coffee shop where Martin sent Jenny an email.

The group followed Mustafa up narrow twisted lanes, past spice shops that smelled of mystery, fresh poultry shops that smelled less welcoming, bakeries, kiosks where vendors were starting their döner kebab grills, eventually reaching the square containing the ancient wonders of the Ottoman Empire. They toured the Blue Mosque, saw the gilt mosaics of Aya Sophia, and then walked down toward the water into the Topkapi Palace to see the treasure chest, with its 86-carat diamond and jeweled dagger. After touring the imperial kitchens that would feed a thousand people daily, Martin noticed that the Archeological Museum was within the palace grounds, so he insisted that everyone visit there as well. The Greek statues were only part of the story. It was the stone relics of the Hittites that were the most sobering reminders of the extent to which the land on which they were standing had been crisscrossed by civilizations long gone.

By this point, the group was justifiably tired. Mustafa had made reservations at a restaurant near the palace for a buffet lunch, with chicken stews, lamb kebabs, pilaf, flaky börek, eggplant prepared five different ways, and twelve varieties of baklava. The Turkish coffee, thick to the point of being chewable and sweetened like syrup, was a welcome ending to a wonderful meal.

The conference van arrived to drive the travelers back to the Conrad for a well-earned rest before the evening's reception. There was an email from Jenny commiserating over the loss of the phone and acknowledging that she had received Kat's number.

- - -

Conference receptions have certain features in common: too much standing around on jet-lagged tired legs, too little food to compensate for the liberally-supplied alcohol and too many false greetings amid those that were genuine. Several of the wives of the Turkish professors wore head scarves, which surprised Martin and made him wonder about the wine bar, but Carl reminded him that while Turkey was drifting toward more fundamentalism, it was still secular. The head-scarf battle had been fought, and the religious folks had won — they could now be worn at some official functions.

Martin led Kat around the room, introducing her to everyone — his friends, his competitors, and the few whom he viewed as enemies. In each case, he said kind words about the talk she would be giving on Wednesday morning, with exciting new results. Nagging at the back of his mind, though, was Jenny's challenge. Was this kind of support necessary?

- - -

The opening session began right on time. Following short speeches by local dignitaries, including the mayor of Istanbul and the head of the Turkish Materials Society, Mustafa provided some details about coffee breaks and meals, the Wednesday night conference banquet and touring opportunities. Carl then took the podium to introduce Martin as plenary speaker.

Martin was an old hand at these talks, combining a brief history of the field of semiconductor surface modification with some recent results: two highlights from the Wojtowicz Catastrophe and a slide with the images from Christina's now-accepted SMSC paper. After the talk, Andersen asked about some experimental details, which Martin outlined before he stepped down.

Hans Burgomeister was the next speaker, presenting some new results on selenium effusion cells. At the conclusion of his talk, Carl said, "We have time for a few questions." Martin had already come to the aisle microphone. "Martin? Of course. You're first, as usual. Yes, go ahead."

Martin asked a detailed question about the method used to sense the selenium vapor pressure, and Hans beamed as he answered with chapter and verse. Kat was right behind Martin at the microphone. "Hello. I am Katarina Rodriguez from CTI in Boston, and my question is this: Have you ever seen any indication of quantum interference effects in the beams from your cell? I'll be talking about this on Wednesday morning, not with selenium, with different elements, but I was curious whether you had ever looked for it."

Bingo. Kat had done it. Not only had she asked a really good question to which Hans did not have an answer, she had managed to plug her own paper as well. Martin couldn't have done it better. When she returned to her seat Martin gave her a pat on the arm. "Good job. Do it maybe once more today, and once tomorrow afternoon. Well done. By the banquet, everyone will be talking about you."

The rest of the day was uneventful. Martin had dinner with Andris and they invited the quiet man, Fujita, to join them. Kat had begged off;

she wanted to grab a bite in the hotel café and then go over her paper. The threesome went by taxi to Taksim Square where they found a quiet restaurant with excellent food. Martin ordered Hünkar Beğendi, a dish that in English is called Sultan's Delight, lamb ragout with a smoked eggplant sauce. Fujita ordered grilled fish, while Andris had the shish kebabs with pilaf.

Fujita turned out to be a very interesting fellow. When he was a student at Kyoto, he had taken a class in Ancient Western History, very unusual for a Japanese science student. He had read Thucydides! His English was challenging to understand at times, but he was eager to talk about their sightseeing adventure and the Archeological Museum, especially. Martin was delighted with his new friend and asked him whether he would like to join him after the conference to visit Troy. Fujita drew in his breath, making the quiet hissing sound so characteristic of the Japanese when they must disappoint. He had to continue to England immediately after the conference for a scheduled visit to Cambridge University. Martin turned to Andris and asked whether he would like to join them. "Kat's going," said Martin.

Andris smiled. "Sorry, Martin. I'm booked back home on Thursday morning. Just the two of you, is it?"

-   -   -

Kat's talk on Wednesday morning went well. She had an attentive audience, and when she showed the evidence of successful atomic deposition exhibiting a quantum interference pattern, there were murmurs in the room. Phelps asked a question about whether she had found any effect on transport properties. Kat said that it was active work, and she hoped to have results by the end of the summer. Koppin congratulated her on her persistence with the atomic beam apparatus, and asked about the accessible range of de Broglie wavelengths, a question which Kat crushed. She left the stage to a more genuine round of applause than one normally hears at these things, bringing music to her ears and a quiet tear to her eyes.

She stayed in the session until the coffee break, but then went to her room. She put the "Do Not Disturb" sign on her door and sent Carly an email telling her of the good reception for her talk. Then she removed most of her clothes, lay down on her bed, and allowed her mind and her hands to transport her where she needed to go, a blurry vision of Carly's lithe body helping her along, after which she drifted off to sleep.

She woke to the sound of the room telephone. It was Martin. "Are you okay?"

Flustered, she replied, "Yes, yes. I'm fine. I think the jet lag finally got to me. And the stress. I needed a nap. What time is it? Lunch time?"

"Hardly. It's four thirty. The afternoon session just let out. The buses for the banquet start loading at five. We're going to this place on the Bosphorus north of town. Will you be coming?"

"Sure. I need to wake up, but I'll be there."

- - -

The bus ride to the restaurant took almost forty minutes in the crazy Istanbul traffic. Café Bosphorus consisted of a huge low-ceilinged room, set up for tonight with six long tables, each holding twenty. The menu was classic: braised fish with a hint of clove and cinnamon, boiled potato, and a delicately simmered vegetable medley seasoned with thyme. The wine was good. Spirits were high.

Some conferences are stuffy, full of pomp. The ESM crowd was more fun-loving. One of the things they did was award a few silly prizes at the closing banquet. Carl Urquhart served as master of ceremonies, making an impassioned speech about how the Program Committee had spent hours deciding on these awards, making allusions along the way to the various talks that had been presented so far. He ended up by announcing that Hans Burgomeister would be awarded a prize for his selenium cells, with the prize certificate reading, "The Man Mostly Likely to Poison the Rest of Us." Fujita, who had given an excellent talk on a newly discovered vacancy defect in cadmium telluride semiconductors, was given a prize for "The Man Who Made Something out of

Nothing." Everyone enjoyed the banter, and the wine flowed. But there was always one serious prize, for "Newcomer of the Year." Kat won it.

-    -   -

Thursday morning at the crack of dawn, Martin sent Jenny an email saying they were off to Troy and that he would let her know how to reach him once they got settled. He packed a few overnight things, leaving the rest of his luggage in his room, and went to the lobby where he and Kat were greeted by the tour company's guide, who escorted them to his minivan. Kemal was a slight man with a bold curly mustache. He kept up a steady banter about the Dardanelles region, including the history of the World War I battle at Gallipoli. That's where Ataturk gained prominence and went on to become the first leader of the modern Turkish state. Kat dozed off, with her head drifting onto Martin's shoulder.

After several hours, including a ferry-crossing of the Dardanelles, the bus finally reached Troy. Just outside the entrance was a big wooden horse, ugly as sin, maybe thirty feet tall, with a staircase full of children scampering up and down. Martin was disgusted, but suddenly Kat was crying. "It's just like the model my father brought home," she said, snuffling up her tears. "He must have got it here. It's beautiful." She snapped a photo with her phone.

Kemal led the group into the archeological area, explaining the nine different levels of Trojan cities, and that the Trojan War corresponded to Troy VI, somewhere around 1250 BC. The first wall was, indeed, a Troy VI wall. Martin had to touch it. He gave his camera to Kat and asked her to record his touching it. And this time, it was his eyes that teared up. Kat, still misty-eyed, linked his arm as they moved on, hugging it to her breast. Arms linked, they continued around the site murmuring 'isn't that wonderful, yes, it's wonderful' all the way through. She never let go of his arm, and her eyes never fully dried.

For Martin's part, after that first teary wave passed, the image of his father at his childhood bedside had appeared, telling him the story of the Trojan War, one episode per night. He now felt a satisfaction of accomplishment, a cleansing, like when he would complete a good solid piece of work. Troy had been on the list of desiderata, and now he was here, seeing it, smelling it, touching it, imagining where the Greek ships had been anchored, where Achilles' tent had been pitched, and where Helen would watch the battles from the tower. He wished his sister could be here.

Kat also found it satisfying, but in a more sensual way. This week had been her debut, a personal introduction to the international leaders of her field, and she had scored. Her father would have been so proud of her. The rush that gave her was intense.

At the end of the tour of Troy, Kamal took them to their hotel and saw them properly checked in. Their rooms had a connecting door that the bellboy started to open for them, which made Kat giggle. "He thinks we're sneaking off together." Martin told the bellboy to leave it locked. "I want to change for dinner," said Kat. "I'll knock when I'm ready to go down."

Dinner was a big hotel buffet, a sample of everything, with an abundance of spiced lamb and chicken dishes, savory baked eggplant and stuffed zucchini, amazing cheeses and rich, creamy yogurt with a dazzling array of desserts. Martin and Kat didn't eat much. They were both in a daze, with images of Troy and their fathers winding in and out of consciousness. Martin asked about Kat's father, what he was like.

"He was the sweetest man. He believed in education. Not just for me, for everyone. It was the only way to cure the ills of society, even though he knew it didn't always work that way. And he encouraged me, all the way. When I wanted to go the university, he said yes. When I wanted to study engineering, he said yes. And when I wanted to go the grad school in the U.S., he said yes, even though he knew that I might not come back home to live. And I miss him so much." Kat fell silent, looking down at her plate, gradually losing her composure, and finally, dissolving into tears. "You know, he died just after, I mean like days after I got my Associate promotion. Shortly after his visit to Turkey.

Did you know that?"

"No, I had no idea. I'm really sorry," said Martin.

"He would have been so happy that I came here, to Turkey, to Troy. He would say," pausing to blow her nose, "he would always say that the stories of the world come alive when you visit the places where those stories happened."

Martin said, "That's just what my father would have said too, but I would never have called him sweet. He could be quite harsh. I don't think he was ever satisfied with me. He died just a few months ago, in April."

Kat put her hand on Martin's arm. "That's so sad. Was it sudden?"

"He'd had a bout of pneumonia, but what killed him was a stroke, so it was pretty sudden."

"Were you close, you and your father?"

"Yes and no. He knew I admired him, and I think he loved me, but it could be hard to talk to him. It got easier when he started feeling old."

"And do you have other family?"

The talk moved back and forth between their two families, sharing stories, some happy, some sad. They finished their meal and continued the story-telling as they walked in the hotel's waterfront garden, basking in the magical twilight.

As they headed back toward their rooms, Martin asked what it's been like for her to be at CTI, so far from home. What Kat said surprised Martin. "It's not the distance from home that bothers me. It's the awful family life. Nobody at CTI seems really happy unless they are bragging about their work. So many people are divorced. I almost never hear about children, or family weekends. Why is that?"

"I've thought about that a lot. I don't think the academic life at places like CTI is good for most families. Too much pressure. No boss telling you to take a vacation, so you work all the time. I'm one of those divorced guys, and I didn't even have kids. But families take time. We cut corners at home and end up with unhappy wives and, finally, in divorce court."

"Is that what happened to you?"

"Sort of, but it was complicated by some bad behavior on my part. You never heard about it? It was around the time you joined the faculty."

"I was too busy and too scared to notice anything like that. But you're happy now, aren't you, with Jenny?"

"Yes, although she's not happy with how much time I spend working. It never seems to change. There's always something more you can be doing, so you do it. What about you? Are you looking forward to having a family?"

Kat hesitated before answering. "Well, the idea of having a child appeals to me, but everything you have to go through before that happens — it's just impossible now."

"You mean there's no husband candidate on the horizon?"

"No," said Kat.

They had reached their hotel rooms. Kat looked up at Martin and said, "This has been a spectacular day, actually, a spectacular week. Thank you so much for everything." She stood on tiptoes and hugged Martin, giving him a soft kiss on the cheek. Martin, safely confined by the rope, hugged back.

-    -   -

The next morning, Kat knocked on Martin's door when it was time to go down for breakfast, after which they came back to collect their luggage. While Martin was in the bathroom for one last pit stop before leaving, the hotel phone by his bed rang and rang. Martin yelled for Kat to come in and get it, assuming it was the guide telling them to come down. "It's for you," she said. It was Jenny.

"Where the hell have you been? I've been trying to reach you all evening. The number you gave me for Kat's phone wouldn't connect. We had to take JJ to the hospital with a high fever — they're worried about pneumonia — and it's taken me hours to find out where you were. And is that who answered the phone? Was that Kat?"

That's when Martin realized that he had forgotten to send Jenny an email last night. "Yes, it was Kat," said Martin. "We were just getting my luggage on the way to the bus."

"Kat? In your room?"

"Yes. We were getting my luggage. I'm sorry. I forgot to send the email last night. I'm really sorry." Jenny hung up.

On the way to the bus, Kat asked who had called. "It was Jenny. My son had spiked a high fever, and Jenny was calling from the hospital. I forgot to send her an email last night telling her where we were staying. She couldn't reach you, and she had a hard time finding me, so she was upset."

"Oh my God, Martin. I turned off my phone last night, by habit I guess, and I haven't turned it on yet. Let me look." And there, in the list of missed calls, was Martin's Maine number, listed ten times. "This is awful. I wasn't thinking. I'm sorry. It's my fault. I'm really sorry. She must be terribly upset."

"She is upset, but we'll manage. Don't worry about it."

But he did worry. As they drove to Gallipoli, toured that grizzly scene of carnage, and then headed back toward Istanbul, he was absorbed in thoughts of the what-if. On their return, Martin found an email from Jenny that JJ was already out of the hospital. It wasn't pneumonia, just a short-lived bug of some kind. Martin replied, saying he missed them both and would be home tomorrow night.

-   -   -

It was early Sunday evening by the time Jenny, Grace and JJ met Martin at the Brimfield Junction bus station. JJ was bubbly, hugging his daddy around the legs. Jenny was cool, silent. Grace's bus to Boston was due in an hour, so they stopped off to say hello to Helen and the kids before putting Grace on the bus. Once they reached the cottage, Martin gave JJ a wooden model of the Trojan horse, supervised his bath, read him a story, and tucked him into bed.

When he returned to the living room, Jenny was sitting in the easy chair, laptop open, working, not even looking up to acknowledge him.

Martin sat on the sofa, waiting. Finally he spoke up, "Nothing happened, you know. Nothing at all."

"Why didn't you tell me where you were? How am I supposed to believe…"

"Nothing happened. It was Troy. The visit was hugely emotional for me. I was thinking about my father and the stories he told me growing up. I was in another world. I forgot. That's all. I forgot. Why can't you accept that?"

"Because she's not trustworthy, and in your past, neither were you. That's why. You forgot? About your pregnant wife and your sick son? Give me a break."

"But it's true. I was transported."

"And I think having Kat hanging on your arm was part of that transport. How can you deny how attractive she can be?"

"I don't deny it, and, yes, she was hanging on my arm while we were walking around Troy. But that's absolutely all. Well not all. Full disclosure. She kissed me. Once. On the cheek."

"She what?"

"She kissed me. It was like a thank-you kiss. For getting her to ESM, to Troy. She was in some kind of far-away emotional state and before we went to our rooms, she reached up, gave me a hug and kissed me. Just like that."

"And what did that lead to?"

"Nothing. Going to our separate rooms. Did you know that her father had gone to Troy and got her a wooden model of the Trojan Horse? Like the one I brought JJ? It was huge for her, to see it. Her father died shortly after he gave it to her. We both missed our fathers. I can't describe that feeling, how powerful it was. But maybe you're right about one thing. Maybe the fact that the emotion was shared is what made me forget to write you. But it wasn't sexual. It was personal."

"In a shared room?"

"It wasn't a shared room. The hotel gave us two rooms next to each other. Apparently Kat turned off her cell phone when she went to bed, so you couldn't get through. And in the morning, when we went up to get our luggage, I was peeing when the phone rang. I thought it was the tour guide telling us to come down, so I asked her to come in and answer it." Even while he was saying this, he knew it would sound false to Jenny. The more Martin protested, the more skeptical were Jenny's responses. The gloom that had descended into their marriage around this trip had now turned into a brutal chill wind, raging in off the ocean, blowing fog and rain clouds into their world.

-   -   -

Martin took two weeks of total vacation, but the storm clouds remained. As her belly had continued to swell, Jenny developed severe sciatica, sometimes to the point that all she could do was lie on her left side on an air mattress. She continued to work with her active clients over the internet, but she posted a note on her website that while she would welcome inquiries from new clients, she was taking a pregnancy leave until December. Her major problem at this point, beyond her fury at Martin, was that the painter for the Berkeley Place house had broken his ankle when he tripped over a curb, and the job was now two weeks behind schedule. And the Roentgen game table, purchased at auction for $223,000, had been slightly scratched in transit. Jenny got her favorite Boston antique dealer to recommend a restoration expert who could do the repair, but there was now a squabble between her client and the shipper's insurer on, first, paying top dollar for a repair job and, second, compensating the client for the loss of value in needing to have the piece restored in the first place.

Martin found himself doing all the shopping, cooking and JJ care. He relished the temporary shrinking of his life down to the basics — exploring the marsh in the canoe, picking wild raspberries, clamming on the mud flats, and, hooray, hooray, taking the training wheels off of JJ's bicycle. But as the end of two weeks approached, he begged Jenny either to shift to the Brimfield Junction house where Helen could help or return to Cambridge where Martin could get some child-care help during the day. He needed to get back to work. Jenny refused. She wanted to stay at the cottage through the end of August.

Biting his tongue, Martin stayed in Maine, and went on a schedule of round trips to Cambridge on Tuesday, Wednesday and Thursday, rising at four, laying out breakfast and lunch fixings for Jenny and JJ, leaving by five to beat the worst of the southbound rush hour into Boston, spending five hours with his grad students discussing progress, thesis editing, paper writing, journal editing and grant writing, then driving the two-and-a-half hours back to Sagadahoc Point in time to fix dinner for the family. Through it all, Jenny remained remote, unmoved.

* **22** *

It was on the Thursday of the second week of this regimen that he was hit with gut troubles. He wasn't very hungry at lunch, so he ate only the fresh grapefruit sections, a huge bowlful. By three o'clock he had the first of what became seven episodes of violent bowel emptying, the last five of which took place at the rest stops on the way back to Maine. He had the sense to hydrate along the way, but even so, by the time he got home, he felt totally wasted. He recognized the symptoms, his irritable bowel acting up, but this was worse than what he remembered from previous bouts. The first step, he knew, was to shift to a liquid diet until things calmed down. He had only tea for dinner, even while cooking for Jenny and JJ. Bedtime for JJ was compressed — no bath, and only a very short story. "Daddy has an upset tummy," he explained.

"Want me to rub it?" said JJ.

"Thanks, bud. Give it a try."

JJ quietly put his little hand on Martin's midriff as he sat on JJ's bed, rubbing gently. "Does it feel better now?"

"Yes, bud. It does. Thanks."

But it didn't feel better, and Jenny wasn't helping. She spent each day with her attention on JJ, taking care, of course, that another adult was around when he went swimming in the bay or walking out on the mud flats. By evening, she was worn out. No matter what her state of anger or forgiveness might be, she simply didn't have the energy to be Martin's caretaker. But they did talk about his troubles once JJ was asleep.

"It could be just a bug. Or something you ate," offered Jenny, her voice timid and hopeful.

"I hope it is. But the last time I felt this bad was years ago, during that horrible time. I'm willing to wait it out over the weekend, but if it doesn't recover quickly, I'm going to see the doc at CTI on Tuesday."

"You mean the horrible time when you were in the midst of a nasty divorce? I hope your body isn't saying that's what's going on here."

"You tell me," said with a rising edge in his voice. "I begged you to go to the Brimfield Junction house, and you refused. I begged you to go back to Cambridge, and you refused. Except for forgetting an email, I didn't do anything wrong at Troy. Why are you still so goddam angry?"

Jenny's jaw trembled as she said, "I don't want to be angry. I love you. But I just can't get over the image of you and that woman sharing a room. It haunts me at night. I'm sure I'll get over it, but something like that doesn't just happen. And I'm sorry you feel bad. Really. I want you to feel better, but I want to feel better too. Do you realize? Do you have even the slightest idea how terrifying it is to be carrying a child and not be confident about your husband, about his commitment?"

"Jesus, Jenny. We never shared a room. And I'm as committed as I can be. I'm cooking, shopping, driving more than five hours a day. What on earth more could I do to show my commitment?"

"I don't know. It's just that the doubt has been planted, and I can't get rid of it. I hear your words, and I believe you. My brain says you're faithful. But my imagination sees the two of you in a bedroom together. Without telling me. And my imagination wins right now."

- - -

The weekend brought no respite, neither to the awkward marital tension nor to Martin's bowel. The liquid diet helped calm things a bit, but he was still cramping and making multiple trips to the pot. On Monday morning he called the CTI Medical Department and made an appointment with his doctor, Michael Okowande. After reviewing Martin's record, Dr. Okowande said, "You've had a history of IBS, right?" Martin nodded. "When was the last serious episode, before this one I mean?"

"Serious episode? Gosh. Several years ago. Maybe five, six years."

"Were you under particular stress then?"

"God, yes. Dreadful."

"And now?"

Martin sat mute. Stress, for sure. Not just stress. Terror that he had irrevocably destroyed Jenny's faith in him.

"Martin?" asked the doctor. "You still with me here?"

Martin looked up. "Sorry, yes. I'm under a lot of stress right now." He described his hideous schedule and his worries about Jenny's pregnancy.

"I want to do a colonoscopy. You're a bit young for this, but just in case. Dr. Feld is our gastroenterologist. Ever had one?"

"No, but I understand it's pretty gruesome."

"Not so bad actually. We give you some liquids to clean you out, which takes a day, you go over to Mt. Auburn Hospital, he gives you a sedative and does the procedure. Takes only a couple of hours. The only thing is, you need to have someone able to drive you home. Can you manage that?"

"It's a bit complicated, because I would have to get someone to stay with Jenny and JJ in Maine. Or maybe I can get them to come down while I do this. Let me talk to her. In the meantime, you should go ahead and get it scheduled."

-   -   -

Jenny agreed to stay with Helen for the two nights that Martin would be away. Martin dropped them off on Monday evening so he could start the internal cleansing in Cambridge on Tuesday morning. On Wednesday, Colleen drove him to the hospital, leaving her cell phone number for when Martin could be picked up. He met Dr. Feld for the first time just as the sedative was beginning to take effect, and the next thing he knew, the recovery room nurse was giving him water and telling him that, during the procedure, they had pumped his colon full of air so he should expect to pass a lot of gas. She actually encouraged him to do it, saying that it wouldn't smell.

Blowing noisy farts and gradually waking up, he asked for more water. It was delivered by Dr. Feld, who had just come in, handing him three sheets of printed instructions. "I found some lesions, so I took samples for biopsy. Doesn't look like cancer, but definitely some abnormalities. Stay on a liquid diet for another few days, and then introduce solid food very slowly. I think you know how to manage that based on the IBS history. I want to see you in my office next week, Tuesday if possible. I'll have results by then. My assistant will make a slot for you."

At that Tuesday session, Dr. Feld said, "Ulcerative colitis. An inflammation of the lining of the bowel caused by your own immune system, an autoimmune situation. Not a bad case. It should be treatable with medication. After you get it calmed down, we'll start you on aminosalicylates."

Thus began a new regimen for Martin — medication, Metamucil, and multiple small meals instead of three big ones. Avoiding citrus, of all things, which Dr. Feld thought might have been the trigger for the outbreak of cramping. But, he said, the irritation had been present long before that. Martin was to keep a food diary for at least two months and use his scientific skills to see if he could spot a pattern of foods that should be avoided. It might take two or three weeks before things settled down enough for him to feel approximately normal, and he should expect more episodes, without much notice, for quite some time. His level of disease wasn't life-threatening, more a nuisance than anything else.

Thinking back to his recovery at the time of his divorce, Martin knew that somewhere within him was the discipline to beat this new challenge. But he needed Jenny's help. He hoped she would come round.

-    -   -

It was the thirteenth of August when Martin got his answer from DARPA. The CTI-led proposal was not selected for funding. Martin's gut reacted in an instant, and he ran for the rest room. How could this have happened? This was the first time he had lost a major competition. He knew the field better than anyone and had brought together a first-rate team with first-rate ideas. What happened?

When he returned to his office, he sent emails to his colleagues telling them the bad news. There was already plenty of chatter about who won. One award went to the Stanford-UCLA-Cal Tech team of Chrysostomides, Andersen and Koppin, and the other went to the Cornell-Michigan-Georgia Tech team led by Covington and Blaha.

Ever the pragmatist, Martin got out his budget-planning spreadsheet and looked at the impact of this body blow. The simple fact was that he was going to have to reduce his group size, or at least their level of support, by the equivalent of either one post-doc and one graduate student or three graduate students. There were options on how to do this, considering how far along each student was and what their prospects were for successful completion of a degree. Of his two post-docs, Khalil's project was funded through the following July, but Evan's was about to run dry. Since it wasn't possible to fire a post-doc without notice, he was going to have to reduce student funding by three slots. Kevin, thank goodness, had finally graduated, and the money for his four remaining doctoral students, Ahmed, Yu-Chong, Christina and Natasha was secure. But two Master's students, Byung and Latisha, would have to get shifted to TAs, at least for a semester, at which point Evan would have had sufficient notice to find another position. He contacted Evan and asked him to come see him and emailed Byung and Latisha, telling them that since they would be doing at least one semester of TA along the path to their degrees, he wanted them to do their first TA this fall, so they should please apply ASAP. He also notified his department's Graduate Office that due to a funding snafu, he needed to shift two of his students to TAs, or to a spare fellowship for a term, if they had any open.

With the student-support impact digested, Martin sat back to think. The irony of having your friends as your competitors in this high-stakes funding game was poignant. In the old days, DARPA did one-investigator projects at the level of 150 to 200 K per year, but now they insisted on these big multi-investigator multi-university centers. The problem was that not only were the sizes of the awards bigger, the contrast between winners and losers was bigger. For the amount of effort Martin had spent on this one proposal, he could have written three individual grants, each one of which would have been competitive under the old model. But now, tied to his partners at other schools, he could no longer be master of his own destiny. They competed as a group, and they won or lost as a group. The best he could do in the short run to restore the lost funds was to carve out his portion of the DARPA grant and send it to the National Science Foundation. It wouldn't take much work, and it might staunch the bleeding.

He thought back to Seamus's question about whether he found his teaching worthwhile, given his research success. On days like this, he wished he was, like Seamus, just a teacher.

-   -   -

Martin and Jenny went about their daily lives in a perfectly polite but withdrawn state. Martin would report on his days at CTI, and Jenny would ask about his gut, commiserate over the DARPA decision and report on JJ's activities and on her project. But the issue of Istanbul remained buried like a landmine, both of them afraid that stepping on it would lead to something neither of them wanted.

Martin spent many hours in the car on the back and forth trips between Maine and Cambridge, providing ample time to think. About Jenny. About Kat. About his insistence on going to Istanbul. About his assertion that Kat needed his presence.

Since he and Jenny weren't in discussion mode, Martin tried taking both sides of the conversation. It was a slow business, this self-analysis, but his entire career was devoted to testing hypotheses. It was time to practice on himself, positing what-ifs, then chewing them over and over and over until the muddle cleared.

What, he would ask himself, would have been the worst outcome if he hadn't been there? Perhaps Kat might not have asked such a good question during the first session. On the other hand, he could have primed her to do so. Did he really need to be there? What about his introductions during the day of touring or at the conference reception? Did they matter? Was she so shy that she couldn't have introduced herself? He couldn't know for sure, but she probably would have made the rounds. After all, her tenure depended on being known. She wouldn't travel all that distance and then shrink into a corner.

So what was his real motivation for insisting on going with her? Was it an infatuation? Clearly not. They had been colleagues for years, and there was no infatuation involved. She had never indicated any sexual interest in Martin, or vice versa. And that one brief kiss was the result of emotional overload on both their parts and didn't mean anything other than 'thank you.' Thinking back to Peter Dempsey's cut about freshman girls, though, was Istanbul just one more example of reaching out for ego-stroking? From Kat? Maybe so. From his international peers? He didn't need to go to Istanbul for that. He was already one of the key players, worldwide. However, what if, thanks to Istanbul, Kat gets tenure? Clearly, Martin will get some of the credit, not just from Kat, but from his colleagues on the Personnel Committee, including Morris, for so brilliantly managing her mentoring. When he finally got around to this thought, his nerves jangled, all the way through his elbows to his hands wrapped around the steering wheel. Was that it? The PC? Is a good reputation in Personnel Committee more important than Jenny? Said that way, it's clearly fatuous, and a dreadful mistake in priorities.

-    -   -

His first attempt to discuss it with Jenny didn't turn out so well. After getting JJ to bed on the last Friday night before they were to return to Cambridge, Martin asked Jenny whether they could talk about things.

"Things? What things?"

"Us. The two of us."

"I'm sure there's plenty to talk about, but I'm just too tired. Does it have to be tonight?"

Martin was sheepish. "I've been thinking a lot. About Istanbul."

"I should hope so. You were totally wrong to go."

Martin bit his lip, trying to stay calm. "Yes, and I'm starting to agree with you. Can't we be friends again? Can we talk?"

Jenny cracked a weak smile. "That's my line. 'Can we talk' is what the woman is supposed to say. The Joan Rivers thing."

Martin risked his own smile. "Yeah. So I'm Joan Rivers. Doesn't that make you Fang? Can't we get your fangs withdrawn a little? It hurts me that you're still so angry."

"And I don't like it either. I don't like it one bit. The problem is I really am too tired tonight. Maybe tomorrow. Maybe tomorrow we can talk for real."

But they didn't talk, at least not on Saturday. But Saturday night, in bed, Martin was startled awake by what felt like a kick in the back. He looked over his shoulder to see Jenny nestled up against his back, her belly with its precious cargo providing the kick. As he turned back to try to go to sleep, Jenny's arm snaked over his chest, and the two of them (wasn't it really three?) slept, back to baby bump.

Sunday was a warm and calm day, and before packing up the house for their departure, Martin took Jenny and JJ to Sagahadoc State Park, which was a bit farther down the point. It had a huge beach, where JJ could explore to his heart's content, looking for shells and lobster buoys and anything else the tide had served up. Jenny took Martin's hand as they walked, watching their son. But, still, neither of them was quite ready to risk stepping on the landmine.

During their drive back to Cambridge, after confirming that JJ was sleeping, Martin finally launched into the speech he had been rehearsing for days: "I've had a lot of time to think this summer, and I finally realize you were right. The red card. You've been right all along. It was a horrible mistake for me to go to Istanbul with Kat. I was swept up by a damsel-in-distress fantasy and by trying to impress the Personnel Committee with my dedication. I behaved as if her career and my reputation with my colleagues were more important than your needs. This was wrong. I'm deeply ashamed for that, particularly because it's so obvious and because it's taken me so long to understand it. But I sold you short, and I'm sorry. Truly sorry. I think I've learned something from all this — especially about how life at CTI can poison your priorities. It won't happen again. The next time you show a red card, I will listen."

Jenny was quiet for more than a minute, during which Martin wasn't sure his heart was still beating. Finally, she said, "Thank you, Martin. I needed to hear that. And it's also time I said something. You have been a real trouper this summer. I've been so scared you were drifting away from me, even though it was clear that you weren't. Being scared is like that. It's... just scary. And the pregnancy. I've felt so lousy for so long, I just wasn't able to think about you, what you've been through. I lost touch with how disruptive this has been, especially with the colitis. So let me say it now: I'm also sorry. And thank you. For giving me time, some space, some breathing room to eradicate that nightmare of a shared bedroom. It really mattered to me. I've been, whatever it is... like they say in Maine... away. I've been away long enough. I'm ready to be back from away." Filmy tears dribbled down her cheeks.

Martin said through gritted teeth, "For you, my love, I will do whatever it takes."

As they were approaching the final exit on the Maine Turnpike, Jenny asked if they could stop at the Kittery Outlet Shops for some baby gear. "Among other things," she said, "I need to get you a practice doll so I can teach you the right way to hold, change and bathe our baby."

"Aren't there a zillion videos on YouTube I could watch?" asked Martin, relieved finally to be talking about events future instead of events past.

"I'm sure there are, but you can't feel a properly supported baby's head on a video."

"Okay," said Martin, laughing. "Bring it on. If I can learn to tickle atoms, I should be able to learn to bathe a baby."

That night, even though the possibility of reigniting the sciatica made her cautious about intercourse, Jenny found a way to welcome Martin back into her love nest.

PART III: Fall Term, 2013

186

* **23** *

Gina returned from her Portland summer at HP looking much less girlish. Her carriage had more poise, and her speech, even, was less valley-girl. While Martin was privately curious as to whether it was the experience at HP or the experience with her boyfriend that was responsible for the step-up in maturity, it really didn't matter. She was an eager and capable student, and their relationship, thoroughly professional as it was, made Martin feel like a proud parent.

At Gina's request, Martin had become her academic advisor. During their course-planning meeting, Martin asked if she was still committed to the idea of becoming a teacher. When Gina gushed a yes, Martin made two suggestions: First, she should take Probability and Statistics to give her the background necessary to interpret all kinds of data. Second, and this was only if Gina felt she could handle the time commitment, she should hire on as one of his undergraduate graders in C&E. "The best way to learn how students think is to see the astonishing variety of mistakes they make, and the most efficient way of doing that for a large group of students is by grading their papers."

"How much time would that take?" asked Gina.

"The normal load for a grader is two sections, about sixty students, but since I want you to be the liaison to Harry's fall project as well, I would give you just one section, about thirty students. Might take you three to four hours per week. Think you could handle that?"

"And what is Harry's, I mean, Professor Huang's project?"

"I sent Professor Huang your report from the spring term. Based on that twelve percent deficiency in the MOOC final exam scores, I persuaded him to set up a fall-term trial, which he did. Sixty of the fall-term C&E students will be allowed to take his MOOC version for Pass/Fail credit, provided they would also take and pass, with a grade of C or better, the written final examination from my in-class version. We will be monitoring how many of the regular students also sign up for the MOOC, and track lecture and section attendance, like we did last term."

"Will we know their majors this time? Of the MOOC ones?"

"Oh yes. Half are EE and half CS. Anyway, if you want, we can set up an RP to work both with Angela Fremont, the new head TA of the MOOC, and Garrett Chan, my head TA, collecting the data on class attendance and student progress through the MOOC, looking for patterns."

"Oh, that sounds exciting. I'll for sure do it. Both things. Thanks so much."

"And we need to set up your schedule so you're free Thursdays at one o'clock when we hold staff meetings. You can attend all of them, except when we discuss quizzes and the final exam. I want you to see as much as possible about how teachers actually function."

"That is so cool," said Gina. "But if I'm a grader, will I be able to tutor in the dorm?"

"Of course. And as a grader, you'll be in demand. You'll experience the conflict that all of us teachers feel between the support we give to help students learn on the one hand, and the painful necessity of evaluating their learning on the other. You might as well plunge into that discomfort zone."

-    -   -

Susan Zeltzer paused outside Kat's office door. The plan for her PhD research was to make measurements on the effect of the new deposition pattern on the carrier mobility, the thing that would determine how fast a transistor could operate. She knocked, and hearing 'C'mon in,' entered. "Hi, Susan," said Kat. "What's up?"

"I'm having a real problem," said Susan. "I've been trying for weeks to repeat Leah's experiments. I can't seem to get the implant pattern to agree with what she had. I even called her at Rutgers and we went over the procedure, step by step. I think I need some help."

Kat was still in shock, having just returned from three weeks in Merida. In mid-August, her mother suddenly became very weak and was now mostly bed-ridden, staying with Carmen and Alejandro. The cancer had not returned, but her body was gradually shutting down. Much as Kat hated to leave, the stakes were too high just now. She promised to return as soon as she could, but realistically, it probably wouldn't be until Christmastime.

Kat knew that it would take only one tiny detail for a procedure as complex as Leah's to fail, so she agreed to go into the lab with Susan for preparation of the next set of samples. Perhaps she could see what was being overlooked. She was sure Leah's results were correct. It must be something small. But as September morphed into October, whatever that small thing was, it was eluding detection. Leah's results could not be reproduced.

-    -   -

As the first PC meeting of the fall approached, Martin got a call from Rebecca to pick up his notebook. The Associate and Full promotions, the first agenda items for the fall, were going to serve as Martin's basic training so he would be able to present Kat's tenure case toward the end of November. When he picked up his notebook, Rebecca also gave him three folders containing selected papers by the candidates. It was a lot to read.

Back in his office, Martin tackled the notebook. There were three tabs separating the contents, one for each Associate case. He started with Edward Jones, a computer science person he knew only by sight. He skipped the CV pages and began reading letters. He had only the vaguest idea of what Jones's research was about — something about control of message latency in multi-processor architectures — but the set of eight letters already told him a lot.

Three of the letters were from CTI colleagues: one in computer science that focused on the meat of the research, one from the EE side of the house talking about his willingness to teach in the elementary undergraduate courses, and a third from a faculty colleague in the History Department who chaired the Task Force on Equal Opportunity that Jones served on, and according to the letter, served admirably well. Right. Research, teaching, service. The remaining five letters were from senior computer science faculty from all over the world: Stanford, University of Washington, Cal Tech, the Technion and Kyoto University. Even at the Associate level, Jones was being evaluated by a United Nations of experts.

Two of the letters got very specific in comparing Jones to others in his professional peer group, ranking him among the first three in a list of five or six, each list being different. One letter said Jones was clearly in the top ten of his age group in his field. Two made no such comparisons, but one of them said Jones would be worthy of promotion at his own institution.

Phrases like 'worthy of promotion' caught Martin's notice, phrases he would learn to parse with great acuity. One was, "I am pleased to recommend this promotion." Was this strong or weak? How can you tell? The other was, "Jones represents an opportunity that CTI should take." Martin found that last one particularly puzzling. Was it a sign of enthusiasm on the merits or was it a reference to Jones's being African-American?

Martin turned to the letters for the other two Associate candidates: Shmuel Goldberg, who had done something important in the theory of encryption for the internet, and Alexi Kerensky, a communications theorist. Goldberg, an Israeli educated at the Technion and Hebrew University, was described in the outside letters as brilliant, equally so with the inside letters but with a tinge of disappointment over his unwillingness to pitch in and do any of the down-in-the-trenches work that the department needed, like teaching undergraduate sections, advising undergraduates, and serving on committees. It was like he got a genius pass, so smart he could define his own heavenly workplace. Martin wondered what CTI would be like if everyone did that. The letters for Alexi were similar to those for Shmuel, a wonderful, brilliant researcher, but not so committed to the nitty-gritty of serving the needs of a large undergraduate population. But Martin had seen him up close while teaching sections of the Signals and Systems class. Alexi had an almost magical command of the issues, with a crispness and clarity that made Martin envious, because in spite of the adoration of the Gina Farrell's of this world, Martin had to work hard to make his legendary lectures so polished.

Closing the notebook, Martin was shocked to realize that he had already ranked the three cases: Alexi best, Shmuel second, and Martin Jones a weak third. How could he do this? He hadn't even looked at their CVs or tried to read their papers. Nothing. Just the letters and the little he could add from personal contact. Was this the way it worked? He would have to wait until the Wednesday meeting to see things in person, but in the meantime, he needed to go back, study the CVs, and at least try to read his colleagues' papers. He got out his new iPhone, the replacement for the one sitting on the bottom of the Golden Horn, opened the cloud-saved calendar and blanked out all of Wednesday morning for PC reading.

-    -   -

"This is utter crap," said a disgusted Carleton Heppelwhite. "This draft does exactly what CTI has been doing for years, claiming one thing and doing another."

"But Carleton," said Marsha, the author of the Tenure Review Panel's draft report now under discussion, "CTI's mission really is complex. We need to be a top research school, extending the frontiers of knowledge. That's a key part of our mission. It's our research prestige that brings us our students, and without the best students, we would slide downhill. For our grad students, of course, mentorship during research is almost the entire story. The classes are clearly secondary.

And for the undergrads, a lot of what we do is in projects like the RP program, with personal mentoring by our faculty. When we did our grading of cases, we were using only classroom teaching, not mentorship. But if you're going to consider education, fully and broadly, our entire educational mission, it simply can't be done without first-class research."

"Are you done?" asked Carleton.

Marsha smiled. "Yes. I guess that was something of a speech. Sorry."

"What you said is true enough, but it's a question of balance. Why can't CTI be an educational innovator as well as a research leader? Why don't we value the Sharon Gillespies of this world as highly as, say, our Nobel Prize winners?"

Marsha fought back. "CTI is an educational innovator, for God's sake. Look at FIE. Look at how we're pioneering new technologies. Putting complete sets of lectures on the web for free. Making the syllabus in almost every course available…"

Phil Galsworthy interrupted. "Look, Marsha. The data we collected don't lie. The fact is that without an 'A' in research, tenure is denied, almost without exception, and thanks to Martin Felt or whoever that is, the whole community knows it. Those exceptions are most likely to come in the Humanities, which is not where our primary student research opportunities lie. I'm with Carleton in this. Your draft twists things in the wind to make us look different than we really are. What would be wrong with saying, 'It is true that our award of tenure does weight research excellence more heavily than excellence in classroom teaching, but much of our teaching is done through the individual mentoring of research. Without strong research programs, we could not provide our students a complete and balanced education. Furthermore, CTI's track record in educational innovation is as strong, or stronger, than any school in the country, and that innovation is being led by highly creative teachers and researchers who have come through our promotion process.'"

Marsha looked down and replied, "I hate to say this, Phil, but I sort of agree with you. I like data, and I like telling the truth, and our data really do say exactly what you indicated. But Alberto just won't buy it. Your sentence just won't fly. He'll deep-six our report if that's what we say."

"So why the hell are we meeting and doing all this if the Provost is going to write our report?" Phil smacked his hand on the table. "I won't sign this piece of crap." He slapped the draft report onto the table, got up, and walked out.

Carleton looked around the table, got up, and walked out too.

-    -   -

At five to three, Martin gathered up his notebook and the folders with the three Associate candidates' papers and headed for Department Headquarters, almost crashing into Julian Kesselbaum as he emerged from the stairs. Julian apologized for the near-collision, saying he had been called to the EECS computer node, just down the hall from Headquarters, to help with a glitch problem.

"You mean you still work on our system?"

"Oh, yes," said Julian. "But only when things go wrong. You'd be amazed at how often bad stuff happens. The job at IT is to keep the rest of you guys insulated from all that, and I help whenever I'm asked."

"Well, keep up the good work," said Martin, as Julian entered the department's computer center.

Martin grabbed a coffee and took his usual seat in the PC conference room. He had done his homework: CVs, letters, and even an attempt to read the research papers. Now he would see how things really worked.

Most of the committee members were already in their seats when, promptly at 3:00, Morris entered with Bill Burke and Ellen Zefrim. They took their seats, and the meeting began. Morris said, "Welcome to the fall season. There's plenty to do this term, so we need to dive in. Of the three Associate cases, we have most of the letters on Kerensky and Jones, and only a few on Goldberg, so let's look at them in this order. Moshe is Case Manager for Alexi. Why don't you get us started?"

Moshe Felsenthal, like Alexi, an expert in theoretical communications, recounted Alexi's educational history, his hiring dates, summarized his research into algorithms for increasing the data rate in wifi systems, and paused for questions.

Mary Lewinsky, who worked on optical tomography, asked, "Moshe, I'm probably revealing my ignorance here, but I thought issues of data rate were already fine-tuned to the point where there was little more to be done. Is Alexi's stuff making a difference?"

Moshe responded, "You know that when you fly these days, you see those bent up wing tips?" Mary nodded. "Those tips provide a few percent reduction of the air friction, called the drag. In today's competitive airline environment, a few percent of drag reduction creates fuel savings, so most of the airlines are paying the capital cost of changing to the new wings. Alexi's work is a bit like that, that extra few percent. As for impact, maybe the thing to do is turn to the letters." The letters were clear. Everyone was in awe of the intellectual depth of his insights.

Kiyoshi Abe, a robotics expert, said, "He's clearly a brilliant theorist. We acknowledge that. But will his stuff be used? If not, what good is the brilliance?"

Moshe answered, "It can take ten years or more for an idea to get implemented. Remember, these communication systems have to handle immense traffic without failure. You can only introduce modifications after very careful testing. The Hennessey letter, the one from Verizon, addresses that." Amid the shuffling of notebook pages, Moshe quoted:

> "We anticipate that Kerensky's Maximum-Efficiency-Spread-Spectrum scheme will be piloted on one of our internal networks over the next two years, where we can subject it to some brutal in-field testing. If everything passes muster, we would be leading perhaps to first deployment in the 2017-18 time frame."

Prakash Singh, a computer languages researcher, cracked, "What an acronym. Maximum-Efficiency-Spread-Spectrum. It's a MESS." Everyone laughed.

Morris said, "Actually, having Verizon pilot your stuff is, for my money, good enough for an Associate promotion. I'm quite comfortable with all this. What about teaching?"

Roger Ericsson, who studied bioengineering informatics, had been assigned to examine the teaching case. "He has taught sections in Signals and Systems four times, with decent but not overwhelming reviews, and is now time-sharing the grad communications course with Moshe. The only comments that rang a bell were that he was very dry in class, no animation, and this could make things boring. But there were no really ugly comments. His average rating by the students was a four, not star status but not a problem either. Sort of middle of the pack."

Martin added, "I taught S&S sections with him once, and I was simply bowled over with how crisply he could put things. It made me a bit envious."

Rachel Pless asked, "Is he an undergrad advisor? How does he do in that arena?"

"No," said Moshe. "We haven't been able to get him involved in advising. And, since someone is sure to ask, no, he doesn't serve on any committees, but he has been tapped to be an Associate Editor on the *Journal of Theoretical Communications*. So the world out there knows about him and respects him."

"Okay," said Morris. "I think we have the picture here. Pretty decent case. We'll return to it for a final review before we vote. Are we ready to move on to Jones?"

Ellen Zefrim presented the Edward Jones case. The order was the same as for Kerensky: a review of background, education, followed by a summary of research. Then a letter-by-letter scorecard, identifying substance, pro or con. Considerable time was spent on the peer lists and the zinger lines, just what Martin had noted in his own reading. A few minutes before adjournment, Abel Blaine, from artificial intelligence, asked about the last line in Griswold's letter, the one that read, "Edward Jones represents an opportunity CTI should take."

Abel asked, "What's with this letter, anyway? Is Griswold saying promote, or not? What should we make of it?"

Ellen answered, "It's sort of vague the way it stands. I'm sorry our colleagues don't know how to write clearer letters."

Dieter Tannhauser said, "I think he's being clear. He's clearly ambiguous."

Ellen responded, "He's a she, Dieter."

Alex Papadopolous, who worked on auditory acoustics, asked, "So does that mean she's telling us we should keep going as a diversity thing? Like when we hired him in the first place?"

Ellen objected: "He wasn't a diversity hire. He was head and shoulders above the rest of the pool, regardless of race, color, creed, or, for that matter, gender or sexual orientation."

Alex said, "Now don't get heated up, Ellen. He may have looked like a star when we hired him, but…"

Ellen interrupted. "Listen. We've got a few more letters coming. How about we hold off over-interpreting one sentence until the case is in. Okay, Alex?"

A chastened Alex agreed, and the meeting was adjourned.

* **24** *

The October concert went better than expected. The Menotti had been a surprising success, and Martin's rendering of the Schubert *Impromptu* had delighted the audience. Jenny's Berkeley Place project had also gone well. The client was thrilled, bubbling with superlatives, and was scheduled to move in the following week. The dispute over the damaged Roentgen piece was now in the hands of an arbitrator. Except for having to provide an affidavit regarding the state of the piece prior to its shipment, Jenny could turn everything over to her client's lawyers and to their expert witness on antique appraisal.

The Columbus Day weekend was Martin and Jenny's last chance for a visit to Maine before the baby would be due. It was a hot time for the Red Sox, having just made it to the American League Championship against Detroit. This was good news, but even better was that the games at Fenway Park would be on Saturday and Sunday, meaning that if the family travelled up to Maine on Friday and back on Monday, Martin and JJ could watch both games via streaming video on his iPad. JJ was becoming quite knowledgeable about the game, even understanding tagging up after a fly ball, a very sophisticated concept for a five-year old.

They packed up the car on Friday morning, picked up JJ from his Montessori School at noon, and headed north. Jenny's sciatica had resolved itself during her seventh month, so a few hours in the car were now tolerable. But it turned out to be more than a few hours. The road, at least as far as Portsmouth, was crammed with leaf peepers heading for the White Mountains, and even the Maine Turnpike was full until Portland.

They arrived at the Brimfield Junction family homestead just in time for dinner with Helen and the kids. The meal was chaos. JJ was tired and crabby, Jenny was in pain and had to lie down, and Carlo was hyperactive and aggressive. Martin took a plate to Jenny and helped her eat lying down, while Helen spent dinner dealing with tears, most of them from JJ, but with a good dose from Angela as well. Ice cream for dessert seemed to calm the kids down, giving Martin and Helen a chance to catch up with news. Helen had found a new job as the office manager for the State Farm Insurance office right on Maine Street, and she had assembled a team of three Bottlesworth students who time-shared the after-school daycare. Her finances were stable, her mood was much improved, and she was making progress getting Carlo to calm down, thanks to weekly sessions with a behavioral therapist. In answer to Martin's explicit question, no, there were no men in her life. She was too busy to worry about that.

After dinner, Martin helped Jenny into the front seat, strapped JJ into his car seat and drove them the final miles to the cottage. There was a chill wind off the bay when they arrived, so after opening things up and turning on the lights, he fired up the electric heat. He lugged a sleeping JJ out of the car seat and into the house and was helping Jenny up the three steps to the porch when the lights went out. No moon. Pitch black. JJ woke up and started yelling for help. Martin told him to stay where he was, that everything would be okay. He retrieved the emergency flashlights from the kitchen, one of which he gave to JJ, and returned to Jenny, guiding her into the cottage and to the bathroom. Without power, the pump from the well wouldn't work, so she didn't flush. After clothing reassembly, he helped Jenny wince out of the bathroom and onto their bed.

The main fuse box had no thrown circuit breakers, so Martin called Central Maine Power to report the outage. The customer service rep, with a classic down-East accent, asked, "You tahn on a big load?"

"We just arrived," said Martin. "Turned on some electric heat."

"That fig-yahs. Probably ovah-heated the transfahmah. I'll send a truck out yah way."

Martin went to the storage shed to retrieve three kerosene lanterns, filled and lit them, put one in JJ's room, one in their bedroom, and one on the table in front of the fireplace. He got JJ to brush his teeth without using any water, persuaded him that was okay to pee into the toilet that already had Jenny's pee in it, loaded him into his PJs, read him a short selection from a story book about King Arthur, and got him nodded off to sleep, covered with an extra layer of blankets.

Jenny was still in pain. Martin went out to the car and got one of JJ's precious juice boxes so she could swallow a Tylenol. He helped her undress, get into pajamas, and climb into bed for the night. Finally, he brought in the duffels of clothes and the two bottles of wine, leaving the cooler with their food in the car until they had power again.

And then, silence. Martin's adrenaline level began to subside. He started to relax into the glow of the lanterns, the peace, the isolation, the quiet. As he waited for the power truck, fog crept in from the ocean and the mournful music of the foghorns began, a mix of the odd notes of Charles Ives with the long silences of Jonathan Cage. It was his first chance in many weeks to think about Jenny's pregnancy and her fears about his commitment, but unease over life at CTI kept intruding, with visions of lemmings running toward the cliff of online education, Kat's tenure case swinging by a slender thread, and the failure of the DARPA proposal. He wondered how long he could keep the merry-go-round twirling.

Martin opened one of the wine bottles, a California merlot with, as the blurb on the label said, a 'hint of strawberry.' He enjoyed the first glass and was midway through the second when he was finally able to feel at peace. Martin imagined himself transported into an environment where he could really enjoy his time with Jenny, with JJ, with the new child. He would teach, really teach, face-to-face, in small classes, unencumbered by the pressures of an international reputation and the frenzy of his research lab. He wondered if this was just a dream, or whether he would someday have the courage (or poor judgment, perhaps) to make the move to a small college, maybe one without even an engineering program, go back to teaching physics, find time to write his book. Even thinking about the upset of tonight, it was so easy and rewarding to deal with a power outage compared with the political intricacies of a multi-investigator multi-university DARPA grant.

Around midnight, the power company truck showed up. Martin went out to talk to the serviceman, who said that the transfahmah on the pole a hundred yahds up the road had ovah-heated and needed a reset. Sometimes a sudden load could do that. If Martin would tahn off all the heatahs in the house, he would do the reset, and then aftah a minute or two, he could tahn on the heatahs, one at a time. Which he did.

* **25** *

On the following Tuesday, Martin and Gina left their meeting with the Educational Policy Committee, walking together toward Martin's office. Gina asked whether all faculty committees were so full of arguments. Martin answered with a sigh. "Yes, unfortunately," he said. "I thought I would be able to get a serious discussion going on educational philosophy, but it seems that the Provost wants to save money and the math and physics guys don't want to bother with teaching undergraduates, so they all advocate for MOOCs."

The meeting, stimulated by Martin's having sent Gina's report to the Chairman, had turned out to be more of a slug-fest than a discussion. The three representatives from engineering and science departments were intrigued with the opportunity to reduce staff in the large undergraduate courses to free up time for more advanced graduate subjects. Marsha Collins, representing the Provost, was excited that MOOCs could be taught with such a small staff. Even Vladimir Tchernoff, Martin's chamber-music partner, was enthusiastic about possibly creating an on-line tutorial for harmony and counterpoint lessons. Only Tamara Eliot from the English Department put up any fight, focusing on the issue of student interaction, something Gina had highlighted as a major weakness. Lars Hoogeboom from Mathematics dismissed the twelve percent difference in test scores as an improperly controlled statistical study, saying he would wait for the result of Professor Huang's test project.

But Gina, in response, had said, "Actually, Professor, I think there's a problem with Professor Huang's study too. Y'see, I'm a grader in C&E this term and I also do a lot of tutoring in my dorm. So I see, like, a ton of students with difficulties. When one of the MOOC students is confused by something, she goes to one of the regular students to talk about it. I mean, there's always groups of students working on homework together. At least in McGonigal, where I live. So working in groups, like what Professor Quint said, may be more important than the MOOC versus non-MOOC students."

As they neared Martin's office, he grinned at Gina and said, "You really have learned a lot, you know. That remark about the mixing of student groups in the dorms was right on the money. It hadn't occurred either to Harry or me that this could undercut the validity of his study. Good job."

Gina smiled and blushed. "I thought what you said about that Harvard guy was very interesting."

"Mazur, you mean?"

"Yeah, him."

"As I said, he's suspicious of MOOCs because he is convinced that peer-to-peer discussion is what cements understanding. And MOOCs can't do that. I'm really disappointed that both the math and physics guys seem to want to cut corners by going to the MOOC format."

"But," said Gina, "I thought Professor Kimble was a fantastic physics teacher. And he was enthusiastic, like, every lecture. And Professor Stefanos does the labs in physics. Everybody tells me they're terrific."

"Labs are one thing; they're hard to replace with online. But lectures? I predict that Kimble will be pressured to slice his lectures up into ten minute segments and put them online. Would that be the same for you?"

"No, but I might like being able to look at them on my own schedule."

Martin sighed. "Of course. That's really the point, isn't it?"

- - -

Ethel McKinsey, now a senior and still the co-moderator of *The Flame Thrower,* put up the following topic:

TEACHING v RESEARCH REVISITED

The Provost's review committee has turned down
Professor Gillespie's tenure appeal. So we ask: How
can we make teaching more important in the award
of tenure?

CTI students, being smart, recognized that flailing through the
ideas from last spring, especially given Mark Felt's disclosures, would
not be of much interest. The Gillespie protest, cut short as it was by
the tragedy of the Marathon bombing, had failed. But a spark of life
appeared on the blog:

Here's an idea. How about we figure out who's going
to be up for tenure this year and create a thread
on each of them where students can report on
their teaching.
notpresuming

Great idea. But is there a list? How can we find out?
muffin3

A few days later, this idea took hold:

We should look up the details on Prof. Gillespie,
maybe from the Widgit. Her tenure was mandatory. If
we find out when she was hired, we can calculate when
somebody comes up, and if we look at old catalogs, we
can see when people are hired.
qwibble

Sixth year is the normal time.
trojanhorse

That agrees with Gillespie, who came up in her sixth
year on the faculty. We should look at the old
catalogs to find out everybody who started teaching
in 2007.
notpresuming

```
But remember, some of the new people are hired at
Associate rank without tenure, and they probably are
on a different schedule. So just Assistant Professors
hired in 2007.
qwibble
```

That afternoon, 'rogerrabbit' posted a list of seven names of faculty members from the Engineering School who appeared in the 2007 Catalog as new Assistant Professors. Within a few days, the list was expanded to a total of thirteen, the seven from the Engineering School, three from the Science School, and one each from the Architecture School, the Business School, and Humanities. After seeing these postings, Ethel McKinsey and her co-moderator, Ralph Aiken, discussed whether they would be putting *TFT* in some kind of institutional danger if they created threads on individual faculty members. They decided to consult with Marsha Collins.

Marsha's view was that as long as the threads clearly stated that the purpose was to collect student input on teaching, and that personal attacks would be viewed as violation of the blog rules, she saw no reason not to go ahead. Thus assured, Ethel and Ralph went to work.

For example, the thread on Kat read:

```
KATARINA RODRIGUEZ TEACHING THREAD
```

```
The purpose of this thread is to collect student
input on the teaching of Prof. Katarina Rodriguez of
EECS, who is believed to be a candidate for tenure
this academic year. We hope you will take this oppor-
tunity to make your voice heard as CTI makes such an
important decision.
```

Manny Encarnacion, now Editor-in-Chief of *The Widgit*, was thrilled to see the new threads. He asked Susannah Gilpin, a junior in Biology who reported on CTI issues, to contact each of the named individuals to see if she could check the accuracy of the list of names. It was surprisingly easy. Of the thirteen, twelve confirmed that they were up for tenure, some of them joking about it, others expressing what a rough year it was going to be. Only Anna Heidelberg said she was not yet up because she had taken advantage of the CTI clock-stopping for one year when she gave birth to her son. Susannah notified *TFT,* and the thread on Anna was removed. She also contacted Marsha Collins to see if the Provost's Office had any opinion about the threads. The *Widgit* then published a signed opinion piece.

FLAME THROWER TO COLLECT
TEACHING INFO ON TENURE CANDIDATES
By Susannah Gilpin and Emmanual Encarnacion

This week, *TFT* created a new set of discussion threads with the explicit purpose of collecting student feedback on the teaching record of twelve professors known to be candidates for tenure this year. We applaud the creation of this opportunity for the Department Heads, Deans and the Provost to see first-hand what students say about their experience.

We asked Prof. William Burke, Associate Department Head of EECS, and one deeply involved in these discussions, about his department's practice in monitoring classroom activity. He said, "It is important to recognize how disruptive it can be to a teacher to have a senior faculty member sitting in on his or her classes, knowing that the senior faculty member would be weighing in on promotion. Therefore, our policy is to assign a 'teaching buddy' to advise new hires on teaching. The teaching buddy typically attends a few classes and provides private feedback, but the teaching buddy is not part of the personnel evaluation process."

We understand Prof. Burke's point about the intrusiveness of having senior faculty monitor classes if those faculty members also provide evaluations. This makes the potential utility of the *TFT* threads even greater. Students sit in on every class, and they make evaluative judgments day by day. Why not provide a pathway for collecting those judgments in real time, day by day? The students really know what goes in in class. Let's hear from them.

Marsha Collins, reading this piece, said a silent Hallelujah. She was sure that most of the student comments would prove that CTI faculty members were, on the whole, excellent teachers, and that the students would come out in force to support their tenure cases. Better to get the support out before the tenure decisions are made than have screaming protests after the fact.

∗ **26** ∗

Carly and Kat were seated at Carly's kitchen table. As Carly poured scotch over ice for the two of them, she said, "I hate it, this fucking schedule of yours, or the lack of one."

"But, listen, *cara*, this experiment has to work or I'm outta here. We just can't find the problem. It's driving me nuts."

"Oh, I know. You say that all the time, and I understand. Intellectually, that is. You need to find the problem. It's just that I hate that you're never here. Or when you are, you're totally preoccupied. Or too tired. I mean we haven't made it in weeks. It's like that Susan person is more important than me."

"Now that's just not fair," Kat growled. "Susan is my student. My *student*, for God's sake. Suppose my student was named Sam? Would that make a difference?"

Carly sputtered, "It probably would, even though you're right — my feelings make no sense. I don't pretend to be rational. After all," giggling and sniffling, "I'm a woman. It's just that I hate being so alone after what we've had together. And, by the way, can you stop thinking like an engineer? I'm just telling you how I feel. I'm not asking you to fix it. Just listen, and be sympathetic."

Kat took both of Carly's hands, an echo of her remark to Martin about the difficulties of family life ringing in her ears. "You're right. Listen, *cara*, it's probably going to get worse until we find the problem. I wish it wasn't so, but it is, so I've gotta ask you to stay patient. You're so precious to me, but I can't stop now. Some of our experiments run all night and then I have to teach. It's crazy. And the students have just started a blog where they will be posting stuff about my teaching performance. More stress, just when I don't need it."

Carly looked up, suddenly serious. "Really? Students can post about you?" The sniffling stopped and Carly got a tissue to blow her nose. "You should be able to use that. Get them to post good stuff. Make them fall in love with you and tell them, right out front, that you're up for tenure. The Cambridge pols I work with all know how to turn those kind of situations to their favor. They're always looking for votes. You're in the same boat. You want your students to vote for you."

-    -   -

That quotation from Bill Burke in *The Widgit,* where everyone had a teaching buddy who didn't participate in evaluation, had infuriated Kat. Martin had been her teaching buddy, knew all her weaknesses, and now was definitely part of the evaluation process. So much for teaching buddies. When the reporter had called her, she readily confirmed that she was up for tenure. Why hide it? Now that it was public, why not, as Carly suggested, take advantage of the situation?

She strode into her classroom as the students were arriving, lowering the screen as she usually did and connecting her laptop to the projector. Most of the students were present. As she said her good mornings, she launched PowerPoint, landing on the title slide for today's class: 'Designing Photomasks for Lift-off Processes.'

"I have a question before we start," she began. "How many of you have been following the discussion over Teaching v Research on *The Flame Thrower*?" Six hands went up. "Then you are aware, I mean, it is now public information that I am up for tenure this year." Heads bent together, with murmurings. "Yes, it's true. My tenure case is being discussed by my department this fall. If I don't get tenure, I will have to leave CTI." More buzz in the room. "And thanks to *The Flame Thrower,* you have all been invited to post comments on their blog about my performance as a teacher. That's fine. Post away. And, for that matter, email me a copy of what you post." A few students chuckled. "Seriously. I am not afraid of criticism as long as it's done with respect. And criticism will have absolutely no effect on grades. That's a solemn promise. But there's more to this than respect. So instead of today's class on lift-off photolithography, we are going to have a discussion about teaching and education."

Kat closed the PowerPoint, and with a visible flourish, dragged the icon for the file to the Trash bin, evoking a gasp or two from the group.

"I now have another question. How many of you think Professor Quint is a good teacher?" Every hand went up.

"Okay," she continued. "Why? Why do you think he's a good teacher?"

It took a few moments, but then comments flew in from around the room.

"He's entertaining. I mean, he explains stuff, but he's fun to watch."

"Doesn't need notes. It's all in his head."

"Knows his stuff, and says ahead of time what he's going to teach each day."

"Cute," from a woman in the back, followed by giggles.

"Sexy," from a woman in front, followed by laughter.

"Seriously, ladies. I mean, he, like, talks to us. Pauses. Like he wants us to think about what he's saying. It's easy to follow him."

Kat took the floor. "Good, okay. Leaving aside issues of cuteness," (a few laughs) "you have hit on two important aspects: he's entertaining and he's clear." She wrote on the board 'EDUCATION' and 'ENTERTAINMENT'. "I want to ask you about these two words: education and entertainment. How important is the entertainment aspect of teaching to you?"

This produced an awkward silence. Finally, a pimply student in the front row said, "I guess the way it works is, if the teacher isn't entertaining, going to class is like murder. Boring. A struggle. If the teacher is entertaining, going to class is fun."

"That's well put, Tom," said Kat, "but if all you want to be entertained, why not just go to a movie? So there's got to be something more, right?"

"Of course there is," said Tom. "We want to learn stuff. I mean, duh… that's why we're here."

"So think, for a minute, about what an entertaining teacher has to do to get you to learn stuff. What do you think his preparation consists of? Is he just thinking up jokes to keep you entertained?"

Stephanie, the source of the 'sexy' comment, said, "Of course not. He has a plan, a list of stuff he wants us to learn. He has to think about that. The content."

Elmer, seated next to Stephanie, said "Not just a list. He has to have a conception about how to make the ideas clear. That's where Professor Quint is really special. I mean, it's just so easy to see what he's talking about."

Kat replied, "So you're suggesting that planning a class, in fact, a whole course full of classes, is a serious intellectual enterprise, yes?"

Murmurs of 'yes,' 'sure,' 'of course.'

"Then what is it, specifically, about the entertainment part? Why is that so important compared to what we could call the intellectual part?"

The students were clearly struggling with this. Elmer said, "It's like he's connecting with us somehow, getting us to nod our heads, or laugh, or something. Inviting us to be part of a conversation."

Kat wrote 'CONVERSATION' on the board. "Yes, conversation. Let me tell you a story. When I first joined the faculty, I was the kind of teacher who prepared extensive notes and followed them to the letter. I used to get very nervous, and the students could tell. The classes were not good, so I asked Professor Quint for help. He was amazing. He told me about his theory of education as a conversation." She wrote and underlined the phrase. "Education as conversation means that the teacher and the student need to be speaking the same language. Professor Quint came to my classes. He even took over for me once so I could watch him teach my recitations. He demonstrated an amazing gift for engaging students in a two-way conversation. I believe it is that gift, in combination with his intellectual vision about the subject, which makes him a great teacher. Not only does he have a plan for ordering the pieces of content to make them learnable, he has a way of making sure he's connecting with his students. When that connection happens, students feel engaged, entertained." She underlined 'ENTERTAINMENT'. "I would argue," she continued, "that there is a legitimate role for some amount of entertainment in classroom education, but it is subservient to the really important things — the content, and a conversation about that content. What do you think?"

Tom said, "I hadn't thought about it that way, but it makes sense."

Stephanie added, "Yeah. I'm kind of sorry about that 'sexy' comment, by the way. I was trying to be entertaining, but there wasn't much content to go with it." She giggled.

Kat smiled. "As I said, I'm quite happy to have you comment on my teaching, on everyone's teaching, but I would like you to be thinking about what is involved — the pyramid of ideas, with the overarching concepts at the peak, broken down into an orderly set of building blocks, each one developed through a real conversation, with the entertainment part just being a pathway into that conversation. But there's more. How many of you have done some kind of undergraduate research, whether as an official RP or just working with a research group?" Most of the hands went up.

"Would you say the RP experience was education?" Heads nodded. "Okay, let's try to describe the nature of that kind of educational experience and talk about the role of the teacher."

After a ruminative pause, Tom said, "It's like an apprenticeship. Like learning a trade. Sort of."

Stephanie disagreed. "No. It's more than that. I had an RP with Professor Campbell, and he was helping me plan an experiment, I mean, my own experiment. So I had to think about what to do."

David, from the back row, said, "But we have to learn how to operate the equipment, and that's done with the grad students, not the professor."

Tom responded, "Yeah. That's what I meant about the apprentice thing. Learning to do all the stuff yourself."

"I had an RP with Professor Van Rijks," said Alice. "We had tons of data from his neural arrays, and he had me looking at the data to try to find patterns. It was really hard, but really interesting."

Kat asked, "Did he give you any guidance?"

"Yeah. That's the cool part. He had me learn how to use R, you know, the statistical language, to look for correlations and stuff like that. It was really neat."

Kat paused. "Now let me ask this. In your various research experiences, how important has entertainment been, in terms of either your engagement or your learning?"

"The stuff itself is entertaining," said Tom. "The prof doesn't have to do anything special. I mean he talks to us and shows us stuff, but it's pretty low key." Murmurs of agreement floated around the room.

Kat waited for them to quiet down. "So here's another question. Try to compare the content part of your classes with your experiences in research. Is the class content the goal of your education?"

"Not really," said Alice. "It's what you need to know in order to do stuff. In the lab, I mean."

"So is it fair to say that our education here has several components? You've mentioned them, but I want to underscore the ideas." Kat wrote in large capitals: 'CONTENT, SKILLS, EXPERIMENTAL DESIGN, DATA ANALYSIS' and then said, "and there's one more that summarizes a lot of what we do." She wrote 'CRITICAL THINKING' on the board, and continued, "The entertainment component we talked about shows up only in making the delivery of content more fun." She circled 'CONTENT' in red. "So please don't be hoodwinked into evaluating your teachers only by their entertainment value. There's a lot more to teaching than classroom charisma." Kat paused to allow that to sink in. "Does anyone want to add anything to this list?" She looked around the now silent class. "All right, let's get to work." She opened the trash bin on the computer, recovered the PowerPoint, and opened the file. "We have enough time to cover at least part of today's class."

- - -

The *TFT* blog about Kat's teaching performance began glowing a few hours after class:

> I want to thank Prof. Rodriguez for a really great
> class today. We discussed what education is all
> about, and it was very revealing. Most important is
> not to confuse entertainment in the classroom with
> education. Terrific class.
> tomtom

> I agree with Tom. She was great today. And she is
> usually quite organized and knows her stuff. But the
> best thing was she put some balance around teach-
> ing in a research mode and teaching in a classroom.
> They're not the same.
> steffie2014

> It was a wake-up call. Lots of profs here are kind of
> dull. They know their stuff, but it can be tedious.
> Prof. Rodriguez helped me appreciate that classes
> need two-way communication, even in big lectures,
> and so entertainment can help. But it's not every-
> thing. Cool.
> alicefromLA

> When we have classes like the one today, it makes me
> appreciate a live teacher - somebody who talks to
> you, and listens, too.
> elmerfudd

> We talked about Prof. Quint, too. We all agreed he
> was great.
> davidthehutt

Kat sent Martin an email, asking him to take a look at her *TFT* page. She also included a link to a YouTube video. One of her students had broken his leg at football practice and was having trouble making it to class, so his friend had asked permission to video the lecture. Since it was such an unusual class, he asked if he could put it on YouTube, and she had agreed.

Martin watched the video, taking the ego-strokes directed his way in stride and grinning with delight over Kat's performance. He forwarded the link to the entire Personnel Committee.

* **27** *

Kat had spent nearly a month in the lab with Susan Zeltzer, going over and over Leah's procedures and comparing them with what Susan was doing. On their fifteenth attempt at getting the quantum-interference deposition to succeed, Kat noticed that one of the vacuum gauges was not recording a steady pressure. It was jittery. She shouted for joy. At last, something to go after.

They immediately shut down the rig and spent the next three hours warming the apparatus to room temperature and beginning the disassembly. It was a tedious job. Every high-vacuum seal was secured by as many as twenty bolts, and the mating surfaces had to be handled with exquisite care, because even the slightest scratch could eventually develop into a leak. The problem at hand was whether they had a leak or a faulty gauge.

Kat's instinct was to go for the gauge, in part because it was easier to test. They had a spare, swapped out the questionable hardware, and began the reassembly process, cleaning each vacuum seal and torqueing each of the bolts to the exact same level. By this time, it was midnight, but there was no question of stopping now. They put three different starting samples into the air-lock, transferred the liquid nitrogen to start the cool-down of the beam-shield section, then the liquid helium, and brought the atomic source to temperature. It took a different source setting to get the new gauge to the right pressure. This was exactly what they had hoped for. The defective gauge had been causing them to miss the correct source setting. By four AM, they had three implanted samples ready for test.

It took until seven to get the apparatus shut down. Kat offered to buy Susan breakfast at the student center and then drove her across the river to her apartment in Back Bay. Kat returned to CTI, freshened up in the ladies room, and went to teach her microelectronics class. Susan would check the samples later today, and maybe, finally, their nightmare would be over.

- - -

While Kat was driving Susan to her apartment, Jenny experienced her first contraction. She elbowed Martin and said, "Martin, love. Wake up. It's not supposed to happen for two more weeks, but this feels like it." She waited until she could get Martin to stir, got out of bed and waddled into the bathroom, at which point a more intense contraction coincided with the breaking of her water. "It's definitely time," she shouted. "Call Dr. Rosen."

Martin flopped out of bed, checked that Jenny hadn't fainted, and called the doctor. His answering service said he would be at the hospital today and that a nurse would call back. He woke JJ, got him into and out of the bathroom and into his school clothes. He called Colleen, who had agreed to take care of JJ for the day. Jenny had already packed JJ's overnight bag, so when JJ came in to give her a hug, she said "It's time for your brother or sister to come out of mommy's tummy. This is an exciting day." But JJ wasn't buying. He was scared and sniffling.

Colleen collected JJ just as the nurse from Dr. Rosen's office called. Martin reported that the contractions were coming at six-minute intervals. The nurse said that they might as well come in now, before traffic clogged the roads.

Martin called Steve Campbell, asked him to take the class, helped Jenny into the car and headed for Mt. Auburn Hospital. They fidgeted through the registration and admission steps and into a labor room, and then began to wait. Five minutes. Four minutes. Five minutes. Six minutes. Five minutes. Dr. Rosen came to examine Jenny, and said she was only partially dilated. "Might be a long labor," he said, "but it looks like today's going to be the day."

By three in the afternoon, the pain of the contractions, still about five minutes apart, had gotten so intense that Jenny asked if she could take something. The nurse examined her, said she could have a Tylenol, and went out to call Dr. Rosen. Dilation wasn't proceeding, and the baby had shifted with the head now sideways. Dr. Rosen arrived an hour later, did his own examination, and suggested that because of the shift of position and the lack of dilation, it would be much less risky for the baby if they did a C-section. The appropriate release was signed and Jenny was wheeled toward the delivery room.

Martin was invited to scrub up and see the operation, but he was afraid of his reaction on seeing Jenny cut open. He asked her permission not to watch. She patted his hand and said it was okay; she knew that women were the brave ones in this world. He went to the old 'wait and pace' lounge set up for expectant fathers, but he was the only one there.

He got out his iPhone to work on email. He found an early message from Kat telling him about the faulty vacuum gauge. Scrolling down, he found another saying that the new implants showed exact agreement with Leah's results and that Susan was preparing one of their samples for the transport measurements. Martin replied:

```
Bravo. Within a few minutes, I'm expecting news on
my son or daughter, being delivered as we speak.
Will check in with you on Monday. Good luck with
the measurements.

- Martin
```

An hour later, a nurse's aide came into the lounge to tell Martin that his baby daughter was fine, a little underweight at just under five pounds, but everything looked fine. His wife was still in the recovery room, but both would be going to a room on the maternity floor to which he was directed. You can see them then. "Helen," thought Martin. "We could name her Helen."

He fidgeted until Jenny and the baby were wheeled in. Martin gave Jenny a big kiss and picked up his baby, swathed in a blanket and a little cap. This was the first time in his forty-three years he had held a newborn. Tears leaked from his eyes, tinged by wondering what things might have been like if he and Katie had ever had a child. But this, this was a miracle, a birth and a rebirth, all in one. Gently laying the infant in Jenny's arms, he said, "You're a genius to have done this, and I love you beyond the price of rubies." After an hour admiring the drowsy mother and sleeping child, he went home, collected JJ from Colleen's house, told him the good news, made dinner, and got him quietly and happily to bed.

The next few weeks would be complicated. Colleen volunteered to do some day-time child care once Jenny got home, and Jenny's mother, Grace, was coming from Worcester to stay for a week or two. She would sleep on the sofa-bed in the study, so Martin moved his computer setup to the living room. That night, with the memory of his father's words about children ringing in his ears, he played the piano for two solid hours before turning in.

-    -   -

Martin delivered JJ to school on Friday morning and drove to the hospital to check in with Jenny and the baby, who now needed a name. They agreed on Ellen, the name of Jenny's paternal grandmother and suitably Hellenic for Martin's need to honor his father's passion for the Greek legends.

Martin then went to CTI. He told his research group and, by email, his teaching staff and Kat, that he was going on a new schedule starting next week: full day on Wednesday, but otherwise, half days from mid-morning to mid-afternoon. He also emailed Bill Burke that he would be taking advantage of the CTI paternity leave, meaning that he would not be teaching in the spring. The Semiconductor Tools Corporation, the equipment manufacturer for which he did regular consulting, was alerted that while he would be reachable by email and phone, there would be no two-day trips to Silicon Valley until January at the earliest.

—   -   -

Since Jenny might have trouble with stairs until she healed from the Caesarean, Martin and JJ went shopping on Saturday for a folding daybed and a second changing table, both to be set up downstairs. The two of them visited Jenny and the baby that afternoon. The obligatory photo of a swaddled Ellen in the lap of a puzzled but smiling JJ was recorded for the birth announcement. For dinner, he took JJ for pizza and ice cream, wondering whether his son had any idea of what had just happened and what it would do to their domestic life. After getting JJ to bed, he played the piano before turning in for what would be the last decent night of sleep he was to enjoy for many months.

On Sunday morning, he left JJ with Colleen and went to Mt. Auburn Hospital to pick up their little miracle. While unloading the car, Martin documented the big event with his iPhone. He would prove to be a relentless documenter, from big yawns to the changing of poopy diapers, but for now, just a few shots of Ellen's arrival would do. He removed the infant car seat with its priceless cargo just as JJ and Colleen came over from next door. He handed the car seat to Colleen and turned to help Jenny wince out of the front seat. JJ asked, "Can I hold her again, Daddy? Can I hold her?"

"You can hold her when we get inside," said Martin. "It's better if you're sitting down."

With Colleen's help, Martin shepherded everyone inside and got Jenny installed on the living room sofa just as Ellen started to fuss. Colleen gave her to Jenny, who opened her blouse and began nursing. JJ was wide-eyed. "What's Mommy doing to the baby?"

Jenny laughed. "Babies need to eat, silly boy, and when they are very young, they get milk from their mother's breasts. You've seen pictures of kittens nursing, and puppies nursing, and even baby cows nursing. Well, this is baby Ellen nursing. This is how she eats."

"Did I do that?" asked JJ with wonder.

Jenny laughed, "You sure did. Sometimes you sucked so hard I thought you would swallow me."

"I couldn't swallow you. You're too big."

Everyone laughed, including JJ. The family was home. Martin thanked Colleen for her help, expecting her to leave, but she said she could stay around until Jenny's mother arrived. It had been a long time since she had to deal with an infant, and she enjoyed the hustle and bustle.

After Ellen had drunk her fill, Martin picked her up and tried to encourage a burp by softly rubbing her back. He got the burp along with some of Jenny's milk, safely caught on a towel on his shoulder. Then he changed her diaper, for real this time, not just on the doll he had used for practice. He could barely believe that this little creature, so recently out in the air, was already capable of processing nature's bounty and re-emitting the parts she couldn't use. He cleaned her up using the irritant-free baby wipes, being careful to stroke in the correct direction, positioned and then hitched on a clean diaper, and leaned down to kiss her little belly. This felt like fun.

Grace called to say she expected to be there by three in the afternoon. "Who wants lunch?" asked Martin, "We've got salami and turkey and lettuce and tomato, just name your choice." He gave Ellen to Jenny as he went to the kitchen to get the food, but before opening the refrigerator, he checked his email. Nothing new from Kat.

He and Colleen made up a plate for everyone, even JJ's choice of PB and J. He brought Jenny's sandwich into the living room just as she was drifting off to sleep. He stood, staring, admiring, astonished in hindsight at her determination and courage to go through a pregnancy, his pulse banging in his ears like a bass drum.

Colleen left shortly after Grace arrived. Having visited many times before, she was familiar with the house. She picked up Ellen and cooed a bit, but then took her overnight bag upstairs to the study and returned to usher JJ into the kitchen for milk and cookies, leaving Martin and Jenny some quiet in which to digest the wonder of their new arrival. Grace was a welcome guest, especially to Martin. She not only enjoyed

her own moments with her second grandchild, she also liked to help
— with cooking, dishes, laundry, shopping, bathing and diapering.

* **28** *

Martin couldn't sleep when Jenny was nursing. It wasn't just the twice-a-night disturbance and the fact that Jenny was too sore to bounce out of bed to collect her. It was the miracle of watching this tiny creature sucking away on those very breasts he loved to caress and nibble, with Jenny looking like the Madonna. Martin begged for and got a little taste, but that was it. Jenny's milk was spoken for.

Sleep deficit notwithstanding, there was work to be done. The Associate cases were through the PC. All three were sent on to the Engineering School with a positive recommendation. So were the three Full promotion cases. Now it was tenure time. On Friday, Ellen's eighth day of life, Martin got his updated notebook. All of Kat's letters were in. Not counting Martin's, there were fourteen — four from inside and ten from around the world, with the inside letters first, in alphabetical order, followed by the outside letters, similarly arranged.

He took the notebook home to digest the contents between play episodes with JJ and the fascination of diapering, cuddling, and just plain staring at his newborn. Thank goodness Grace was there to cook and to bathe the baby. Martin was still a little clumsy at bathing a live wriggler instead of a doll.

There were no surprises with the inside letter writers but Martin was shocked to find that Wolfgang Schultz was one of the outside writers, and also his own PhD advisor from Stanford, Dimitri Chrysostomides, someone he had quietly hoped would not be writing because of his stated skepticism about Kat's quantum-interference idea. Maybe Morris knew that, maybe not. At any rate, there was now a Chrysostomides letter in the packet and a letter from Wei-Li Hung from National Taiwan University, a poor choice in Martin's view because he was at or beyond retirement age and was probably not keeping up with things. The others were from Kat's list.

As he had come to understand from his boot-camp training with the Associate and Full Professor cases, the key to reading these letters is to look between the lines for hints of either criticism or genuine enthusiasm. He highlighted key sections as he read.

Epstein wrote, "I am always delighted to see new ways of using quantum effects in manufacturing. Prof. Rodriguez has taken bold new steps in this direction. It would be a loss for CTI not to award tenure."

Fitzgerald's summary read, "Her basic idea is really very clever. Prof. Rodriguez has already demonstrated successful execution of the required implant, a tour-de-force of experimental technique, but we do not yet have confirmation of its effects on transport. And I would have liked to have seen more of this work out in the peer-reviewed literature, but I am aware of how difficult a path she has selected, which means things may take time. I support the award of tenure."

Ulster's letter was a bit lame. "Prof. Rodriguez taught sections of Electricity and Magnetism with me and did a credible job. Her student reviews were good and her contributions to the staff discussions on pedagogy were stimulating. And while I do not understand all the details, I find the prospect of using quantum effects in ion implantation very intriguing. Prof. Rodriguez meets the standards of tenure, and I support her promotion."

Visconti had a different approach. "Prof. Rodriguez, as one of the few Hispanic professors in any technical field at CTI and the only Hispanic woman doing real engineering, has injected fresh air and new points of view into our consideration of women's issues at CTI. She will be a fighter for women, for Hispanics, for proper treatment of everyone. I consider it critical to the integrity and future of CTI that she be awarded tenure. To fail to promote her will send such a negative message, it will push back our progress in broadening the diversity of our faculty by decades."

Martin sagged visibly after reading the Visconti letter. If it was one thing Kat did not need, it was dragging the Hispanic-woman card into the promotion case. Gabrielle was, in effect, daring CTI not to award tenure, which was the wrong thing to do, especially given the lukewarm zingers from the other inside letter-writers.

He turned to the outside letters, starting with Andersen's letter, then flipping back and forth at random. Things got both better and worse. Andersen, not surprisingly, was totally supportive — imagination, capability, intellectual depth, future promise, go for tenure with no reservations. The international writers who had met Kat at ESM were generally supportive, even if some of them were guarded.

Fujita wrote, "Very clever work, perhaps of great importance. I strongly support tenure."

Urquhart noted, "She captivated the ESM workshop with her presentation on quantum-interference effects and stimulated many others to look into this. I wish there were results from the transport effects, but the direction she is going on looks very interesting."

Burgomeister's letter said. "Control of atomic beams to precise enough conditions to get quantum interference effects is very difficult. I am impressed. Based on the work to date, she probably merits promotion." Martin gulped when he saw the 'probably.' Not a helpful word.

Of the domestic writers beyond Andersen, Phelps was the best informed since he had both hosted her seminars in June and seen her presentation in Istanbul. He ranked her among the top five or six in her peer group, tossing in the names of P. Y. Chang at Texas A&M, S. J. Chang at Minnesota, Nishigawa at Kyoto (protégé of Fujita), Benson at Berkeley (protégé of Paderewski), and Frederickson at Uppsala, among others. It was clear from the letter that Kat had captured his support with her Istanbul performance.

Blaha and Covington, who had also hosted Kat seminars in June, liked her vision but were cautious about the lack of transport effects. Blaha was more specific in his peer rankings, putting P. Y. Chang first, S. J. Chang second, Kleppner at Georgia Tech third, and Kat fourth.

Covington threw in the name of his own protégé, Amos Levin, as ranking ahead of or on a par with Kat, both of whom were ranked below P. Y. Chang. Their zingers were lukewarm.

The Hung letter was pretty useless, as Martin had expected. It was polite, clearly uninformed, and said that "Professor Rodriguez has a strong enough record to consider for tenure." It was the kind of zinger that Martin had learned would be read as negative.

It was the three remaining letters that were really troubling. Chrysostomides was openly skeptical about the importance of Kat's idea, while Paderewski was disappointed that she had been unable to prove there would be any transport benefit, citing Benson and Nishigawa as having done more exciting work. And Wolfgang Schultz dropped a bomb:

> "In my opinion, the widespread enthusiasm for the direction Professor Rodriguez is taking in her work seems misplaced. While her former student, Dr. Carillo, has proven to be well-trained and very inventive in his work with us at COD, I cannot imagine that industry would ever adopt Professor Rodriguez's methods, which require extreme cryogenic control of deposition chambers. So even though the insight into transport would be interesting from a physics point of view, provided that it turns out to be real, of course, the impact on high-speed transistor manufacture is probably going to be zero. In terms of peers, I would rate Professor Rodriguez toward the low end of this list: Chang at Texas A&M, Nishigawa from Kyoto, Phillips at Eindhoven, Chang at Minnesota, and Benson at Berkeley. I would be cautious about the award of tenure."

Martin kicked himself. In his careful compilation of letter writers with Kat, he had neglected to suggest any industry leaders. He now realized, thinking back, that every case he had seen discussed in the PC had at least one industrial reference. Several had two or three. Morris, quite correctly, in the absence of a suggested name from industry, had to choose someone and he chose Schultz. There were better choices at IBM and Intel, but it was Martin's fault, a rookie mistake, that he hadn't fed Morris those names.

- - -

Martin soon learned that he was not going to be able to sleep even when Jenny was done nursing. The first episode of endless crying hit on Saturday, the sixteenth night of Ellen's young life. An hour after her eleven PM feeding, she started screaming. Jenny poked Martin, who dragged himself out of bed, looked at the clock in disbelief, picked her up and patted her back, with no effect. Jenny, who by this time was awake, tried nursing her, but Ellen wouldn't take the nipple, arching her back, clenching her little fists, and wailing.

"Is she sick?" asked a nervous Martin.

"Might just be a tummy-ache," said Jenny. "JJ had lots of them when he was little. Try rocking her a bit and see if that helps. I need to try to sleep some more."

Martin took the little bundle down to the living room, where a Shaker-style rocker had been added to the furnishings. He laid her on his knees and rocked, and rocked, and rocked. Ellen kept crying. He rubbed her tummy, and rubbed, and rubbed some more. Ellen kept crying. After an hour, he got up and carried her back upstairs and woke Jenny. "Do we need to call the doctor?"

Jenny groaned out a big yawn, "Not yet. Take her temperature. If she has a fever, we can call. If not, let's ride it out. She'll wear herself out and go back to sleep."

Martin pried off the singlet and diaper and used a suitably lubricated thermometer to take her rectal temperature, although with Ellen screaming, it wasn't as easy as with the doll they used for Martin to learn on. The temperature was normal, but the screaming continued.

"Maybe it's just colic," said Jenny. "JJ had colic."

"Like this?" asked Martin.

"Just like this," yawned Jenny.

Martin took the bawling infant back downstairs and rocked and rocked and rocked. At three AM, she finally fell asleep, but woke again at five, hungry for the nipple. The same thing happened on Sunday night. Martin understood for the first time how a bleary-eyed parent might shake a bawling baby to death. He was determined to see it through, but this was hard. At seven, after only a few hours of useful sleep, Martin got up to get JJ ready for school, having forgotten that today was Veteran's Day. A good day to skip CTI and just sack out.

-    -   -

That afternoon, Susan came running into Kat's office without even knocking. "It works! It works! Finally. Mobility of the implanted sample is fifteen percent higher than the uniformly doped one, and this is after including the correction for average doping level. It works. You're a genius! I'm so fucking pumped!"

"Whoa. Whoa. Slow down, Susan. This sounds good, really good. Lead me through it, one step at a time."

The two women sat at Kat's conference table and went through the details. This was their third set of samples after finding the faulty gauge, but the first set with decent results from electrical measurements. Susan had been careful, checking calibrations and standards along the way. The work looked correct and the result was exhilarating. As each confirming step appeared, Kat's pulse went up five beats. By the time Susan had finished, it was going through the roof, but she knew what needed to be done. "This is great. Better than great, it's fantastic. Now we have to do it again. From the beginning. Make four new samples, use two for confirmation of the implant pattern and two for a repeat of the measurements. We need to prove this wasn't a fluke."

Their conference ended with a celebratory hug, and Susan went off to start the replication. Kat sent Martin an email.

Good news. First transport measurements show fifteen
percent improvement in mobility. Susan is starting a
new run with more samples.

Martin's reply arrived that evening:

Couldn't have come at a better time. I need details.
Tomorrow at 9?

Martin met with Kat at nine on Tuesday after dropping JJ at school, and, operating once again on only four hours of sleep, struggled to give a coherent lecture and to manage his group meeting. Tuesday night was just like the others with three hours of crying and no chance for sleep. Jenny was still too exhausted to sit up for hours rocking Ellen, and they needed Grace to sleep at night so she could be useful during the day. By Wednesday afternoon, having lost particularly badly to Peter Dempsey at squash, Martin's head was spinning. He had barely enough time before the PC meeting to grab a snack at the Lobby Coffee Bar. Fizzy water and a cookie. His copy of Kat's new results was tucked into the notebook in his backpack. Astonishing. It looked like she was right. It works.

He deposited his backpack and the cookie on a lobby table and took a seat. As he opened the water bottle, it bubbled up, splashed the backpack and formed a spreading puddle on the table. Martin jumped up and ran to grab some napkins at the coffee bar. By the time he ran back, the backpack was gone.

He ran into the main lobby area, but saw no one carrying it. He yelled, "Who took my backpack?" A few people in the lobby area looked around, but no one responded. With his gorge rising, he did the only thing he could think of. He called the Campus Police, emphasizing that the backpack contained highly confidential material along with his iPad. He then called Rebecca and asked her to tell Morris. Shaking with rage and embarrassment, he waited.

Officer McGraw arrived ten minutes later and took Martin's report. He said that whoever took it was probably looking for a laptop or money and that he would probably toss the backpack in the trash. Yes, the backpack had Martin's name on it, with a phone number. Yes, the entire force had already been notified. The notebook and papers would probably be just fine. When there is news, Martin would be called.

He dragged himself away from the lobby, heading for EECS Headquarters, stopping in a men's room where he vomited violently. When he entered the conference room, he was greeted with a stony silence. Martin went to his seat, and as he sat down, he said, "I am so mortified. I can't believe…"

"How did it happen?" asked Morris.

"It was so trivial. I was at a table at the Lobby Coffee Bar, opening a bottle of soda, and it bubbled up and made a spill. I got up to get some napkins and, boom, my backpack was gone. Somebody must have been watching for an opportunity. Couldn't have been for more than fifteen seconds."

"Let's hope it's found with the notebook in it," said Morris. "I can't even think about the consequences if… if the letters. Ugh. It's too awful even to…"

No one else said anything.

Finally Morris spoke. "We had planned to discuss Rodriguez today, but I don't think Martin is in shape for that. Let's see what we can do with Van Rijks. Roger, you're the case manager. The floor is yours."

With pretended normalcy, the PC got to work, reviewing Van Rijks' program on creating micro-brains — neurons grown onto microfabricated cell-culture substrates that included junction regions where synapses could form and microelectrodes for stimulating various axons. They then parsed the fine points of each letter.

That evening, after dragging himself home, Martin was starting to tell Jenny about his disaster when the phone rang. It was Campus Police. The backpack had been turned in by a student who found it on the Student Center steps. No, there was no iPad in it. No, there was no notebook. Just what looked an umbrella, a wool cap and some kind of rubberized canvas thing. Yeah, could be a rain cover. Martin said he would pick it up in the morning. He put his head down on the kitchen table and wept.

The nightmares started that night. A wraith straight out of that Edvard Munch painting, with a gaunt face and long gnarly fingers, followed Martin wherever he went, grasping for the bundle Martin was carrying, a bundle that looked like a swaddled baby. As he walked, the ground gradually turned to soft sand, then mud, miring his feet at every step as he dodged the wraith's flailing arms. He tried to run, but he was too tired. He faltered, and put down his bundle for a moment to rest. The wraith seized it ran off. Martin woke in a sweat.

* **29** *

Rebecca's phone rang at 9:01 AM. A voice said, "You need to look at *The Flame Thrower*. The read-all-about-it post under Teaching v Research Revisited." Then silence.

Rebecca went to the blog's webpage and looked for the topic. There was a post with the headline 'Read All About It.' It contained a link, which she clicked. It took her to *Dirty Linen*, a notorious website hosted in Romania where whistle-blowers are invited to upload whatever they want. The specific page, below a headline that read 'College Tenure Revealed,' contained a series of more than forty links, each bringing up a scanned copy of one of the tenure letters from Martin's notebook.

With Morris away in California, Rebecca called the Provost's Office, explained the problem, and got connected to Marsha Collins. Marsha said she would get the post taken down, at least the one at *TFT*, but they both knew that it was already too late. No one, not even the U.S. government, had ever succeeded in getting *Dirty Linen* to take down a post, even major Department of Defense security breaches. Rebecca put in a call to Morris and woke him up in his hotel room. Morris's comment was: "Now we are in deep trouble. I'll get home ASAP. Send an email to everyone on the PC and tell them to make no comments to anyone about any of this. Refer all inquiries to me."

Of course, universities being nearly discipline-free zones, Dan Cranagh and Roger Ericsson had been chatting about Martin's loss of the notebook in the corridor after the PC meeting. They were overheard, and within a few days, at least a third of the EECS faculty would know it was Martin's notebook that had done the damage.

-   -   -

Marsha Collins sent emails and texts to Ethel McKinsey and Ralph Aiken telling them that the post contained stolen confidential materials and it needed to come down immediately. She also asked for the name of the student who had posted them.

Ethel's texted reply arrived within minutes.

```
Post is taken down. Posting logon is daniel.ellsberg.
We don't have access to student names. Must get
from CTI-IT.
```

Marsha contacted the User Accounts section of CTI-IT. The name on the account was indeed Daniel Ellsberg, but there was no one at CTI by that name — no student, faculty, employee, affiliate or anyone else, even alumni. The account listed a home address that turned out to be fake and a home phone that was a disconnected line. The account was bogus. Another hacker. Or more likely, the same one.

She called her contact at Google to get the *Dirty Linen* link taken down, or at least taken out of the search space, but Google could only do so much. It was one thing to remove a cached page with things like homework answers, a request they regularly cooperated with, but the contact said they had no control over the Romanian website and could not force them to remove the materials from the internet. However, they were willing to make some tweaks in its search criteria to lower the visibility of the link to the site. That was all they could do.

While she was on the phone trying to reach David Rittenhouse, CTI's General Counsel, things started getting crazy. Within the space of only a few minutes, Marsha had four urgent messages from the CTI News Office. Someone had to field calls from the *Boston Globe*, the *New York Times,* CNN and Fox News. Marsha's answer to all of them was that she had not yet read the letters and could not comment on their veracity. But she knew. It's one thing for videos of cats playing pianos to go viral. It was quite another thing when tenure letters did.

From a quick scan of *TFT*, Marsha learned that the link to *Dirty Linen* was now freely available on more than a dozen Facebook pages, and the Twitter messages were spreading it like oil on water. Student reaction was mixed.

```
At last we can see what a tenure case is. Almost all
research. just like I suspected.
truth46

These are private letters. it's wrong to have them on
the internet. Somebody should take them down.
muffin3

You can't unscramble an egg. Ask Humpty-Dumpty. The
whole bleeping world has them now.
binkie29

I read them all, and I counted only eighteen para-
graphs on teaching, mostly of the BS variety, in
fifty-eight pages of letters. Teaching matters, prof
burke? SUUUUURRRREEE it does.
rogerrabbit

This just confirms what I said last spring. It's
only research.
trojanhorse

lawsuit city. wouldn't want to be prof wong just now.
aretwo
```

-   -   -

That afternoon, Alberto Ricci, short, wiry, with almost an afro of tightly curled graying hair, was pacing the floor of his office. Marsha Collins and David Rittenhouse were seated at the small conference table near the window, with its view of the courtyard, the river, and the towers of Boston beyond.

"We need a damage-control plan, David. A map. It's a shit storm. We've got possible lawsuits from letter writers, lawsuits from tenure candidates, lawsuits from the tenure candidates against any negative letter-writers, and, in the midst of it all, we have to decide whether we can go forward with these cases. If we do, we're walking naked in the park, and if we don't, we're screwing the tenure candidates for something that wasn't their fault."

David, who had taken notes, responded. "Okay. First, I realize that the letter-writers are upset, but I don't think there's much risk of suits from them. When they write this kind of letter, they do so with our explicit promise in our solicitation request to take all reasonable precautions to keep their reply confidential, but we never use language that guarantees confidentiality. I expect that every letter writer will raise a stink. I would, in their shoes, but their lawyers would tell them that they would lose if they try to sue for damages especially given that disclosure was the result of criminal activity and not negligence on the part of CTI.

"As for the tenure candidates suing us, there's little risk of that unless we deny tenure. If we do deny someone, he could probably make it very unpleasant for us due to alleged damage to his reputation, and it wouldn't surprise me if we would have to buy him off. Or her, buy her off. I need to get Larry's input on this though. He has much more experience in these kinds of things. I mean, he managed to get Gillespie to settle, and that was a big relief."

"Have you spoken with Larry?" asked Ricci.

"Left a message. He's in court on the west coast for the next three days. He offered to send a junior associate over, but I said it was best to wait for the senior guy. Okay to wait?"

"I guess we can wait on him. But what about the tenure process. Can we go ahead?"

"There's one more thing you mentioned first, the possibility of suits against negative letter writers. I think they're protected. When someone responds to a request like with a tenure letter, they have an implied privilege, a legal protection against libel or damages. That doesn't mean an angry tenure candidate can't sue, but they surely can't win anything. I suggest that right away, today, we send each of the letter writers an apology over your signature. I can draft it. We may want to follow that up with something Larry could draft that explains the implied privilege. We'll see what he says. He might prefer to say nothing until someone threatens a suit."

"Yes, let's do the apology. Lord knows, we need to apologize. But what about the tenure process itself. Can it proceed?"

"That's the one where we need some time to think. I would need to do a careful review with outside counsel of the pros and cons of going ahead and what other options may be possible. It seems to me that we have some exposure if we don't go ahead, exposure based on the difficulty of getting new letters given this breach of confidentiality. I'm likely to come out for going ahead, but I'm not sure. We will sure as hell look awful if we go ahead, deny one or more cases, get sued for it, and lose."

Marsha asked, "Has anyone here besides me actually read the letters?"

Alberto looked to David, and both shook their heads.

"My concern is with the Rodriguez case, that it might run into problems. The letters are kind of mixed, and I'm just not sure. We might have a Gillespie case all over again. It's different because she has clearly made some important progress on research, and she's Hispanic, from Mexico. But apparently not everyone agrees about the importance or the level of success."

"Well," said Alberto, "we sure as hell don't need another Gillespie case. If there was ever a time when we needed to do things right, this is it. It involves the face of CTI to the whole goddam world. Prendergast needs to be consulted also. David, get Larry Barr on this as soon as you can. In the meantime, Marsha, you should tell Wong that they can discuss the cases internally, but they shouldn't vote. Try to see which way they're leaning, on Rodriguez especially. And get those IT Security people in here again, goddamit. We need a secure system here."

Marsha contacted Morris, who echoed her concern. The Rodriguez case was likely to be on the margin but the other two looked okay. Morris asked, "Since the letters are now exposed, do we have to treat things differently? I mean with a little more latitude?"

"I'll have to discuss this with Alberto," said Marsha. "I suspect what he will say is, deal with the case on its merits and let the chips fall. But I'll confirm that before your group needs to vote."

Marsha again consulted the IT security manager, who recommended setting up a super-secure FTP site where future promotion letters could be deposited electronically. On-line read-only permissions would be granted to those needing access to the letters. No printed copies, no emailed copies, no more notebooks. Like direct deposit of a paycheck. The security manager suggested that their consultant, Julian Kesselbaum, had set up systems like this for a number of banks and he could probably do this as well.

- - -

Morris arrived in Boston that night. His email inbox was jangling with unhappiness.

```
Dear Professor Wong:

I was most distressed to receive an email this
afternoon from a bogus address, presumably a proxy
of some kind, which contained a scanned copy of the
letter I sent with regard to the tenure of Professor
Rodriguez. I'm sure you are aware that this breach of
confidentiality thrusts a dagger into the heart of the
kind of honest opinion sharing that is so essential
to the promotion and tenure process.

Until there is a complete explanation of how this
happened and convincing assurances that this will not
happen again, I must decline any further requests to
comment on promotions at CTI.

Regrettably,
Carl Urquhart
```

Wolfgang Schultz was less polite.

```
Hey, Prof. Wong.

What kind of a sloppy shop do you people run?
```

My letter on Rodriguez is posted on the fucking
internet. How did this happen? You better warm up
your lawyers.

Wolfgang Schultz
Director of Advanced Semiconductor Research
COD

But amid the heaps of scorn and upset, there was one that
was different:

Dear Professor Wong:

As a Department Chairman, I sympathize with the
dilemma you now face with the disclosure, malicious I
assume, of a set of tenure letters. I wish I could do
something to help, but the cat is totally out of the
bag at this point.

A member of my Promotional Advisory Committee, who
had looked at the names of the letter writers on the
Dirty Linen website, decided to read the one from
Wolfgang Schultz of COD, who has written with regard
to Katrina Rodriguez. The reason is that Dr. Schultz
also wrote on one of our pending cases. There is an
odd discrepancy between the peer group rankings in
the two letters.

I would like to discuss this by telephone with you at
your earliest convenience.

And, yes, I am related to Moshe. He is my cousin.

Isaac Felsenthal
Professor and Chair,
Materials Science and Engineering
Texas A&M

-   -   -

In the history of CTI, there had never been a time in which candidates
for tenure were able to read their own tenure letters. Here was Kat,

patiently working through the entire set, not just her own, but all three cases. She had been repeatedly told that a tenure-track position was not internally competitive. Every tenure-track position would be evaluated on its merits. There was no quota or restriction. All three candidates could get tenure. But Kat didn't believe it. As she read the cases, it was clear that she would rank third out of three based on the letters. Her critics were right, at least in part. She had not demonstrated the transport benefit in time for the letter writers to see it. But she had it now, dammit.

Just as she was finishing, Martin arrived at her office, yawning with fatigue. He was crestfallen and embarrassed over the letters, fumbling an apology as best he could. He said he could get her new experimental results into consideration for the tenure case, but he absolutely had to have proof that it was correct. Kat said that Susan was pushing ahead with the new samples. It would take a few days, but not more than that.

Kat asked Martin what the PC was going to do now that the letters had become public, and Martin didn't know. He said Morris didn't know either. Decisions were being made at the level of the President and Provost. But the new results would be critical, no matter what.

Kat tried to swallow her anger over the negatives in her letters and focus on fighting back with data.

* **30** *

Dr. Alvarez, the pediatrician, did as thorough a check of baby Ellen as her young age would permit. He proffered that her nightly crying spells looked like colic and that within three months or so, it would be over. In the meantime, he said, the only thing to do was for Jenny to try dropping dairy from her own diet, or better yet, keep a food diary and see if there was any relation between diet and Ellen's episodes. Failing that, keep Ellen as comfortable as possible during an episode and be patient. It often took a few months for an infant's digestive systems to get the kinks worked out, but colic, if that's what it was, usually went away on its own.

But it wasn't just Ellen's crying jags that disturbed Martin's sleep; it was that recurring nightmare, clearly a replay of the incident in the Lobby Coffee Bar. But in the nightmare, the bundle was a baby, not the notebook containing Kat's tenure case. Was the tenure case his baby? Was that what Istanbul was all about? Carrying his baby to safety? And who or what was the wraith? Was it Schultz, with his toxic letter? And what was the sand? The mud? Was that Ellen? The real baby? Causing his feet to drag? Could he have prevented the theft? Of course. But did he have reason to suspect a wraith was watching? Of course not. He tossed and turned, trying to reconstruct the event, seeing if there were any familiar faces, maybe someone who was angry at him, but he kept coming up empty. He could understand if a random thief stole the backpack for the iPad, but not for the notebook. And why publish the letters? This wasn't just a prank. This was sabotage. It was malicious. It was the work of a wraith.

- - -

Grace and Harvey were off to Italy on a tour that they had purchased almost a year ago, adding to Martin's overload. He now did the shopping, the laundry and the cooking, as well as JJ's school chauffeuring, except for Wednesdays, when Colleen filled in. Now that Jenny could do stairs, they started bickering over who should rock Ellen when she had one of those nighttime episodes, especially since Martin was spending his evenings keeping JJ entertained. Jenny would shower every night before going to bed, but it wasn't because she wanted her boobs nibbled. Lingering discharge problems with her post-partum feminine hygiene demanded two showers a day, something Dr. Rosen said would clear up within two or three more weeks. Sex was, and would remain, off the table for the foreseeable future.

The cumulative fatigue took its toll. Martin stopped doing morning treadmill and weights, and most nights, he skipped the piano. His lectures lost some of their crispness and bright enthusiasm, and his teaching staff noticed. His acuity in judging research results and advising next steps seemed fuzzy and his grad students noticed, muttering among themselves, wondering what was wrong. His promptness in dealing with his editorial responsibilities sagged. He looked gaunt. Felice noticed. Gina noticed. Peter noticed. While Martin would, with a laugh, pass it off as the fatigue produced by the new baby, he knew that his failure to protect the letters was eating at him like a cancer. Flying in the face of his rational self, something inside him was beginning to blame baby Ellen for his inattention to the notebook. Every time he would plant a sloppy kiss on her belly after changing her, he wondered what kind of hell she had gotten him into.

- - -

"In his letter on Pin-Yen Chang," said Isaac Felsenthal, speaking on the telephone with Morris, "he ranked the peers like this: Nishigawa, Phillips, S. J. Chang at Minnesota, and your Rodriguez, all ahead of Pin-Yen. But in his letter on Rodriguez, the one he sent to you, he moves Pin-Yen to first position ahead of the others. This doesn't look like an innocent mistake. This looks like intentional mischief. It's as if he doesn't want us to give tenure to Pin-Yen, even though he thinks highly of him."

"Well, as you saw," said Morris, "his letter on Rodriguez was pretty negative. Was the letter on Pin-Yen also negative?"

"Surprisingly negative, especially in light of ranking him first in your letter. Do you have any idea what's going on?

"I'll have to ask Martin Quint. He knows Schultz. I'll get back to you."

The call ended, and Morris summoned Martin to a meeting for the next day.

-     -   -

"One possibility is that he's pissed off at me," said Martin, sitting with Morris and Bill Burke in Morris's office. Martin stifled a big yawn. "Sorry for that. My new baby, she's up a lot at night. Anyway, he and I had an unpleasant run-in over a publication. It involved the Chang from Minnesota. But why he would take that out on Kat is beyond me, especially since he's had a good result with hiring her student, Carillo, so I don't think that's it."

Morris agreed.

"The only other thing I can think of is a pretty ugly concept. Maybe Wolfgang wants to hire Pin-Yen Chang, so he's sabotaging his tenure case." Morris and Bill Burke sat silent as Martin continued. "I can't believe that he would actually do this, but it's the only other thing I can think of. He knows who's who out there. When he talked to me about it that paper, he asked whether it was the Chang from A&M, so I'm sure he knows about both Changs, Pin-Yen and S. J. He wouldn't make those jumbled lists by mistake. I've heard stories about his aggressive recruiting in the past, in fact, from Andris Andersen at UCLA, if I remember right. But regardless, doesn't the A&M info give us a way to discredit the Schultz letter? That would really help Kat's case."

"I don't think we can use the A&M letter. They can use ours, of course, because it's public now. But theirs? I don't think we can cite it. At least not directly, but maybe we can build some kind of fence around Schultz's letter. We'll have to think about how to do it and maybe consult with what's his name, the General Counsel. Ritter, or something."

"Also, by the way," said Martin. "Kat has new results on transport. I was going to present them at the meeting... Well, you know, the meeting where it happened. Her stuff is very encouraging. She's repeating them now with new samples. If it comes through, I think her case will suddenly look a lot stronger."

"If we can do the case at all. I'm still waiting for a judgment from on high. Apparently even Prendergast is involved on this one. Ugly, Martin. Really ugly."

"I know. I feel like it's my fault."

"Unfortunately, it sort of is your fault. I don't like to say it, but..."

-    -   -

Marsha Collins didn't get to be Associate Provost without having certain skills. With the patience of Job and the persistence of Earl Warren, she managed, after a series of one-on-one meetings with each of her Tenure Review Panel members, to craft a compromise on language that would allow them to issue a report without dissent. The key paragraph was published in *The Widgit*:

EXCERPT FROM PROVOST'S REPORT
ON TEACHING v RESEARCH

The standards for the award of tenure must take into account CTI's multi-faceted mission. We need research excellence, excellence in student-mentoring and excellence in classroom and laboratory instruction. Not every member of our permanent faculty need be a world leader in all three, but we do generally require demonstrated strengths in more than one. Excellence in research is judged, to a great extent, by letters solicited from world leaders in the candidate's research field. These letters also document the extent to which a candidate is growing into a leadership position within that field, through service as conference organizers, journal editors and highly valued consultants. Excellence in student mentoring is judged, in part, by outside comments on the post-graduation careers of a candidate's students and, in part, by internal testimony from CTI colleagues. Excellence in classroom and laboratory instruction is documented by each department in their cover letter to the tenure case, based on evidence gathered from student evaluations and from teaching colleagues. It must be stressed that each tenure decision is an individual one, taking fully into account how, based on all the evidence, the candidate's projected future contributions will serve CTI's complex mission.

Once again, Emmanuel Encarnacion commented.

PROVOST'S REPORT DISAPPOINTING
by Emmanuel Encarnacion

The denial of tenure to Professor Sharon Gillespie last spring led to a firestorm of student comment on *The Flame Thrower*. The unauthorized disclosure of the confidential internal review of past tenure cases as well as the more recent publication of letters of recommendation from three EECS tenure cases threw more gasoline onto that blaze. The Tenure Review Panel headed by Associate Provost Marsha Collins has now issued a report (see highlight box) that is, to some extent, responsive to the questions raised on these pages, but it is still silent on the apparent down-weighting of teaching in the final award of tenure at the Institute level. While we agree that research mentoring is an important component of a CTI education, it is not a replacement for, and should not be ranked ahead of, inspiring classroom instruction.

-    -   -

"No, goddamit, no!" Martin sat up in bed, his shout waking Jenny.

"No, what? What's wrong?" she asked.

Martin, dazed, looked at his wife as if she were a stranger, and fought back tears. "I'm so sorry. It's not your fault. He was reaching for the bundle…"

"What are you talking about? Who? Reaching for what?"

"It's not your fault. She didn't do anything."

"Who?"

"Ellen."

"Ellen? What on earth could be her fault?"

"She won't stop crying."

"Oh my God, Martin. I know. She has colic. What is all this?"

Martin finally woke up. He shook his head and wiped away the remains of a lonely tear. "It's so hard when she cries and won't stop. And this dream makes me crazy. I end up blaming her… and you."

"Blaming me for her crying? This isn't making any sense. What dream?"

"Sorry. I'll try to explain." He described the nightmare, the wraith, the bundle, the sand, the mud, and the theft. He added that he understood the bundle was the tenure case, or at least the notebook, but he couldn't understand the sand and the mud. All he could come up with was the fatigue, and Ellen was the cause.

"Fatigue? You don't think I get tired too?" said Jenny. "Try giving birth someday. And have your belly cut open and your breasts on call 24 hours per day."

"Fair enough. But I try. I cook and shop and do the laundry and God knows what else, and take care of JJ to boot, something you have pretty much abandoned. My work is going to hell and everybody jokes about it."

"That's nonsense. I pay attention to JJ all the time."

This made Martin snicker. "I don't think you have any idea how JJ complains that Mommy won't play with him."

This made Jenny cry. "I hate this. We shouldn't be fighting. It's true, I don't spend the same time with JJ as before. But I don't shut him out either."

"Well, he feels shut out."

"So what were you imagining when we were making a baby? That it would be like one of those idyllic TV shows? Babies demand attention. You wanted this baby, at least you said you did, in spite of how nervous you were."

"Nervous? As I remember it, I proposed right after you said you wanted another child."

"Yes, but when I told you I missed my period, I could smell how nervous you were. It was creepy. That's what made me so frightened when I was pregnant."

"Okay. Yes, I was nervous. Is that why you made such a fuss over Kat? Because I was nervous."

"Yes, and I told you so. She made me nervous, the whole time I was pregnant, partly because you were nervous and you have a past."

"Goddam it, Jenny! Have I done anything that justifies bringing up my past, as you call it? I've been totally honest about it. About Camille. Even about the little peck on the cheek Kat gave me in Istanbul. And as for being nervous, sure I've been nervous. I've never been a parent before, not counting with JJ, who's bigger. But being nervous doesn't mean I didn't want a child. I did. I do. She's a miracle. But I'm too goddamned tired to enjoy her right now. It's scary how angry I get when she cries like that. I'll never hurt her, but I get so angry..."

Jenny, still sniffling, snuggled up to Martin. "Of course you won't hurt her, and I'm sorry you had a bad dream, but this is what being a parent is all about. A crying baby. A poopy baby. A hungry baby. Wait 'til you see that first real smile, though. I promise you, you'll melt. I love you, goofus, and you love Ellen, so don't worry. We're in this together."

Martin felt comforted, but he lay awake a long time.

* 31 *

Within the week, Jenny recovered well enough to do the daytime baby care, the cooking and the laundry, but Martin still did the shopping and the dishes and as much JJ care as he had time for: dressing him in the morning, making his breakfast, packing his lunch, driving him to school, and each evening, managing the bath, reading and bedtime.

At one level, he relished his home duties. It was like a replay of his post-Katie domestic life, but now with purpose and, best of all, with a baby that, as the Bible might say, he begat. But between caring for Ellen's fitful sleep and his own bad dreams, he was getting so exhausted that his body was rebelling. His ulcerative colitis had flared up, badly.

After getting JJ to bed that night, he put a yellow card on Jenny's pillow.

"What's this for?" she asked, coming to bed after her shower.

"I know you will hate this, but for the next few days, I need you to take care of Ellen at night."

"Martin. I can barely get through a day. You know that. And you want me to do night, too?"

"Yes, until I'm done presenting Kat's tenure case, which I'm hoping will be next Wednesday. Just a few days, but I need to tend to my awful guts and get a solid night's sleep. I have to be sharp with that committee. I can't do it in the state I'm in now. Too foggy in the head."

"Still Kat is it? The latest intrusion?"

"This is not her, goddam it. This is me. Me. I need your help. It's not Kat. It's me. Can't you understand that? I need to sleep better."

"And I need a maid."

"Seriously, you want a maid?"

"No. I'm sorry. I don't. I meant, as a fantasy, I like the idea of having someone we could give Ellen to when she's fussy. It wears me out too, but I don't want a maid. Yuck."

"Could we ask Grace to come again, for a week or so?"

"Might be smart. I'll ask her if she's willing to do the night shift for a bit. I'm sorry for that crack about Kat. I guess I'm tired too. And thanks for thinking of the yellow card. It's better than fighting."

-   -   -

The apology letters had been sent and the Provost's consultations with outside counsel Lawrence Barr, senior partner at Barr, Galinsky, and Stevens, had been completed. Five of the letter writers had threatened legal action against CTI, but Larry Barr sent each of them a carefully constructed explanation of (a) the limits on the guarantee of secrecy provided by CTI and (b) the fact that what they wrote was covered by an implied privilege. He also said that CTI would assist them if they found themselves challenged by the tenure candidate on whose behalf they had written. So far, no actual suits had been filed. After three long meetings of the Institute Council with Messrs. Barr and Rittenhouse in attendance, the decision was made to proceed with the three EECS tenure cases. The alternative, to declare the cases flawed by publication of the letters, was simply unacceptable, mostly because it would be impossible to get new letters that were as objective as the set they already had in hand. The risks were understood. Denial of tenure to anyone risked a lawsuit.

Martin, refreshed from five nights of real sleep — thanks to Grace and Jenny and a gut-calming diet regimen — began his presentation of Kat's case to the PC. Now well-schooled in how these things are done, he reviewed Kat's educational background, and her thesis work with Andris at UCLA. He went on to explain her bold decision to attempt the implementation of atomic-beam quantum interference effects to enhance transistor performance. The idea was her own invention: if the impurity atoms could be deposited in just the right pattern, then in theory, one of the mechanisms that slows down electrons would be suppressed. Therefore, transistors made with this particular method would be faster than conventional transistors, meaning that computers could run faster.

He recounted the successes of grad students Frank Carillo and Leah Wiesenthal, which demonstrated the correct atomic pattern, and then passed around the room a brief memo that summarized Susan Zeltzer's most recent experimental result, showing a fifteen percent improvement in electron speed in one test devices. But it was clear that the committee was skeptical. Only one sample so far was a pretty tenuous result. "But," argued Martin, "there are more samples in process, with results coming out daily. The validation of her entire concept is right at hand. Of course the letter-writers haven't seen this. It's too new. But it's goddam important. She deserves the chance to make her case."

Morris interrupted. "Martin, I think we should go through the letters, keeping in mind that Kat may now have some transport results in hand." It took well over an hour, parsing each letter for its hidden, or not so hidden, meanings. Martin tried, like in the old Chinese fortune cookie game, to get the committee to re-read each letter, adding Kat's new results at the end, changing the negatives into positives. He thought it worked, but he wouldn't know until they voted after the holiday break.

The Schultz letter got special discussion. Martin, having cleared with Morris ahead of time what could be said, and Morris having also cleared it with the Dean, said that they must ignore the peer rankings in the Schultz letter based on confidential information provided by another school in which a Schultz letter on a tenure candidate had a completely different ranking of the same peers. This produced quite a stir.

Abel Blaine said, "You're kidding, right? He used different lists?"

"Yes he did," said Morris. "I have confirmed it with the Department Head at the other school. I guess this is the only benefit from the publication of the letters. The other department saw the discrepancy and contacted me."

Moshe Felsenthal said, "Maybe we throw out the letter altogether."

"I don't think we can throw it out," said Bill Burke, "but we should be able to build a fence around it in our cover letter."

Dieter Tannhauser sat up in his chair. "Personally, I like the fact that she is trying to exploit quantum effects. I don't care if Schultz thinks it can't be adapted to manufacture. What she's done is scientifically intriguing. It's too early to judge the engineering importance. We should just ignore the Schultz letter altogether."

The discussion continued all the way around the table, Martin watching each person for any hints of where they stood. Only Dan Cranagh and Alex Papadopolous abstained from comment. Martin had been watching Alex, in particular, for any sign of his interest or leaning, but Alex had donned a poker face. What surprised Martin was that Dan, normally quite animated in the discussion, had also demurred. Why? Was his mind already made up?

Morris turned the discussion to Kat's teaching record. Prakash Singh, recalling that her teaching case had been mediocre at the time of the promotion to Associate, seemed happy and quite surprised to report how strong it had become, especially the most recent postings on the TFT blog, all of which were hugely supportive. Mary Lewinsky, who had not only looked at the blog, but had viewed the entire video, said that it sounded as if Martin rather than Kat had led the class the students were raving about. Martin laughed. "Well," he said, "it is true that I spent a lot of time with her earlier, and I do tend to get preachy about teaching philosophy. Perhaps some of you have noticed this?" Everyone laughed. "I wish I had been at that class. She struck a blow for intelligent consideration of what education is all about. I recommend the video."

By the end of the meeting, Martin knew he had done as much as he could to paint Kat's record in shining terms. But he also knew she would rank third among three. The question was whether the new results would manage to inch her over the top and get her at least as far as the Engineering School. He had spent almost a year with her promotion as one of his top priorities, to the point where it felt like it was his promotion to win or lose.

- - -

After dinner that night, with JJ tucked into bed, Jenny was at her desk nursing Ellen. Martin came in and asked, "Something at today's meeting really bothered me. Can we talk about it?"

"Of course," as Jenny switched Ellen to the other breast.

"It involves Kat. Can you deal with it?"

"I'll try," said Jenny, smiling.

"I think I need to tell Morris about Alex Papadopolous and Kat. He's on the PC, and he didn't say squat during my presentation of her case. Usually, he's one of the more talkative ones. But only if you're absolutely sure. I don't want to be spreading rumors."

"Charlotte ought to know who her ex was dating, so I'm pretty sure it's true."

- - -

The next day, Morris ushered Martin into his office, directing him to a chair while he took the sofa. "What's up?" he asked.

Martin paused before answering, his head hung down. Finally, he looked up and said, "I think there may be a conflict-of-interest problem in Kat's case."

"Conflict? You mean you have a conflict?"

"Not me, no."

"Then what?"

Martin fidgeted. "The problem is that I'm not sure, but I have learned through a third party that Kat may have had an affair with Alex Papadopolous. It may not be true, but if it is, I wonder what his judgment might be over her tenure. I mean, I was watching him during the discussion of the Schultz letter, and he didn't say a word. He didn't even move a muscle. He's not usually silent like that. So it made me think."

"Who else might know about this rumor?"

"I have no idea. It came to me via Alex's ex-wife, who is friends with my wife, who passed it on to me. I can't imagine why Charlotte would say such a thing without any basis."

"Well," said Morris, "it could be serious or it could be nothing. May I discuss this with Bill and Ellen? Just between the three of us?"

"Sure," said Martin. "As long as it's clear that I'm not sure about the facts."

Later that afternoon, Morris, Bill Burke and Ellen Zefrim met and agreed to take no action until after the PC had voted. If Alex remained silent and his only action was to vote, even if he submitted a low vote, they agreed that this could be managed. One vote does not a tenure decision make. But Ellen said, "You know, I noticed during the discussion of Kat that Dan didn't say anything either, and that's not like him. So maybe this is all just rubbish. Not talking in PC doesn't have to mean anything."

* **32** *

As was his custom, Martin used the last few days before Christmas to clear the paper piles from his desk. With his grades turned in, his students scattered for the holidays, the Personnel Committee in recess until the mid-January vote, incoming emails reduced to a trickle and Kat off to Merida to spend two weeks with her bed-ridden mother, he could put away the detritus from the old and prepare for the onslaught of the new.

Thanks to baby Ellen, the new this time around would be simpler, with no teaching in the spring. But his research group would return after New Year's, the journal papers would still need editing, and the grant writing would once again be a high priority, especially in light of today's depressing email from the NSF. Thanks to congressional penny-pinching, each program manager at the NSF was experiencing a sequestration cut, and that translated to fewer opportunities to fund new grants. Today's email said that while the proposal that had been carved out of the failed DARPA grant was worthy of funding, there was no money.

It struck Martin as ironic that CTI's paternity-leave policy got him out of teaching, the one activity he thoroughly enjoyed, and kept the pressure on research and service, things that right now felt like burdens. Oh well, Helen and the kids were coming for Christmas, their first chance to meet Ellen. Time to turn off the computer, turn out the lights, and go home for a few days.

- - -

Helen, Carlo and Angela arrived in the late afternoon of Christmas Eve just as Martin was putting a duck into the upper oven. The plan was for Helen to sleep in the study and the two children to use sleeping bags on the floor of JJ's room, a prospect that did not thrill the five-year-old. Martin helped Helen unload the luggage while Jenny, who had just finished nursing and changing the baby, collected Carlo and Angela to meet their new cousin. Angela seemed fascinated with the little creature and stayed with Jenny, but it only took a half-minute before Carlo was asking where JJ's toys were and only a few minutes after that before JJ started yelling that Carlo wasn't playing fair.

Helen, coming down from stowing her bags, played umpire and negotiated a sharing of cars and blocks and Legos while Martin assembled the casserole of candied yams and put it, along with a sheet pan of oiled and salted winter vegetables, into the lower oven. He then unwrapped a wedge of brie, sliced a baguette, poured out a bowl of goldfish crackers for the kids, opened sparkling cider and a bottle of cabernet, and invited everyone into the living room for their traditional carol sing. No one in either family was religious, but they loved the Christmas songs, especially when led by Martin at the piano. Helen and Jenny shared a book of carols and sang with more enthusiasm than intonation, while little Carlo surprised everyone by knowing the words to almost every song. JJ did really well on 'Jingle Bells' and got at least the tune right on 'A Dusty Fidelis.' Angela munched on the goldfish, her eyes glued to Ellen, swaddled in a wooden cradle with Snow White carved in bas relief at one end. Jenny had herself been laid in this cradle some thirty years earlier.

Dinner was only mildly traumatic. Carlo wouldn't eat the duck or the vegetables, but Helen kept him calm with a combination of goldfish and the tiny marshmallows off the top of the yam casserole. Angela spilled her milk, and while Helen reached over with a napkin to catch the spill, her elbow caught Martin's wineglass. Martin laughed and said not to worry, praising Jenny's wisdom in getting water-resistant table pads for the Queen Anne. Helen's apple pie, supplemented with ice cream, made everyone happy, even Carlo.

After dinner, Martin cleaned up while Helen and Jenny saw to baths and bed for the three children. With fingers crossed, they came down to join Martin in the living room, Jenny carrying Ellen, who was in need of another suckle. Helen seemed in good spirits. Carlo's behavior was improving, her job was going fine, and she had even met a nice man who worked at the college as Assistant Director of Development. He had come over from Colby, where, as a junior development officer, he had learned the ropes during the negotiation of the huge Lunder art donation.

"Sounds interesting. So how far along is this?" asked Martin, with a broad grin.

Helen beamed. "I want you to meet him. Let's leave it at that. "

"C'mon, Poochie. We don't want to leave it at that."

"Okay, if you insist. He's tall like Martin, blond, doesn't smoke, born in Springfield, Illinois, and went to Oberlin, majoring in economics. Okay? Enough?"

"How nice. Does he have a name?" asked Jenny, laughing.

"Oh yeah. Bill. William Engle. His name. And that's enough. So, how's it going with the new baby?"

"How did you meet him?" asked Martin.

"Really, Martin. I said that's enough."

"Yeah, but when you say that, it means there's more to the story. So how did you meet him?"

Helen whooshed out a huge breath and said, "Okay. He came into the insurance office looking for a quote. About a week before Thanksgiving. The agents were out of the office, so I took the information. Homeowner and car combo, what was the discount. That kind of thing. On a whim, I asked him whether he wanted a quote on a term life policy a well. He said there was no family to consider. I guess that's what got me interested. I asked him whether he was going to any relatives for Thanksgiving, and he said no, his parents were now living in Hawaii and it was too far for just a weekend. So I asked him to join us, just me and the kids. For Thanksgiving."

"My God," said Jenny. "So quick? You musta' liked him."

Helen blushed bright red. "Yeah, I guess I did. I guess I do. It has been quick. I invited him for two o'clock, but he called at noon and asked if he could take the kids to the park for some soccer before dinner. So I said yes and he did, and they had a great time. At dinner, we talked about books, and movies, and his family, and Dad and the college and, well, just about everything. I offered him a nightcap, but he said his limit was two glasses of wine, not a drop more. And we talked some more. And then…" Here, Helen paused, and blushed again, "And then I invited him to stay for breakfast, and he did. Okay? Now is that enough?"

"Wow," said Martin. "First date. Wow. You must really like him. How nice. I hope it keeps working. What neat news. You should have brought him for Christmas."

"He went to Hawaii. So now, and I mean it, how's it going with the baby?"

"Ellen's doing fine," said Jenny, and with a sideways look at her husband, added, "and Martin, I'm delighted to report, has been reborn as a daddy. He's fantastic."

Martin sat upright. Jenny looked him square in the face and reached out to take both his hands in hers. "Yes, love, you've been fantastic. With the work load you're carrying, you've just been…" She could see Martin struggling to choke back a tear, so she turned back toward Helen. "He bathes her, does her diapers, plays with her endlessly, and he takes almost total care of JJ. We couldn't ask for a better nanny."

"Martin?" asked Helen, looking toward her brother. "Really?"

"Really," said Jenny. "Yes, really."

"Well, that's different. I'm impressed."

Martin, with a sheepish grin, said, "Remember last spring when Dad had pneumonia and we talked about stuff? I had told him that we were trying to get pregnant and he said that something amazing happens when you have a child of your own. I wasn't sure what he was talking about then, but now I know. If I didn't have to work, I would just stay home at this point."

"Is work that bad?"

"The teaching is great, but I'm having something of a crisis with research funding. I actually had to cut down my group. And, frankly, I'm not enjoying the research as much as I did ten years ago. It really feels like a struggle, keeping my group funded. I like the students, but I don't like the money scene."

"The best thing," said Jenny, "is that he's cut way back on travel. He's home now, most of the time."

"It's true, but that will have to change if I'm going to rebuild my research support. You have to visit sponsors, go to conference, all that. Lots of travel. It used to be exciting, all that running around. But now, it feels like a burden. I'd rather be here, at home with our little miracle. Let Jenny earn all the money."

"Very funny," said Jenny. "Between JJ and Ellen, I've got my hands full. We'll see what happens after the holidays. Whether I can take on new clients. Hey, it's getting late. We'd better put out the presents and get to bed. I don't know about your kids, but JJ is likely to be up before dawn."

Martin and Jenny didn't go for Christmas trees, but they did go for gifts. Between what Helen brought and their own slightly extravagant shopping, they erected a small mountain of wrapped presents in a corner of the living room, ready to greet JJ, Carlo, and Angela when daylight came.

Part IV: Thereafter

* **33** *

Mid-January. Time for the PC to vote. Morris allocated thirty minutes for a review of each case, including summaries of the input from the meetings with senior faculty in each of the candidates' areas. None of these meetings had produced surprises. Each had advocates; none had detractors. When it was time to review Kat's case, Martin reiterated that her experimental results on the transport benefits from her implant pattern continued to confirm between ten and fifteen percent mobility improvement, now with six different samples, but no, the results had not been published and had not yet been formally reviewed outside of CTI other than by Andris Andersen, to whom Kat had sent a short memo and, by email, he had replied saying, "It looks good. Keep going."

The voting scheme used a zero-to-four scale. Four meant a superb case with unequivocal support for tenure. A zero, in contrast, said absolutely no. Two was for fence-sitters — not in favor but not opposed either. The three and one votes meant on balance, yes, and on balance, no, respectively.

Everyone but Morris voted, using secret ballots, which were then tallied for all to see. The votes for Van Rijks were seven fours and seven threes. For DeMaitre, three fours, and eleven threes. But for Kat, one four, seven threes, five twos, and one one. Morris said it was pretty clear he would want to bring Van Rijks and DeMaitre forward, but he was troubled by the Rodriguez vote. He thanked everyone and took it under advisement, reminding everyone that no one was to provide any feedback to any of the candidates at this point. Once he had made his decision, his office would do whatever informing there was to be done.

- - -

A week later, Martin was slumped in the black leather chair in Morris's office. "I just can't bring this case forward," said Morris. "I've never seen a case this weak make it through, and regardless of that, the fact is that the letters are correct. She doesn't have externally reviewed confirmation of the experimental benefit of her implant pattern. I can't go forward attempting to claim that un-reviewed, unpublished experiments on a few samples constitute the basis for tenure."

"But, in my case …" sputtered Martin, but Morris cut him off.

"Before you get going about how your Associate case had a similar situation, there were major differences. First, it was an Associate case, not a thirty-year commitment like tenure. Second, you had already presented your results at a conference. The problem was with repetition. And third, unlike Kat, you had established a track record as a superb and innovative teacher, and here in EECS, we really value superb teaching. And …" gesturing to hold Martin from interrupting, "and while I cannot show you your letters, or tell you what your vote was, I can assure you that your case for Associate was stronger than Kat's present case for tenure."

"You know what's wrong with this?" asked Martin.

"No, what?"

"Suppose Albert Einstein or Richard Feynman came up with a theory that turned out to be wrong. The experimental confirmation just couldn't be found. Would that be a reason to deny tenure?"

"Of course not. How is that relevant?"

"Because nature gets a vote too. Kat had a bold idea and she took a huge risk to try it. She's doing exactly what the Collins report said that CTI values, going to the frontier of knowledge and bringing her students along for the ride. Suppose the idea had been wrong, meaning that the experiments were negative. Okay, maybe that's a reason to deny tenure, but it wouldn't have been a reason for an Einstein or Feynman. You just said so. But — and this is my point — that's not even what happened here. Kat not only had a bold idea, she managed to get the implant pattern to work and she has preliminary transport results that say the theory is right! She's moving in the right direction, but her progress is deemed to be too slow for CTI's tenure clock, so she's shit-canned. It's just plain wrong, Morris. She has done exactly the kind of thing we want our permanent faculty to do — have a good idea and follow it up with good experiments. And she has become a capable teacher, to boot."

"You're right about the tenure clock. It's our clock that made her case mandatory this year, and you're right that perhaps if she had another year or two, the outcome might be very different. But the tenure clock protects both us and candidates from all kinds of abuse. Having a firm deadline on tenure forces us to make a decision, and that's actually good for CTI even if we make a mistake and let go of someone who proves to be outstanding. But it's also good for the candidates. We wouldn't want to drag things out, keeping that kind of tension on the candidates year after year. "

"So what happens now?"

"I will meet with her later this week, and I will tell her that we have decided not to bring her tenure case forward. She'll have a full year after July first to get settled in a new position, and we'll do what we can about reducing her teaching load and helping her transfer her equipment and research programs. "

"She'll sue us, of course."

"Yes, I suspect she will, especially because of the publication of the letters. But that doesn't change my mind. This decision is completely consistent with CTI standards for tenure and I predict that if the Provost does convene a review committee, they will agree with my decision."

"Well, I don't agree. Not at all. She will go somewhere else, and the experiments she has done will be set back by a year, but then she will get her results, get her work into *Applied Physics Letters,* and in two years, I predict, she will get a tenure offer from Stanford and CTI will look like a bunch of jackasses for letting her go. She's the real deal, not some imposter."

"As I've said, if CTI lets someone good go, that's better than keeping people with weak tenure cases. It's the weakest accepted cases that determine the review standard. If we give Kat tenure with this case, the entire system gets calibrated down a notch, and that is not what we want for CTI."

"Can I make a suggestion that might buy her some more time?"

"You can try. What?"

"Since we know she'll sue CTI if she's turned down, there will have to be a review at some higher level. So why not pass the case forward to ES and see what happens? I mean, when all this started, you said 'get her tenure because we need her.' So what's changed? Don't you still need her? An Hispanic female role model, who is, after all, a provably good researcher? Bold idea, and positive progress, even if it's slow? The extra time might get her the results that would answer to the weakness in the letters."

"It's worth thinking about, I suppose. But the irony, perhaps the tragedy, is that the publication of the letters makes it harder to push her through. There is, I agree, some real merit in the case based on a bold program and some progress to date. If the letters were confidential, we could fight internally on the Hispanic woman issue, a rarity in engineering, and maybe win. But with letters out in the open, especially that pugnacious Visconti letter, it would reveal to the whole world that we tenured a marginal candidate for affirmative-action reasons, and that could create all kinds of backlash, including possibly from other candidates who have had tenure denied but might have had a stronger paper case"

"Can you at least ask the Dean and the Provost about that?"

"Actually, I already have. They pushed it right back in my lap, telling me to make my decision based on the case, period. Pushing it forward at this point would be like what Mechanical did with the Gillespie case. She had weak letters, but they moved the case to ES anyway, which promptly shot it down and blamed the department for bringing it forward. This situation is a bit worse, thanks to your unfortunate mishap with the letters. I'll consult with Bill and Ellen, and we'll discuss it, and I'll check again with the Dean and Provost. But there's one more thing."

"What's that?"

"I want you to resign from the Personnel Committee."

"Do I have a choice?"

"No."

"So you want me to leave CTI?"

"Absolutely not. You are highly valued at CTI."

"But not my judgment on personnel cases?"

"Martin, I can't say it was your fault exactly that the letters got exposed, but it certainly happened on your watch, and the fallout has been staggering. Actions, or inactions in this case, have consequences. The PC needs to move on without you."

- - -

Martin, with Ellen tucked under one arm while he ate dinner, told Jenny about his meeting with Morris, and how his year of focus on Kat's tenure had come to naught, including being kicked off the PC.

"If you need a witness, I can say you certainly did your best. You put her way ahead of a lot of other things."

"You mean ahead of you?"

"At times, yes. But I'm managing all that now. Are you still having those dreams?"

"Not so much, but I feel really drained." Martin finished eating, passed Ellen to Jenny, and said, "Hey, JJ. Ready for bath and bed?"

"And story," said JJ. "Don't forget the story."

After putting JJ to bed, Martin practiced for thirty minutes and then went to the study. Jenny was at her desk, reading email while nursing Ellen. He found a green card on his desk chair. "What's this?" asked Martin.

Jenny smiled. "We've got yellow cards and red cards, but those are negative signals. I thought a green card could be different. A happy signal. I've been thinking about everything. Your trouble with sleep, the colitis, the tenure case, the notebook, Morris. You've had a rough time. But the fact is, you've been fantastic since Ellen was born, and I've been mostly too tired to say so. So I'm letting the little card say it for me."

Martin's jaw trembled a bit. "Does this mean we need to talk about something?"

"Only if you want to. I'm happy. That's what it says. We're going to get through this phase, the colic, and start to enjoy our baby more. And calm your belly down. But I do have an idea about your dream."

Martin looked up, quizzical.

Jenny continued. "I think the wraith and the sand and the mud represent your overloaded job, dragging you down, preventing you from becoming the father you want to be."

"I don't get it."

"Think about it. The bundle you are carrying is a baby, not a notebook. The wraith wants to take it away. It's your job that separates you from your baby."

"If the wraith is my job, what's the sand? And the mud?"

"The overload, making it harder and harder to keep your bundle safe. I've seen you in action. When you told Helen at Christmas you'd rather be home, I think you meant it. I think you really do want to stay home. That means the enemy is your job."

"I must say that after Morris fired me from the PC, I felt ready to look elsewhere, but I wasn't sure I should tell you. Is that what you're hinting at?"

"I'm not sure, either," said Jenny, "but it's okay that we talk about it. Yes?"

Talk they did, late into the night. What might happen to Martin's research? Could they stay in Boston? If not, what about Jenny's business? Schooling for JJ and little Ellen?

Martin knew he could get a position at STC or some other major semiconductor company, possibly earning vastly more than he did at CTI. But leaving New England, where both their families were, was unattractive. In addition, Martin was, first and foremost, a teacher. Jenny knew that, and admired it.

At the end, Martin got Jenny's blessing to start making some phone calls, starting with Fred Walsh, a longtime family friend and President of Bottlesworth College. Maybe he would have a suggestion. It was a good thing, too, because the Engineering School did, as Morris had predicted, turn back Kat's tenure case in early March, and that had repercussions.

* **34** *

Kat picked up the phone and called Carly. "I got the final answer," said Kat, "and it's a no. You know a good lawyer?"

It didn't hit her until she got home. Carly brought dinner, but Kat wasn't eating, and fearful that Kat might harm herself, Carly decided to stay the night, holding Kat in her arms as she wept, finally drifting off to a troubled sleep.

The next morning, Carly called in sick, and the two of them talked some more, Carly encouraging Kat to let it out, like the air from a deflating balloon, reducing the pressure to where one could think clearly about options. Over the next few days, there were several such discussions. Had the answer been yes, some of the questions they were now facing would not have come up. But now, anticipating Kat's departure to a new position, possibly far away, each of them had to evaluate where their commitment to each other stood. The emotional drain was enormous, but the process worked.

The first thing Kat decided was that even though she was appealing her decision to the Provost, she thought it unlikely that an appeal would succeed. Assuming that to be the case, her priority was to find a position in the Boston area. This meant Boston University, Northeastern, Tufts, or Brandeis, or, a long-shot, maybe UMass Boston, which didn't have much engineering research going on. No point in considering Harvard, in spite of their new thrust into engineering. No way those snobs would hire a failed CTI tenure case.

The second thing was to find Kat a lawyer. Carly thought Kat should be able to get at least two year's salary as a settlement, maybe a lot more given the exposure of the letters, the harm to her reputation, and things like that. Carly volunteered to research the choices, looking for someone who could squeeze blood from a stone.

Third, Carly persuaded Kat to go home over spring break and spend time with her mother, who Kat knew was likely to die soon. Kat wanted Carly to go too, but she said, "No, there's no need to complicate things just now. You want a peaceful trip, not a confrontation."

Finally, with the tenure issue no longer at the forefront, Kat and Carly decided to get married when the moment felt right.

- - -

Martin heard the conversation in his outer office and got up to open the door. There stood Win Henderson, the Dean of Faculty at Bottlesworth. His six feet of blond solidity were loosely wrapped in a blue down jacket over a red, yellow, and green plaid wool shirt and brown corduroy pants. He was chatting with Felice about his trip down from Brimfield Junction.

"Come in, Win," said Martin. "Hope your drive wasn't too bad."

"Nice to see you," Win responded. "Some traffic around Portland. Otherwise fine."

They entered Martin's office, where Martin hung up Win's coat. "Coffee?" he asked. "Water? Anything?"

"No, I'm fine, thanks. I hear you have a new baby. Congratulations. A daughter?"

"Yes, baby Ellen." He picked up a photo from the desk to show Win. "She's almost crawling now. The joy of my life."

"And it's Jenny, isn't it? Is Jenny doing okay?"

"She's finally getting enough sleep, which is a big relief. Ellen was colicky, crying all night for the first three months, but she's sleeping through better now. I've gone on a work-from-home schedule three days a week, and I'm not teaching this term so I can help out."

"Our second child was colicky," said Win, chuckling. "Been there. Done that. It's a real test of one's humanity. If babies didn't smile, they would all be strangled."

"It does feel like that sometimes. Jenny's mother comes every few weeks, which is good I guess, even though having her underfoot and in the way, especially when she rearranges everything in our kitchen… well, you know how that can be." Win laughed in agreement. "So what brought you all this way? I was kind of surprised to hear from you. Just here to see me, or do you have other business?"

"You're the reason," said Win. "Let me start by saying how sorry I am about that crisis with the letters last fall. Somebody really did CTI dirt. And I understand from your conversation with Fred that it was your casebook that got stolen. That right?"

"Yes," answered Martin. "Afraid so. We've all been told to expect lawsuits, which makes me something of a pariah around here just now, especially with my Department Head. He thinks it was my fault, and maybe it was. I left my backpack unguarded for fifteen lousy seconds, and boom, it's gone. And who knew that the thief would want the notebook? And then publish it? I mean, who could guess?"

"Yeah. Well, Fred and I have been talking. We loved having your father on our faculty. He was just the kind of guy that makes us a great school. So I would like to plant a seed. I, that is, we, would like you to consider coming to Bottlesworth, at least for a couple of years. Take a leave from the mess at CTI. We have a job that we think you are uniquely qualified for, and we know your Brimfield Junction roots run deep."

"My God, really?"

"Yes, really. In fact, it's very real. Our entire senior administration, from Fred on down, is in favor."

"And you have a specific job in mind?"

"Yes. You know about our three-plus-two engineering option? Students take three years with us and then two years at Orono or Dartmouth to get an engineering degree?" Martin nodded. "We're thinking we want to strengthen the on-campus part of that, and Phelps Donahue, who's been in charge of it, unfortunately had a pretty serious health problem a month ago which has really slowed him down. He wants to be relieved of the program responsibility and go on a part-time schedule. It would never have occurred to us to approach you, since you play in the big leagues, but you had called Fred, so we thought, maybe… maybe catching you at a time in your life when getting away from CTI would feel like a relief. We sure as hell can use your expertise. We've both heard you preach on what real education is for an engineer. We want to be able to offer that to our students."

"You mean you're creating an engineering department?"

"No, at least not now. We would keep the program in the Physics Department, which is where your appointment would be."

"I'm dumbstruck," said Martin. "Is this a visiting slot, or are you thinking permanent faculty?"

"We plan to offer you a tenured slot," said Win. "Shit, Martin, any school would. But we would have to start it as a visiting slot, since it might take too long to get a tenure appointment through in time for the fall. We assume you would take a leave from CTI so if you didn't like it, you could come back to Boston. But I know you'll like it. Once you get back to Maine… Anyway, what I want from you is a CV, so we can finalize the visiting offer, and also permission to start a formal tenure case. We would only need five or six letters, and I'm sure you could contact your buddies ahead of time and feed us appropriate names. Normally we don't screen letter writers, but in your situation, world expert and all that, you would need a chance to tell them what's up so they don't flip out when we write them."

"But I would have to shut down my research group."

"Actually, no. We thought of that. We would arrange your schedule so you could spend a couple of days a week in Boston and keep your research students going, at least until you decide whether you want to stay with us for the longer haul. And, oh yes, did I mention? This is a fully endowed chair in Applied Physics we're talking about, donated by one of our alumni. It's an interesting story. He made his money in robotics. Got his Master's from CTI and was debating between CTI and us for a major gift, but when CTI didn't give Professor Gillespie tenure, we got a chair."

"I'm stunned. Let me think about this and talk to Jenny. It's a lot, and this is pretty sudden."

"I think it's less sudden than you do. You're a Bottlesworth guy, born and bred, and all we're doing is enticing you back to your roots, back to where you can be the kind of teacher you talked about last spring. And not just a Bottlesworth guy. As I recall your father saying, your mother was a Bottlesworth descendent, so you're actually a Bottlesworth!" The two men parted, and Martin sat back, thinking about finally having the time to write his book, and how the fog blows in over Sagadahoc Bay.

-   -   -

"It's almost too much to think about," said Jenny. Martin and Jenny were in their study, having put JJ and Ellen to sleep. "I mean, you may want out of CTI, at least for a while, but what about me? My business? My friends?"

"I know," said Martin. "It's a lot. We need to decide this together. There're two issues really, staying at CTI, which I'm pretty sure I don't want to do, and moving from Cambridge, which would impact you a lot. It would depend on where I could find a suitable job. But, frankly, I doubt anyone will step up and match what Bottlesworth wants to do."

"But aren't there other engineering schools in this area? I would think they would want you."

"None as good as CTI. And I have to tell you, I'm really getting tired of the research merry-go-round. What I really want to do is teach and finally write my book."

"So get a teaching job at a good college like Brandeis or Wellesley. Or Harvard? Wouldn't Harvard wet their pants to get you?"

But neither Harvard, nor Brandeis, nor Wellesley, nor Tufts, nor Boston University were interested in making a senior appointment in Martin's area. Northeastern was. Emphatically. When he spoke to the Dean of Engineering, he learned that they were already ecstatic about the chance to land Kat Rodriguez, and to get both him and Kat would be a huge boost to their semiconductor research program. But Martin had had enough of the firestorm around Kat and struck Northeastern from his list.

In the meantime, tantalized by the possibility of making a major change in lifestyle, one that would have Martin at home more, Jenny began her own critique of running her one-person business while raising two children. Since Ellen had come along, she had taken on only two new clients, both modest jobs, and managing even that with the two children had turned out to be more than Jenny could handle with comfort. So she contacted an artisan she had found in Waldoboro, Maine, an antique restorer and superb builder of fine replica furniture. She asked whether he might want her to create a national market for his craftsmanship on the internet, a business she could manage mostly from home. He leaped at the suggestion, and added that several of his friends in Wiscasset and Damariscotta might also be interested. Jenny began thinking more positively about a move to Maine.

Some weeks later, once again sitting in their study with the children safely in bed, Jenny said, "I think we should make two lists, one of why we should go to Brimfield Junction; the other why we shouldn't. Where does money fit in? Can we afford to do it without my income? Or a reduction in your consulting income? Remember, Katie's alimony isn't paid off yet."

"But the royalties account will cover that," said Martin. "One more year and I can buy her out."

The lists got made along with a financial what-if spreadsheet. They concluded that a move was totally affordable, even with no income for a year from Jenny's business. Taking into account rent levels in Brimfield Junction compared to what they could bring in by renting the Cambridge house, they would easily clear enough to pay for Martin's twice-a-month hotels when he would need to stay overnight in Cambridge, and those expenses would be tax-deductible.

As for Jenny's parents, they were very clear: "If the move is right for you and Martin, do it. We enjoy Maine just as much as Cambridge, and it's only a few hours away, not enough difference to matter."

Ultimately, it came down to what they each wanted, deep inside. Martin wanted to teach, to write his book and to stop hustling for increasingly inaccessible grant money. He wanted to be a real father to his daughter, not just a symbolic male who is mostly away from home. The Bottlesworth option met those needs. Jenny, encouraged by the vision of Martin as a fully-present parent, gradually shifted from cautious opposition toward cautious optimism, and once she came on board, Martin's ten-month battle with his ulcerative colitis began to wind down. He became less nervous about the distance to the nearest toilet, gradually returning to a digestive normality that refreshed his enjoyment of food.

Bowel issues aside, life for Martin at CTI had become truly shitty. In response to Kat's appeal of the negative tenure decision, Provost Ricci had set up an ad hoc committee to review the case. The committee had confirmed by late April that the Dean's decision to deny tenure was consistent with CTI standards and would not be reopened. So Kat sued CTI, the EECS Department and Morris. Things were still in the discovery phase, and since Kat had outed both Dan Cranagh and Alex Papadopolous as compromised members of the Personnel Committee and had accused Peter Dempsey of improper sexual advances, the process had gotten personally unpleasant for virtually everyone in EECS.

The most painful part for Martin had been Kat's rejection of his help going forward. "I'm a grown-up," she said, "and I can handle it. I know you did your best. I really do believe that. But unless you want to join me as a plaintiff, it's best if you back off. My lawyer says you're absolutely going to have to testify, and, I'm sorry to say, I hear he can be rough."

CTI was providing Martin with legal representation at no cost to him, since Provost Ricci had determined that Martin, in spite of having lost the notebook, had been a consistent and proper mentor and advocate for Kat during the year between joining the PC and the negative tenure decision. Martin had to appear for deposition and was grilled first about his carelessness — his sneeringly alleged negligence — in his handling of the notebook, and then on the extent to which he knew about Professors Cranagh's, Papadopolous' and Dempsey's relationships with Professor Rodriguez prior to and during the tenure deliberations. Kat's attorney kept at him — why didn't you raise a flag when you heard there might have been a conflict of interest? He had raised a flag, but since it was based on third-hand reporting of what might be a rumor, the only thing he could do, which he had done, was to report the possibility of a problem to Morris. And, no, he never raised a question with Professor Rodriguez because he felt it would compromise the supportive role he was committed to in helping her prepare her tenure case. "What the fuck!" Martin snapped, an oath uttered under oath. "How the hell could I build up her tenure case if I accused her of sleeping around? She would never talk to me after that. Then she would have no Case Manager, and that would be worse. Frankly, I don't really care a fig about her sexual activities, whether with my faculty colleagues or anyone else. That's her business, and theirs. I did my best to get her through, and I'm goddam sorry it didn't work. Period."

* **35** *

Kat's mother died in June, and Carly accompanied Kat to Merida for the funeral. In early July, just after Kat finalized a deal with Northeastern as an untenured Associate Professor with the promise of a tenure decision within two years, Kat and Carly got married in a quiet ceremony, with Amanda and Felicity as the only guests.

Before Kat and her students disassembled the atomic beam equipment prior to moving it across the river, Susan made enough samples to confirm their early positive results. They submitted a paper to *Applied Physics Letters* and jumped for joy when it was accepted. Kat was bringing to Northeastern not only the prestige of having developed a controversial new type of implant structure that might, if her preliminary results become independently confirmed, provide as much as a fifteen percent improvement in carrier mobility. She was also bringing more than a half million in annual research grants plus two superb graduate students.

The person or persons responsible for the various bogus computer accounts had not been found, in spite of superhuman efforts from the IT Security group and their crackerjack consultant. The Provost endorsed the proposed drop-box method where electronic versions of promotion letters would be uploaded, with individual secure portals for every faculty member entitled to see the letters. Julian's team got it up and running by mid-August. But Julian said, as he often did, that "the weakest link in any computer network is the people that use it. If individual faculty members print copies of the letters for their own use and then lose them, the drop-box idea could still fail."

This new super-secure system was carefully explained in CTI's solicitation for promotion letters that went out starting in the late summer, but the fallout from the notebook incident was still keeping CTI radioactive. Fewer than half the requests for letters in support of Associate and Full promotions were resulting in replies, which made Morris nervous about how the cases could proceed. Meanwhile, Julian, logged in as edward.snowden, downloaded and read each letter as it arrived.

-   -   -

Martin's feelings about the implosion of the atmosphere at CTI were a mixture of guilt for having been an unwilling agent, and relief for having the opportunity to escape. Arranging the leave of absence had not been easy. In spite of having kicked him off the Personnel Committee, Morris really did want Martin to stay at CTI. To Martin, that spoke volumes. It pains the CTIs of this world to lose someone of Martin's caliber, especially to a place like Bottlesworth, but Martin was firm. He had accepted the visiting offer at Bottlesworth starting in September. It was not negotiable. He would not be teaching C&E in the fall. Morris had no choice, so he gave in.

Even though this was officially a visiting appointment, Martin knew that he wasn't going back to CTI, no matter what. If Bottlesworth didn't work out, there were plenty of places that might, with enough notice, be eager to have him. He unloaded the journal editing over the summer, telling Callaghan that without his own secretary, managing the review process would be impossible. They agreed that he would finish up the eight papers he now had in review but would not be assigned any new ones. It was a relief. The Chang story still upset him, how the nonsense with Schultz had almost destroyed S. J. Chang's career. Somehow, Chang never mentioned Schultz as a potential problem and Ryszard Pulaski ended up writing to him, who, in character, wrote a toxic letter. Only after it had come in did Pulaski call Martin and ask for a refresher on the story. Martin, biting his tongue, politely reiterated the details of their conversation in Denver and told him to

look up on the internet what Schultz wrote about Kat. Pulaski said he
would build a box around the letter and apologized for having flubbed
Martin's warning. Both Changs did get tenure, but holy smokes. More
generally, taking on reviewers you didn't know was getting dangerous.
In July, a huge scam out of Taiwan blew up. One of the highly respected
journals had been hornswaggled by a fellow who created multiple
email accounts and had wormed his way into the review lists so he was
actually, under pseudonyms, reviewing his own papers. All of them got
published — no surprise there — and at a school where paper count
determines promotion, this served as a cute way for him to write his
own ticket to tenure, at least until it was discovered. Martin knew the
journal editor from the conference circuit and had written him a con-
soling and supportive note when the story went public.

Because he wanted to limit his travel, he not only resigned from two
conference program committees, he told STC that he would make only
one consulting trip per month. All other consulting would have to be
via the internet. Martin knew that in a year or two, he would no longer
be the kind of expert he was now, so this consulting job would eventually vanish, but he and Jenny had already figured that possibility into
their financial plan. If they decided to stay at Bottlesworth, they would
sell the Cambridge house, and if they bought a house in Brimfield
Junction with twenty percent down, they would have something like
two hundred and sixty thousand in cash left over.

Unbundling his research group was especially difficult. He had
an old grant from DARPA, and one each from NSF and NASA. The
DARPA grant was a collaborative one that would be impossible to
manage from a distance, so he persuaded Peter Dempsey to take
it over. The other two were his alone, and he could manage sponsor
relations as the grad students moved along and finished up. He told
his Master's students to plan on switching groups for their PhD's, and
he gave notice to Khalil that he should get his resume out, because his
present appointment would not be renewed. Of his remaining PhD
students, Christina, her over-sexed dressing style notwithstanding, had

proved to be a very sharp student. She was already writing her thesis on the hexagonal surface reconstruction. Natasha's experiments on a combined implant/anneal cycle to control near-surface screw dislocations produced during high temperature processing steps were yielding good enough results that she could probably finish by the following summer.

When he told Seamus and Colleen about the upcoming move, they offered him their guest room any time he wanted, at least when their grandchildren were not visiting. And Horatio volunteered to have his piano fixed up so their music group could meet in his house whenever Martin had the chance to stay over. As an affirmation of continuity, Vladimir had signed up for a November concert in the Little Theater, even though it wasn't yet clear that they could pack enough rehearsals in.

Perhaps the saddest and most wrenching part of this relocation was giving up his undergraduate advisees. Gina was devastated. She even asked, sobbing, if she could transfer to Bottlesworth so she could continue to work with him. She was learning so much. No one else cared like him. Martin recognized the infatuation component of that request, and while it took quite a bit of gentle persuasion, he finally talked her through the upset, convincing her to stay where she was, especially since she was doing so well at CTI.

Through all this, Martin kept thinking about how fast and how far Gina had come in just over a year. No longer a gushing freshman, she had learned to think on her own, to criticize, even to speak up in a committee room full of senior faculty. Mixed in with some pride over his successful mentoring of such a promising student was the hope that little Ellen would someday grow up to become the next generation's Gina — as smart, as pleasant, and as capable.

EPILOGUE

The day dawned bright and clear, with the temperature a pleasant 65 degrees. Martin got up at six, pulled on his workout clothes and went into the basement of the 1920s three-bedroom home they had rented just off the Harpswell Road, a half-mile south of campus. He did his usual three miles on the treadmill while listening to the first act of *The Elixir of Love*, thinking of himself as Nemorino, a besotted youth. But unlike Nemorino, he had needed no special potion to attract his Adina. It was the other way around. She had committed to him with her eyes wide open, his past and all, and in spite of their mid-course struggles, they had made it through to what felt like the Promised Land. Here he was, back in Brimfield Junction, freed from much of the stress of his CTI overload, and never more deeply in love than on this particular day. He went upstairs, showered and dressed, collected Ellen from her crib, changed her diaper and brought her into Jenny, who was beginning to stir. Next stop was the kitchen where he set out breakfast fixings for everyone: JJ's cheerios with a banana sliced on top, hot water for Jenny's herbal tea and a French press of coffee for himself. He popped two slices of high-fiber bread in the toaster, scrambled two eggs and ate them while reading the *Times* on his iPad. After washing the frying pan and putting his dishes into the dishwasher, he went up to wake JJ and get him dressed. By this time, Jenny had finished feeding Ellen, and everyone came down to the kitchen.

"A big day for you, Mr. Goofus," said Jenny as JJ dug into his cereal. With his mouth full, JJ asked, "Why do you call Daddy Mr. Goofus?"

"Because I love him," said Jenny.

Martin gave Jenny, still holding Ellen, a hug and kiss, and bent down to plop a farty kiss on Ellen's belly, which drew giggles from the smiling baby, tangling her hands in his hair.

"Knock 'em dead, my love. The kids deserve the very best."

"Yeah, maybe, if they're awake. The only downside is that it's a nine o'clock class. We'll see if they actually show up."

"Don't forget. Dinner with Bill and Helen tonight. Their place."

JJ said, "We see Uncle Bill tonight? That's fun. He's awesome."

Martin took his leave and walked briskly toward the campus into the network of quads with their sentinel oaks still in full leaf, quads crisscrossed by the paths that would take him to his temporary office in the gray stone Science building. As he walked, he reveled in his good fortune, the lucky inspiration he had back then to call Fred Walsh to ask him for suggestions about where he might find openings somewhere in New England.

Martin arrived at his office at quarter to nine. The details of where to house him permanently were under discussion, but for now, he had a tiny room to himself, sharing the department secretary with the rest of the Physics faculty. He pulled out his sheet of bullet points for his first lecture, wondering what CTI was going to do about MOOC credit. Credit for online classes was running amok, and not just at places like Arizona State. He had read in the paper about a virtual high school that had been set up somewhere or another with no classes at all. The students did everything online. Although the politicians and school administrators made pious statements about preparing the students for the workplace, Martin believed that this was driven by money, not by educational merit.

The CTI Educational Policy Committee, after many stormy meetings through the spring, had recommended, and the faculty had approved at its May meeting, the creation of a new faculty committee whose job was to review and approve transfer credit for MOOCs, whether CTI-based or from anywhere else. Their reasoning was that CTI did accept transfer credit for classroom courses, so why not also consider transfer credit for MOOCs? Tamara was opposed, claiming that the educational equivalence of MOOCs to in-class offerings had not been demonstrated. But she was out-voted in committee, the cost-cutters and efficiency seekers and, to be fair, some enthusiasts for educational experimentation, carrying the day. The first task for this new committee — one that Martin felt was impossible to fulfill — was to write a set of standards for accepting MOOCs. "More power to them," he thought. "I'm well away from it."

-    -   -

At five minutes before nine, Martin went to his new classroom, a bright, well-furnished hall seating forty, with individual desks for the students. Half the desks were full. Martin went up to each student, introduced himself and asked their names, saying it would take him a few weeks to get everyone straight, but he wanted to get started. By the time he had made the rounds and the stragglers had arrived, it was time to begin. He outlined what was expected in terms of homework sets, laboratory exercises and exams, and then began his lecture.

"You are all about to embark on the study of engineering, so it's reasonable to ask: what is engineering? My answer to that is both simple and complex. The words are simple: engineering is the purposeful use of scientific knowledge." He paused to let that sink in, then wrote the word 'PURPOSEFUL' on the board in large caps and underlined it twice. "The problem, and it is a real problem for each and every one of you, " as he glanced almost menacingly around the room, "the problem is that one man's purpose, or one woman's purpose, can be another person's anathema."

At the end of the lecture, the students applauded and Martin smiled. As the group began filing out, three of the young men came up to him. The tallest one, blond with a baseball cap on backwards, said, "That was great, Professor Quint. Great lecture. But we have a question."

"Certainly," said Martin. "Fire away."

"I noticed that FIE is offering a Circuits and Electronics course online, so all three of us signed up for it just to see what it's like. How will it compare to this course? Is there any problem doing both?"

Acknowledgements

I've had a lot of help in crafting this book, most importantly from two people: First, my wife, Peg, who has been a patient and creative sounding board for the past two years, recognizing that when I drift off into another world, it is into the world of Martin Quint and CTI, a world that over time has also become familiar to her. Second, my 'writing buddy,' Susan Baruch, friend of long-standing and a helpful critic, even before what started as a short story grew into this novel. I am also indebted to those who read and commented on early versions or added their professional expertise on certain topics: Gordon Doerfer, Nancy Sizer, Bruce Knobe, Arnold Messing and Loring Conant. Also to MIT colleagues with whom I discussed MOOCs, computer security and the tenure process: Jay Keyser, Gerald Sussman, Harry Hoffman, Larry Bucciarelli and Anantha Chandrakasan. Finally, I owe a significant thank-you to Leah Hager Cohen, who helped me along early in my fiction writing and has been encouraging and supportive ever since.

Stephen D. Senturia
Brookline, MA

CPSIA information can be obtained
at www.ICGtesting.com
Printed in the USA
FSHW011623050720
71801FS